Bug
Trouble

A Cable Counties Thriller

Hartley Stevens

In all respects this novel is a work of fiction.
Names, places, and incidents are either the product of the author's imagination or are used fictitiously. Any resemblance to actual persons, living or dead, or to actual events or locales is unintentional and coincidental.

Bug Trouble

ISBN: 978-1-944941-03-1 (ebook)
ISBN: 978-1-944941-04-8 (print)

Published in the United States of America
By Big Toe Writes, LLC.

Cover design by Derek Murphy
www.creativindiecovers.com

Editing, formatting and layout provided by
Polgarus Studio
www.polgarusstudio.com

Website Design by Sharon Julien
www.sjulien.com

Marketing and Media by Kelly Thompson, April & Scott Schroeder
www.liquidcreativestudio.com

For Jeanie
Love & Life

Contents

Bug, n.1. any insect or insect like invertebrate. 2. any microorganism, especially a virus. 3. a person who has a great enthusiasm for something; fan. A craze or obsession. v. 1. to bother; annoy; pester.

Trouble, n. 1. difficulty or problems. 2. public unrest or disorder. v. 1. causing distress or anxiety. *Synonyms:* worry, stress, bother, disturb, agitate, perturb, annoy, strife, irritate.

Prologue

Facon… clicked on a familiar computer icon. The screen blinked and another glowed to life. A smile crept over his face as he reached up to pull an imaginary chain attached to a phantom light bulb. He did this whenever the idea he'd been chasing around his brain came into focus and he truly saw the light. *It's the electricity,* he thought.

He leaned back in his chair, letting the satisfaction rush over him like the warm Mediterranean Sea breeze he'd loved as a child. In the background, he heard a small squeak, like a tennis shoe catching on a waxed floor. He glanced over his shoulder. It must have been a night noise—a shuffling of inanimate objects. He reached into the bottom drawer of his desk and retrieved a mini-bar sized bottle of Scotch. He twisted the tin cap from the plastic bottle and felt the warm, satisfying liquid flow down his throat. For a moment, he wished there was someone else to share his discovery, but all the other students, scientists, and faculty had left hours ago.

The squeak came again, more faint this time. He looked at the black rows of identical cubicles. Maybe this was his friend and fellow researcher, Larry Red, returning for some forgotten book. Amul Instad Facon, good-naturedly referred to his friend as Larry "the Red," because of his fanatical belief that socialism was the true humane form of government.

He heard a small *tinkling*, as if a test-tube had rolled across the surface of one of the research counters. The noise persisted. Then nothing. A split second later, a tiny crash.

Facon stood and called into the blackness. "Red, is that you?"

No response. The room seemed to inhale. As playful as Facon could be socially, he had no patience for the adolescent pranks many of his fellow researchers played on one another.

The light switch was on the other end of the large bay. He took a tentative step into the darkness. "Larry… Red… is that you?"

Still no response. Facon felt his palms go slick with nervous sweat. He retreated back into the safety of the cubicle and tried to rationalize the sounds. He turned to grab his chair, but instead he found himself confronted by three men, all dressed in black.

Startled, he stumbled, reaching for the edge of the desk to keep his balance. A lightning-quick glimmer of light flashed in the corner of his vision. Before he could blink, Facon had the last thought of his life as his head was severed from his body. He actually saw his own shocked corpse… still standing upright, through eyes that tumbled down in a head that hit the terrazzo floor with a wet splat.

Chapter 1

"Listen, Cloud!

You horse's ass. I didn't call you because I think you're the best. I called you because we have a big hairy cluster of crap that seems right up your alley. I know you're juiced in with all of the local slime. Maybe, just maybe, you can find somebody who may have seen or heard something. Big people are involved, and when this hits the papers, everyone in the state is going testicle-hunting."

My name is Jeremiah St. Cloud. From time to time I solve problems. I was sitting in Carter Wells' downtown office listening to him enjoy the sound of his own voice. Wells is a construction mogul and current mayor of our growing university town. He and I became acquainted a year or so earlier when he was a mere county commissioner and needed some behind-the-scenes work done. The situation had turned out just fine for him, but left me with no desire to trespass on local political quagmires. Carter wasn't known for his charity, or even for his political competence, so this situation must have some consequences that threatened to derail his gravy train.

"I'm not working for you, Carter. People become very unpopular doing favors for you, and I believe some become dead."

"That's out of line, you cheap dick. I don't need some pile of crap like you making disparaging remarks about unsubstantiated rumors that happened a long time ago," he said.

"Disparaging and unsubstantiated in the same sentence. You must be listening to those *How to Increase Your Word Power* tapes again."

"Always with the lip. You want this or not?"

"Who's paying?"

His eyebrows bent towards his sarcastic grin. "Soooo honorable… but still willing to whore if the money is right, huh?"

I brushed the barb aside. "You know how I work. Once I'm hired, I stay with it till I cross the goal line."

"Meaning what?"

"Meaning if you interfere, I'll see you as part of the problem, and I'm the problem solver."

"I do believe I might hate you."

I pooched out my lip.

Carter Wells shook his silver helmet of a head. This conversation was beneath him. "The Cup, which is to say the 1996 NCAA National Championship trophy, was stolen from the athletic department show case last night."

"So?"

He looked horror-stricken, then regained his pompous demeanor. "Oh, I forgot—you didn't attend the University of Florida. You were a little too *good* for our southern university. *You* attended the high and mighty Military Academy at West Point."

"It's a trophy, Carter. Do everyone a favor and just send the trophy company a check for fifty bucks and get a new one. No one will ever know the difference."

Now he looked aghast. "But they would, and I would. The story will surely leak, and our boys didn't sweat their blood and guts out to be shackled with some counterfeit trophy. We would be the laughing stock of the whole South Eastern Conference."

"Why is this particular trophy so important to you?"

"Boy, I bet you don't even believe in God, do you?"

In his estimation, my answer wasn't required. I said, "Are you going to give me the low-down or not?"

"So many of the university faithful see that trophy as the tangible evidence why they send in their annual booster checks. It doesn't sit on their mantle at home, but knowing it sits over at the stadium in that hallowed glass case is the next best thing. Makes them feel like they're one of the team, like they're wearing a goddamn jersey on the field come Saturday."

Oh my, with the huffing and puffing. "What's in it for you?" I asked.

"Team spirit. School pride."

"And my balls drag on the ground when I walk."

"You are one mouthy smear of injun blood. When the team wins, the university prospers. When the university prospers, all of the Cable Counties prosper."

"And with all that prosperity going around, some of it just kind of leaks back into your pockets."

"There's nothing wrong with making a little money. You're certainly in no position to look down your nose at the wealthy. You live quite well from what I hear. An airplane and a landing strip on your own property."

There was no plane, not anymore. But it really wasn't any of his business anyway. "So you want me to get the trophy back?"

"Nothing even so difficult. I just want for you to find out who took it."

"Then what? You send your cowboy mafia to bend the takers up?"

"That's of no concern to you."

"I'll need to cross the goal line."

"You arrogant prick. Do you want this job or not?"

I shrugged. "Goal line?"

Carter looked at me with the kind of pity most people hold for the permanently injured, the crippled, and very small children. "Alright, cross the goddamn goal if you can. Just get me that trophy back."

"Of course, you mean get the trophy back for the university and the faithful alumni, don't you?"

"Just get the trophy."

"Ten thousand up front, no refund. Another ten when the cup is returned to the *hallowed glass case*. I'll assume all expenses unless things get wild."

"Not such a cheap fuck after all, but a whore all the same."

I rested my boot against his desk and retied the laces.

He squirmed, probably figuring out how to shaft me on the back end of this arrangement. "Alright, deal."

With a big, blue company check in my pocket, I left Carter's office. The check was payable from Wells and Johnson, Inc., Carter's own business. I needed to cash it quickly then find out what that missing trophy had to do with a construction company. No way Carter was doing this just to see what team spirit smelled like.

Chapter 2

I headed over to Burrito Brothers for lunch. It was a mainstay for the college crowd, but us super-sleuths had to keep our energy up as well. I'd been looking forward to today's lunch since yesterday, and I attacked the two beef and bean burritos like piranha on a baby water buffalo.

One of the perks of working for yourself is getting to indulge in two and three martini lunches. There were no martinis served at Brothers, but a cold cup of Budweiser was really more in keeping with burritos anyway.

When the food was gone, I pulled out the morning newspaper. The headlines didn't focus on the theft of the Championship trophy—this was a good thing. It would give me some latitude when asking questions. Once a crime became common knowledge, many stories started to fit what people read instead of what they actually knew. On the bottom of the front page was a curious item about a robbery/homicide that occurred on campus at the Biotechnology Research Building. The headline read, "Biotech Break-In Leaves One Student Dead."

"Campus police responded to an apparent robbery/homicide in the early morning hours at the Biotechnology Research Building located on campus. Authorities discovered the body of Amul Instad Facon, a doctoral student from the Middle Eastern country of Qatar. Details of Facon's death are being withheld until the campus police can contact the family. Authorities would not comment on what was taken from the Biotechnology Research Building but are speculating that Facon was killed during the theft."

This seemed odd to me, two crimes taking place on the normally tranquil campus during the same night. Real crimes, too. Usually, most student felonies centered around too much alcohol consumption and too little sexual restraint.

I flipped to the sports pages. The main topic was the upcoming college football season. The University of Florida had captured its third national title a few years earlier and was in the middle of the preseason rankings. I searched the list of colleges rounding out the top twenty-five. Once again the Military Academy was missing. I breathed a sentimental sigh and said, "Go Army."

Chapter 3

I decided to start my inquiry at the top. Crossing University Avenue, I headed toward the athletic department offices stationed within the undercarriage of the football stadium. I'd never had any cause to deal with the University Athletic Director on a professional basis, but we had some common friends, and I knew him pretty well on a social level.

I walked through the double doors and into a large reception area. The walls were covered in heavy, trophy-laden cases, but not an ounce of dust clung to one single trophy or plaque. To my left, a large glass display had been smashed. Yellow crime-scene tape was strung out around it. I surmised this was the lifting scene. We crime-solvers are sharp like that.

A buxom, former cheerleader-type sat manning the receptionist desk. She was answering and directing calls with amazing efficiency. Wearing an operator's headset, her fingers nimbly scanned and pushed buttons. I guessed the alumni faithful had caught wind of the trophy theft. I also imagined the receptionist had endured a very difficult morning handling calls from the most powerful men in the state.

I approached the desk, giving her my many-zeroed kilowatt smile. I got some change back, but no interest on the smile. She ignored the incessantly ringing phone and looked up with saucer-sized gray-blue eyes. She pushed back from the desk and crossed her tanned legs. "May I help you?"

You may domesticate an animal. You could teach a Rottweiler or Pit Bull to salivate for kibbles, bits, and loving pats on the head, but, buried deep in the animal brain, he wants to hunt, kill, and smack bone-crushing jaws over newly dead flesh. The same could be said of all men. Let me say again, *all* men. We're the inferior species, and we all still have a warm feeling for dragging the maiden back to our cave. Fortunately for me, I am very domesticated, and my cave is well-stocked.

"Hello," I said, handing her my card.

"Mr. St. Cloud, do you have an appointment with Director Malloy?"

"It's Cloud… just Cloud. No mister, no saint," I said, laying down my own flurry of eyelash maneuvers. "And, I don't. But if you would tell him Cloud is callin', he might just make time for me."

"The director is very busy. We've had something of a crisis, and he's been taking calls from the alumni all morning."

"Funny you should mention it. I'm here to solve your problem. I've been asked to look into the crisis," I said, motioning toward the broken trophy case.

"Oh, I'm sorry. Are you with the university police department?"

"No, I'm not with UPD. I'm kind of a specialist. Could you see if he would fit me in?"

The cheerleader had heard many lines before. Countless fraternity boys had tried to wear sheep's clothing only to be later exposed as wolves. Knowing seduction was a far more powerful weapon than force, she batted more eyelids than a butterfly garden and tried for flattery. "You're a big one. Did you used to play for Florida?"

She was tenaciously loyal. To tell her I attended another university would have slammed iron doors. So I almost lied. "Yes, I played some ball. Some boxing and wrestling as well."

It worked. She pushed buttons. "Director, there is a Mr. Ahhh, a Mr. Cloud here to see you. I know he doesn't have an appointment, but… yes sir, I'll send him right up."

There was a plastic business card holder on her desk. I picked up one of the cards and looked at it. It was generic, but she'd handwritten her name in below the university emblem: Mary-Ann Lemke.

She beamed the big blues at me again, "Mr. Malloy will see you now. Do you know where his office is located?"

I tucked the card into my Cinch Jeans and said, "Yes, I know the way. Thank you Mary-Ann." Lucky for her, she was sitting. I'm sure her knees would have buckled with the mention of her name. She smiled again, and at that same moment, another call rang through, and she was back to business.

Chapter 4

Jack Malloy was deep in the platitudes of his job when I let myself through his open office door. "Yes, Senator, I know. It is a terrible tragedy, I… Yes, sir, I'm on it. We have every available resource… Yes, sir, I understand, you'll be the first one I call when there is further information… Yes, sir, and it's very good to hear from you. Okay then, goodbye."

He hung the phone up with obvious distaste. The director had lived many political years this morning. I studied several honorary plaques and framed certificates hanging on his wall. I was looking at a large frame that held Jack Malloy's business cards. They were arranged sequentially and showed a well-earned career from the ticket office to University Athletic Director.

"Cloud, it's good to see you. It's good to see any face that isn't condemning me to a slow death."

"Tough morning?"

"I believe these alumni fat cats think I keep the trophy in a vault and spend twenty-four-seven guarding it with my life."

"So the word has leaked, huh?"

"Leaked. I wish that was all it was." He pointed a remote control at one of seven televisions built into the office walls. The set jumped to life on ESPN.

A large vanilla moon pie sat behind a high tech desk, laptop computer within reach. *"Well… what do you think, Chris? The National Championship trophy has been stolen right out from under the noses of the university. And I don't mean figuratively. I mean they lost the hardware. Maybe this is a sign. Maybe this is just a forecast of the upcoming season, and you know Florida was very lucky to escape with the National Championship in '96."*

"I think you're right there, Mike. There is no way the university can do it again. Down in Tacky-Ville, USA, this is a fitting scenario. The Stanley Cup is passed around to every member of the winning NHL squad, and every year the Cup comes back. But these bumpkins can't even hang onto the hardware in their own backyard. Very sad."

The talking heads continued. The university mascot, a huge vicious-looking alligator head hung in the background. Malloy pressed the remote, silencing the nonsense.

Jack spun his chair toward me and said, "What can I do for you, Cloud?"

This man was not up for any word play. "I'm here to get your hardware back."

Malloy surprised me. "Why Cloud, I didn't know you cared. You're an Army man and have something of an indifferent reputation."

"Frankly Jack, you're right. I don't care, but I'm being paid by Carter Wells to bring back the trophy."

"My tired brain can hardly recognize an honest man. I'm sorry if I offended. What can I do to help you help me?"

***

"Well, let's start with who you think might have taken the trophy."

"Hell Cloud, if I could accurately speculate on something like that, I'd quit right now and move out to Vegas."

"I wasn't asking for an answer based on facts. I was asking for your gut feel for the thing."

"In that case, it could have been an over-zealous alumnus. It could have been a rival team trying to cause a sensational uprising. Or it could have been one of our own students in a fraternity prank. But my gut tells me that whoever did this was in the background; they hired some professionals. I don't really have a motive in mind, but I would guess it was vanity or something trivial."

"What makes you say that?"

"The damn thing isn't worth a hundred bucks on its merits. Its only real value is sentimental. Did you know they clubbed some poor security guard half to death?"

"I'm only an hour or so into this, and you're the first person I've talked to, so no, I didn't know anything about the security guard. Is he alright?"

"Yeah, they say he'll be okay. He's over at the university teaching hospital in stable condition."

"What's the security around here like at night?"

"There's an alarm system, of course, and one roving security guard on premises from five in the evening until seven in the morning."

"Did the alarms go off?"

"No, there was a campus-wide black out. The storm last night knocked out the power, and the emergency backup generators are ancient and unreliable."

"I read some time ago the stadium has its own emergency backup generators for football games."

"True, but they're only online for games. The power goes out so often around here we don't want the added expense of additional generators kicking in every other day."

"How about internally? Is there anyone on the staff who could have taken such a liking to the trophy—they just had to have it?"

"I suppose anything is possible, but I can hardly imagine anyone who works here stealing it."

"Anyone you pissed off lately? Anyone you fired that might have an axe to grind?"

"Damn, Cloud. We hire and fire people around here like anywhere else. You do know that the University Athletic Association is one of only six athletic departments around the whole country that's incorporated?"

"Meaning?"

"We function like a business. We're not entirely removed from the university, of course, but we show profit and loss—mostly profit, something else that sets us apart from most athletic departments."

"So your employees aren't subject to the same rules as the other staff and faculty employed by the university?"

"That's the good part. We're not subject to the same stiff guidelines, but all of the employees here get the same benefits."

"Seems very cozy for you and yours. How'd you manage that arrangement?"

"I didn't do it. The University Athletic Program hasn't always enjoyed so much success. There was a time only a few years ago when we had yet to win a single conference championship in any sport besides swimming and golf. During those years, the university was very eager to separate us financially. Now they have to live with the arrangement. It doesn't work out so badly for them either. Last year we donated a million dollars to the library, and the year before that *and* the year before that. All of the savings are supposed to go to the faculty's salaries. So you can see why so many of our engineers and scientists are also rabid sports fans."

The phone on Jack's desk beeped once, and he grabbed the receiver. "Yes? Alright, just give me a minute, then put him through."

Jack held the phone in both hands and looked fatigued. "I'm sorry, I have to take this. It's the governor—the third time he's called this morning. Let me tell you, having the governor of your state as an alumnus might be handy on some fronts, but when a crisis emerges, I'd just as soon he went to that… *you know*, university to our north. Give me a call, if I can help more."

"Thanks, I appreciate the time. The only other thing I need is a free pass from you. I want access to anyone on campus—the coaches, the faculty, secretaries, custodians, everyone."

He opened his top desk drawer and removed a bright orange card. He turned it over and scratched something on the back. "This will give you access to everyone except the faculty. I don't have any control there."

I grabbed the card and stuffed it into my pocket. He was already saying, "Hello again Governor, what can I do for you?'

I stopped at the door and gave him a wave. He returned an imaginary gun with thumb and forefinger.

Chapter 5

St. Petersburg, Florida

An enormous yacht grazed the sides of the walkway as it pulled to a stop. A sun-worn, crusty, gray-haired man expertly steered the boat into the private slip. A very young, very brown boy jumped from the bow and began tying a mooring line.

The diesel engines continued to boil the bottom sands of the luxury liner parking lot. A bold rock medley from the band Seven Mary Three bellowed from speakers on board. The youth mouthed words. He didn't really know the lyrics, but the music was contagious. The marina was awash in familiar sounds, most notably the island crooning of Jimmy Buffet. The old and knowing captain dropped the volume of his craft and Seven Mary Three, gave way to "Margaritaville."

Three men, all dressed in black designer clothing, walked the boardwalk toward the boat. Each man carried a shoulder bag and one trailed a wheeled, carry-on bag. Tourists and even a dock waitress or two greeted the three men. They ignored the friendly greetings and plowed on toward the yacht.

A step before reaching the edge of the yacht, one of the men pulled out a cell phone. A gangplank lowered toward the dock. The man casually tossed the phone into the water.

The men came aboard, and within seconds the gangplank was folded away. The boy quickly released the line, and the boat backed away from the marina.

***

The three men entered an elaborately decorated stateroom. Each of them had dark olive skin and thick, black hair. Watching them arrive, a huge, fat man sat behind a dark teak desk. He looked like Jabba the Hut, only he could have been Jabba the Whole House. He moved a silver tray, bringing fist-sized oysters closer to him.

One of the men produced a cigarette case and clicked it open. The slight noise disturbed Jabba, and he looked into the still sunglassed eyes of the visitor. The man replaced the cigarette case without taking any of the contents. Jabba smiled in approval and grabbed another oyster. The huge mound of fat slurped with the intensity of a vacuum cleaner. It was lucky the crustacean was impervious to sound. If not, the slurping alone would have killed it.

As if on cue, the same young man descended a spiral stairway from the upper deck and took away the spent tray of oysters, vanishing upstairs again.

The newcomers stood rock-steady. The stateroom was dark, but these men preferred the anonymity the gloom and glasses provided.

The Hut motioned toward some chairs arranged in a neat row. They sat down.

He smiled slightly. *How well trained they are*, he thought. "Gentlemen, I believe you have some things for me?"

One of them unzipped his shoulder bag and produced a silver cup. The Hut gave a small shrug and a dismissive wave. "I believe you have something else for me?"

The carry-on bag was pushed forward. One of the men spoke with an Arabic accent. "You must mean this. We have brought you your precious treasure, but we have also discovered its true worth. We had previously spoken of one hundred thousand U.S. dollars. I regret to inform you that the true worth of this treasure is now one million U.S. dollars." The three of them grinned together.

"Yes, I thought people of your breeding would probably gather the true worth of this treasure. I came prepared. Let me summon my assistant. He has the money."

The Hut tapped lightly two times on the stainless steel button affixed to the arm of his chair.

The boy returned. He wore a bright, naive smile. His eyes changed as he stepped off the final stair and entered the stateroom. He flung two silver objects toward the visitors.

The two men sitting on the outsides clawed at the now-shattered sunglasses. A six-inch talon of silver steel gleamed from their eye-sockets. They went to their knees in writhing agony. The man in the middle reached for his breast pocket as the boy produced a huge white smile. Pointed teeth were dripping with devilish strands of saliva. Before the man could bring the Browning automatic up, the youth jumped with savage grace.

The Hut chuckled, his immense belly jumping against his thighs. The boy scissored his teeth into the dark man's neck. There was an audible wet warble as the jagged teeth buried themselves into the throat of the dark man.

Five minutes later, the old captain appeared. He looked at the carnage and dipped his head in revulsion. The boy sat in front of the Hut on the floor. He was still tearing flesh from the open neck wound of his victim.

The Hut dismissively waved a hand at the captain. "Take us to the Strait of Derricks. Our foreign friends have not come to friendly terms with our fine young cannibal."

Chapter 6

The Cable Counties

The analyst on ESPN in Jack's office called our town Tackeyville. Huh.

Mary-Ann still sat at her desk, accepting and directing calls. I had yet another urge to flirt but decided it was better to leave her with a little mystery.

The offices let out onto the street level of the stadium entrance. I groped the orange card in my pocket and thought I should use my go-anywhere license as soon and as much as possible. I was sure the university police would not enjoy my presence on campus and would pass the word to avoid conversations with me.

I turned left and headed into the cavernous underbelly of the stadium. The near wall was painted white and had framed, reserved parking emblems for the athletic director and the head football coach. On the opposite wall, the same nasty-looking prehistoric alligator clutched a football and ran roughshod over the mascots of rival teams within the South Eastern Conference. The alligator wore a jersey with the number one prominent on the front. The jersey was shredded and hung in rags on the beast.

I harkened back to my days at West Point. Our stadium was roughly half the size of this one. And our wall paintings were not even half as vicious.

I went to one of the openings to the stadium and looked out onto the brilliant green grass, inhaling deeply. Nothing says *football* more than newly mowed grass. The turf was a vast carpet, not yet scared by the lines and toils of the players who would follow in the upcoming weeks.

The stadium was empty save a group of twelve or so football players climbing the bleacher seats under the watchful eye of a conditioning coach. I savored their pain. I remembered how much I despised off-season conditioning drills. I was sure at least half the young men dramatized their agony for the sake of the coach. If they could somehow fake the symptoms of heat stroke, the workout would be cut short.

I was reveling in the past when a soggy, wadded ball of paper-towel smacked into the wall inches from my nose. I turned with disciplined slowness and saw a cackling form in the shadows of the tunnel. The man standing there was about six feet eight inches tall but slim as a scarecrow. It was Sal Crimp, a dreaded local redneck hoodlum. Leaning against the wall, two dumpy men joined in his satisfied laughter. I recognized them as Butch Davis and Edvard Garcia, a couple of the losers Crimp had formed into a gang. All three men wore the dingy gray coveralls of the university custodial service. I returned their smug grins.

"Well, well, well, if it isn't our old buddy, Clown. What the hell you doing here on campus, Clown?"

I lapsed without thinking into a barrage of Spanish. "I'm with the humane society and I'm looking for a mean-ass gang of poodle fuckers that's been ravaging the country side."

Garcia had Hispanic ancestry. I hoped he understood what I said. It was obvious from his change of expression he did. With narrowing eyes, he translated what I said to the long tall scarecrow.

Crimp's smile faded and the cackling stopped all together. "What did you say, you injun mutherfucker?"

I spoke in crisp English this time. "I'm hunting the missing trophy, and I was wondering if any of you dog asses had any idea who might have taken it."

Crimp's knuckles grew white around the mop handle in his hand. "Well, I'd say you're trespassing, and these two fellas would back me up. Clown College is in Tallahassee. We don't take to 'tards trespassing on university soil."

I remembered what people called Crimp when they wanted to get his edge up. "Sally… I almost didn't recognize you in your professional attire. I guess all those days in the detention center couldn't rob you of your station in life."

The two dumpy men rolled with laughter at my mentioning Sal's less-complementary street moniker. He shot them a mean look and both stifled their laughter. "That's all I been waiting for. We're gonna bend you up, Cloud. I would've let you go with a warning, but you had to go and call me Sally. Now we're going to fix that high and mighty attitude of yours."

Rule one of street fighting… draw first blood. Without changing my expression, I stepped forward and punched Sally in the throat. His hands immediately were consumed with a light massage of his trachea. Before Davis or Garcia could take in the blow to their fearless leader, I executed a Three Stooges double-eye poke to each man. I took a half-step back. The entire encounter had taken seconds. All three men looked as if they truly were the victims of a very aggressive Stooge.

I kicked the mop handle from Sally's hands, and he fell forward in a face-first dive onto the grimy concrete. The *dumpy's* howled, and both ran to a nearby water fountain to try and rinse the poke from their mangled eye-sockets.

I picked up the mop and stomped on the shaft just above the head. It snapped free, leaving a few strands hanging in long dirty dreadlocks. Sally pulled himself into a sitting position, but he still clung with both hands to his injured throat. He might be speaking again soon, but it would be a little raspy.

I stuck the mop dreads to his loose coveralls. His eyes grew wide, and he fumbled a slap or two at the wet end of the stick. I turned the handle so it caught in his baggy uniform and held fast, fashioning a makeshift joystick. I shoved the stick forward, punching it into his non-existent belly—an attention getter. I pulled him to a standing position and looked into his bulging eyes. "Let's go somewhere a little more private, shall we?"

I led the lean scarecrow behind me like a stray mutt in the noose of a dogcatcher. We left the tunnel for the bowl of the stadium, and I noticed the ball players had succeeded in shortening their workout. They were gone. We had the place to ourselves. I climbed the stadium steps toward the top. Two or three times, Crimp attempted to resist, and his efforts quickly waned when

I pumped the mop handle into his gut again.

We finally stood on the top step of the stadium, some ninety-three rows from the playing field. I pushed Crimp to the back edge and let him get a good look at how high up we were. North/South drive ran about five or six stories directly below us.

"Now *Sally*," I said, "what do you know about the theft of the National Championship trophy?"

Crimp moaned and shook his head. A cornflower of foam formed in the corner of his mouth. Several strands of oily, muddy-looking hair framed his gaunt face. It reminded me of a joke. "You have kind hair there, Sally—the kind that grows wild on a boar's ass. Now tell me what you know, or I'm going to throw you over the side."

A very dim bulb flickered behind his eyes. He measured my intent then swung his head in the same motion. Several dirty wisps of hair clung to his sweaty face. I pushed him backwards with the mop handle to the point where he was bent over the border wall of the stadium. He was standing on tiptoe in order to manage the contortion and still keep his footing.

A hoarse, high-pitched squeal came from the scarecrow. "Don't kill me, Cloud. Please don't kill me."

"My reputation might have exceeded expectations, or, maybe not. You were very rude. I loathe the rude. If you don't have any information for me, then you really don't have anything to live for anyway."

The same high pitch, "No, Cloud. Listen, man. I have something. Pull back and I'll tell you."

"No, I'll have the information now, or I'll just give a little cough, a hiccup really, and your lanky ass will just sail over the top and crack that nice new concrete down below."

"Okaaay… okay. I heard a couple of the other custodians saying Paul Washington saw the men last night."

"Paul Washington? The old man works *here* now?"

"Yeah. Now come on man, let me down."

I saw an osprey riding the high hot winds circling above the stadium. She listed left and came to rest on the edge of a huge nest fixed in the stadium's lights. Watching her, I became aware of something behind me. I turned and saw Butch and Edvard attempting their best stealth-tracking move behind me. I turned and pulled the Colt .357 Python from my shoulder holster and leveled in on the wannabe urban guerrillas.

"Gentlemen! No, that's probably too complimentary. How about assholes? Why don't you two assholes get in a little exercise? Start doing pushups right where you are." The two *dumpy's* minded well. They immediately began pushing up concrete.

With that, I hammered the mop handle with my forearm and it broke in two, releasing Crimp from his precarious yoga. "I appreciate the information. If I need more, I'll know where to look."

I dropped my half of the mop handle and started down the stadium steps. The osprey took off from its nest, and I watched an aerodyne shadow sweep across the field.

Chapter 7

The Gulf of Mexico

The bright white yacht cruised at twelve knots. Painted in deep azure blue letters along the bow was the name, *Big Thunder*. The immensely fat man sat in the stateroom, scraping the very last morsels from the carcasses of nine rock lobsters. A silver gravy boat held melted butter, and a wheel of garlic cheese rested on a cutting board. He first drowned each bite of lobster in butter then added a thick wedge of garlic cheese. The big man wore a tablecloth around his swelled neck, covered in splatters of cocktail sauce from an earlier appetizer and dotted with yellow butter spots and crumbs of rancid cheese.

He was Harry Wyatt Sullivan, a fourth generation South Florida sugar baron. For reasons unknown to anyone but himself, he preferred to be called Wyatt. His ancestors had dredged the Everglades back when they reached as far north as Lake Okeechobee and had been growing sugar cane on the backs of illegal Cubans and Central American refugees since before the days of mosquito spray and air conditioning. Harry Wyatt inherited twenty-three thousand acres of muck only suitable for cane. Several times over the years he had attempted to pocket a politician or two who might give him permission to develop the sugar cane fields into yet more single-family homes. But, big sugar was essential to the market, and the politicians were under increasing pressure from environmentalists to not only let the land be, but to actually turn some of it back to the Everglades swamp.

So Wyatt had given up on developing his cane land. But, he had knowledge of a potentially larger pot of gold than even single-family homes by the beach could provide. This time he was more prepared, and he wouldn't have to deal with public sentiment or even the greed of southern politicians.

Wyatt licked plump doughy fingers and smiled to himself. He looked to the plastic sheet covering an oriental rug on the floor of the stateroom. The young man was curled into a fetal position. He was smeared from head to toe in gore. His belly distended with his gorge, and he clutched two bloody human femurs to his chest as if they were a child's security blanket.

Wyatt clapped his hands twice. The young brown man came awake with lightning speed, and he was standing, almost quivering with energy, before the fat hands broke the second time. He raised a bronzed arm and licked the blood from his sinewy forearm, like a panther washing his jowls.

"Zan, tidy time."

The blood-covered youth looked quizzically at Wyatt, turning his head slightly sideways in a canine inquiry.

The fat man lowered his eyebrows. It looked like two huge black fuzzy caterpillars reaching across a great divide to kiss.

The young man cringed as if stricken. Wyatt clapped again, louder. "Zan, tidy time." This time the command came with deliberate slowness and a threat of things to come if questioned.

Zan knelt to the plastic and began to lap at the coagulating pools of blood.

Chapter 8

Back on Campus

I had known Paul Washington for most of my life. He was a custodian at my high school when I played ball there some years prior. I thought of him as ancient *then* and naturally assumed he was no longer in the land of the living. Obviously, the old man was not only alive and kicking but also was moving up the custodial ladder at the university.

When I was a freshman in high school, I'd been promoted to the varsity team at the end of the junior varsity season. I didn't play, but they used me as a tackling dummy for the big boys that season. One day after practice, the older players had made some sport of taping me inside my locker. I banged around in there for thirty minutes or so trying to get someone's attention. Paul Washington was the only one left in the gym, and after hearing my banging, he came and freed me from the locker and used his pocket knife to cut the tape.

Paul never asked me who did it. He knew I wouldn't tell him, what with honor and all, trying to fit in with the big boys. But remarkably I never had any problems with the older boys after that. They were downright polite to me. I always thought Paul maybe had words with them.

I searched through the tunnel of the stadium until I found a large cleaning and supply closet. I pushed the door open and saw three seasoned men sitting on buckets. I recognized Paul. He truly was the most handsome elder human

I'd ever seen. A fat cigar protruded from the corner of his mouth. All three men looked in my direction. One of the other men said, "This is the custodial office, young fella. What're you looking for?"

Paul looked at his friend and patted his thigh. He turned to me and revealed a huge smile. He might be up in years, but it appeared he'd hung onto all the original dentistry. "It's alright, Mike. I know this young man." He reached behind a small counter covered with clean rags and grabbed another bucket. He turned it upside down and slid it in my direction. "Have a seat, Cloud."

I hitched my jeans and sat down. "How are you, Mr. Washington?"

"It's a might dangerous for a young impatient man like yourself to ask a very old man how he's doing. Mostly you'll get the run down on our busted plumbing and pessimistic outlook for the future."

I smiled at the wisdom I'd forgotten the old man possessed. "Let me try it again. You look real good, Mr. Washington. I'm glad to see you."

A twinkle graced his eyes. "Mike, John, let me have a few minutes with my friend here." It was obvious the old man held sway with the others. Both of his friends got up and shuffled toward the back of the supply room.

"I speck you're here about that trouble we had last night, huh?"

"Still sharp as a tack."

"Well, I tell ya, Cloud, I'm an old man 'cause I always kept my nose clean and out of other people's business. I already been talked to death by a couple of the young bucks from the university police department. I told them I didn't see anything, so why would *you* think I saw something?"

"One of your coworkers, Sal Crimp, said he overheard you mention something to the contrary."

The old man huffed and rolled the damp cigar from one corner of his mouth to the other. "Crimp, huh? Now that's one sorry sack of shit, and he should'a known better than to be telling tales out of school. What happens in the dark here on campus s'pose to stay in the dark."

"Yeah, well this particular happening is pretty important to a whole lot of people. I would surely appreciate it if you could bend your *in the dark* rule and tell me what you saw."

"Wha'd Crimp tell ya?"

"You might say he was under some duress. He didn't have much to say and only told me about you 'cos I was, ahh, very persuasive."

He smiled. "I always know'd you was different. And not 'cos you could play ball the way ya did. By the way, I heard you went up to West Point, played football. Then I got wind you went a little dark, so to speak, in military language."

"Yes, sir."

"You was always a little too slow, but by god, it was fun to watch you hit people."

"I appreciate that, Mr. Washington."

"That's another un. You the only white boy whatever called me Mister. All them years of politeness fixin' to pay off, 'cos I saw them fella's last night."

"What'd you see?"

"Well, for we get to that, do ya know what I do here?"

"No, sir."

Washington's face slackened. He became more relaxed. I reckon not many people refer to him as "sir" either. "I'm the king trash collector here on campus. I spend most of my time around the stadium, but that's just because I like the sports."

I noticed some of Paul Washington's language had slipped from old ghetto country to something much more educated. "So you run the whole campus custodial operation?"

"Yeah, I pretty much run it. I don't get paid for it—they got a white man for that. But yeah, I make sure all of the *pro*-fessors don't have to stoop so low as to dump their own trash baskets."

"That's very impressive. I mean, you are so, ahh, mature."

"Let's not bullshit each other. Old. You mean I'm so old."

Embarrassed, I looked to the polished concrete.

"Well, I didn't tell you all that so you could congratulate a septuagenarian custodian. I told you so you would understand. I saw the man last night who took the trophy. But an apprentice of mine over at the Biotechnology building said she saw two more fella's dressed exactly the same."

Someone thumped the old bulb in my head. "Hey, I read that a student was killed over there at the Biotech building last night."

The old man smiled, very satisfied. He removed the stump of cigar and flicked it into the trashcan at his side. He immediately produced another from a breast pocket. He cut the end with an ivory pocketknife and moistened the tip. He rolled the cut end over his tongue and lit the cigar with a match he raked across the concrete wall.

Chapter 9

Back in my Ram 2500, which I refered to as both transportation and office, I cruised out of the city and toward home. It was a twenty-minute ride, and I used the time to reflect on what I'd learned so far. It wasn't much, but I gathered from my conversation with Paul Washington that the theft of the trophy and the death of the student at the Biotechnology building might be connected.

The events seemed very distant in location and matter, but definitely connected by time. Einstein mathematically proved many years ago that time was the ultimate factor in all situations. To ignore time was to ignore substance. It's a difficult concept to grasp.

Maybe I would run this by my lady friends who lived at roughly the same location as I did. A very wise man once told me that when you are mentally cock-blocked, ask a woman. I was very fortunate in that I would get to ask two.

About eleven miles outside the city, I turned into a short drive. In front of me sat an anonymous forest of pecan trees, the only barrier, a galvanized steel gate on which hung a square metal sign reading, "Posted. No Trespassing."

I pressed one of three garage door openers clipped to the visor. The steel gate swung open, and I pulled through, the gate closing behind automatically. This had been a gift from a past acquaintance who'd recently become a friend.

As always, I felt like Batman passing through the camouflaged entryway to the Bat Cave. The drive took a sharp dip, and I passed through twenty-seven perfectly lined rows of pecan trees that opened into a large field. One hundred or so nondescript cows and one very lucky bull grazed in the field.

I drove through the open meadow and idled alongside the old Angus bull. He raised his huge head and looked solemnly at the truck. I lowered the window and the bull walked over. I took a bag from the passenger seat and produced a wild, double-stemmed carrot. The big Angus rested his slobber-laden face on the side of the truck. I passed the carrot out the window and the bull slowly took it and seemed to grin back in recognition. I waited for him to finish, then passed him the two remaining carrots. I don't think his eyesight immediately improved, but he slapped his tail two long wisps over his ample back then headed for a cow that was obviously in heat.

I drove into the yard of the house through yet another automatic gate and parked in the circle drive. I reached into the back of the truck and removed a block of white butcher paper from the cooler. I was grilling, and this meant beef—thick Black Angus steak. I went to the kennel where our Jack Russell terrier jumped twice as high as his short stature. I opened the gate and Jake dashed from the confines of his lavish home into a dead run. He came back and savored deeply the smells I had picked up during the day. I rubbed his ears furiously and gave him a small piece of steak I cut from the contents of the package. He ran to the tires of the diesel and marked it as his own.

I walked up the railroad ties that served as steps to our home, Jake in tow. I set the steaks on the kitchen counter, gave the dog a true doggy treat, and went to my study/closet to undress.

I emerged wearing gray running shorts. Jake was jumping with anticipation for the coming run. We filed through the fenced opening, a light coat of sweat already gleaming on my forehead.

Chapter 10

I generally kept to the fence line of my property when running. If I completed the entire circuit, it rounded out to about five miles. Emma and Blue, my two lady friends, were both avid runners and kept the path mowed with a large John Deere mower. Having done this for several years, I knew where all of the old potholes and stumps were buried. But the occasional fresh cow pile made for a necessary attention to detail.

I was on the backside of the property halfway through the run. I ran parallel to the landing strip. I no longer had any plane. My Beechcraft came to a fiery death a few months prior. Everything seemed in order and satisfyingly lonely. Running past the small hangar, I entered a small low stand of water oaks and cypress. Jake was the forward cavalry, checking out the fence line and every new, natural obstacle.

Jake pointed to a cluster of fallen limbs overgrown with high weeds. He stretched his lithe body taught and let his curious nose feel out the bramble without endangering his hindquarters. With a fierce batting of wings and a warning warble from the gobbler, a covey of wild turkeys burst from the bramble. Jake launched into a chorus of furious yet unfortunate bitch-like barks.

The sun had just dipped behind the trees and left that curiously southern haze which comes from melting humidity. I was creating my *own* humidity. I was positively drenched in sweat.

I made the turn toward home. Up ahead, I saw the dog find a concrete water trough. He hurtled the three-foot edge of the trough and dived head-first into the shallow pool. Dogs didn't sweat. They panted to relieve themselves of the heat. My dog was also practical. If a cool pool of water was evident, he partook. Emma and Blue disapproved of letting him jump into the troughs, but I thought it was only because he tended to smell moldy afterwards, as opposed to what they said, was a drowning threat.

We passed under the lone palm, which signaled the end of our run. I cooled down by walking back and forth between our house and the palm.

The back of the yard dipped down to a white sand beach bordering Lake Santa Fe. I saw the outline of my Boston Whaler against the dock.

Chapter 11

The yard was an unbelievable hand-made garden. There was every manner of bush, plant, flower and vegetable growing. Many were several seasons old and grew voluntarily. Others were newly planted and required constant attention. Emma and Blue were in the yard gardening, working at the only pace they knew of life—furious.

These were not pretty gardening women by Martha Stewart standards. They were serious, though not particularly talented. They both sported cut-off jeans. Blue wore a sheer black swimsuit top and a bright red bandana. Emma wore a sweat-soaked white halter-top and large floppy straw hat. Both were barefoot and covered in streaks of dirt and plant parts.

Jake announced our arrival by rushing into the newly turned soil, wiggling and wagging, hungry for female attention. I passed through the fence and both women looked up and smiled. They deposited all manner of gardening tools in the wagon attached to the mower.

We met at the end of a long vegetable-laden garden bordered by large lime rocks. Blue smashed herself against me in what she calls a pickup hug. This means that in addition to arm engulfment, she uses her legs to wrap and climb me like a tall pine. Emma's embrace was slightly subtler, yet equally arousing in sticky, sweaty friction. For that moment there was nothing else, just the three of us basking in our mutual love for each other. We collapsed to the ground in a laughing heap. The dog picked up on our intensity and wrestled his shadow in a violent yet playful dance.

Little was said, we mostly just enjoyed the sanctuary. Blue popped up and grabbed three bottles of Budweiser from a cooler. Bumping the mouths of the bottles together I said, "To sweat sex." We all took a long uninterrupted pull from the bottles. I watched their smooth throats swell and relax with each gulp.

I grilled the steaks on the back porch. We sat in the shallows of Lake Santa Fe drinking the cold beer. The steaks crackled and wept a pungent aroma of pure animal lust. I vaguely remember eating the steaks. I long remember the ample dessert.

Chapter 12

The Middle Eastern Country of Qatar

The slight, dark form of Jamil Rancon Facon stood beside an open well. Ripped and shredded rags of sackcloth lay about his ankles. He repeatedly swept a rough horsehair whip over one shoulder and then the other. His back was streaked with blood from open wounds. He was a Muslim, and he was in mourning. The tradition was to dress in a common garment made of flour sacks and to continuously inflict pain on oneself for a period of twenty-four hours. The body was to be made pure and free of grief by exacting physical punishment for an extended period of time. Facon was in his twelfth hour of the ritual.

It was common for the mind to wander to thoughts of revenge. This was not the intent of the practice. A man was to purge his thoughts of anything but the pain and torture associated with the death of a loved one. You were to allow all of the sorrow to seep out through the lashed, bleeding areas of your body.

Jamil Rancon Facon was a disciplined man and adhered to the teachings of Allah. Yet, he could not keep his mind from wandering to the torment he would visit on the men who killed his only son. He'd desperately tried to convince his son to forgo an education in the United States. America was surely a land of opportunity, and the educational system was of the highest caliber, but the U.S. was also the land of greed, low disposable values, and violence.

Tales of savages on other continents kept children in America in line. Their bedtime stories included tales of Arabian knights who truly practiced the Old Testament. An eye for an eye and the severing of a hand that stole. But nothing in the old storybooks and fables could compare to the real-life drama that played out on Main Street USA. He had begged his son to matriculate into the fine universities of Europe if he felt he must leave home. But Amul Instad Facon was as stubborn a young man as his father had been. He believed a man's education wasn't only science, literature and math, but travel, diverse cultures, and a sense of the social barometer around the globe.

Now he was dead. Dead, never to live the life of a prince, the destiny which had awaited him in his native Qatar. Jamil's hatred of the Americans boiled hotter than ever. He also reserved a large dose of the white-hot rage for himself at not being able to convince his naive son. He should have forced the lad to stay home no matter what.

The bunched muscles of his forearm swelled against the leather of the whip. He increased his intensity and speed. Perhaps he was not inflicting enough pain to purge his soul. Twelve hours more, maybe, then he could forgive and follow the teachings of Allah.

Chapter 13

Strait of Derricks, The Gulf of Mexico, Florida

The yacht idled to stop, easing into a ready slip alongside a pumping oil derrick. The derrick wasn't one of the king-sized monsters which lay off the coasts of Texas and Alaska, but it was the largest in the Strait of Derricks—and the largest in Florida waters. It was built long ago, but with excellent engineering to protect it from the seasonal hurricanes that swept through the Gulf.

In a ready animal crouch, Zan sat on his haunches near the bow of the *Big Thunder.* The moment the boat came to full stop, he leapt across and tied the lines fore and aft. He pounced back to the deck and grabbed a plastic garbage bag, weighted with a cinder block. He leaned over the railing and threw the bag of bones and dead tissue into the eraser that was the Gulf.

A faint *whupping* sound emerged from somewhere overhead. Zan turned his eyes toward the sky and made out a small dot on the far reaches of the horizon. He tilted his head slightly sideways to get a better ear on the encroaching noise.

The captain came on deck. He made the approaching helicopter and looked with hesitant dread toward the boy. "Zan, crate."

Zan curled his lips and showed his filed teeth. The captain, Deke Joyner, held little sympathy for the young man, but what he did feel paled in comparison to his fear of the savage beast. He produced a key chain remote from his pocket and pressed a button. The steel collar around the cannibal's neck lit up with a powerful shock wave. Zan collapsed to the deck, both hands and feet trying to pry the collar from his neck. It was of no use; the collar was soldered tight around his muscular neck.

Zan writhed with agony for a long moment. Then he jumped to his feet, his chest huffing. Tendrils of sweat streaked his body and he quaked with anger. Deke Joyner widened his eyes and gave a shrug as if to say, *See? That's what you get when you don't obey.*

Joyner dangled the remote between thumb and forefinger. Again he gave the command. "Zan, crate."

With a sneer of hate, Zan turned and trudged toward the steps. He went downstairs and to a large wooden crate at the end of the hallway, one door away from the galley. He gripped the wooden posts lining the door of the crate and clinched his fingers as tightly as possible around the splinter-ridden timber. He bit deeply into his lower lip and a trickle of blood drooled down his chin. Zan opened the door, stepped inside, and pulled the door shut. A faint electronic beep came from the lock of the crate.

A single tear ran down the face of the young brown man.

Chapter 14

The helicopter hovered over the platform of the oil derrick. Thick wisps of saltwater caught in the wind circled the landing pad. Deke Joyner waved an orange flag, signaling for the craft to land. A moment later the helicopter bounced on the pad and eased back its engines.

With the blades slowing, a dark-haired woman unfolded from the cockpit. She wore opaque octagonal sunglasses and a confident smear of greed across her acne-dimpled face. Her face was not attractive in any way, and she didn't pretend it was. Instead, she possessed a stacked body. *Power* was her aphrodisiac.

Kari Vilano-Lobos was a shark hunter in the most extreme manner. She didn't seek the sharp-finned, perfectly evolved space in evolution that ran wild in all the earth's waters. She hunted opportunity and weakness. She was at the top of the food-chain of lawyers and at the bottom of humanity. Over the past nine years, she had worked for four different oil companies. She had built a sizable reputation for bringing fear, intimidation, and a willingness to do whatever it took to get what she wanted.

Vilano-Lobos was the signature counsel when the British Petroleum catastrophe wrecked the Gulf coast. Needless to say, she was the defense's most potent weapon.

She covered the distance between the chopper and the gangplank of the yacht with determined grace. Deke Joyner felt an arctic wind blow towards him as she approached. He was definitely more afraid of this Medusa than even the ravenous cannibal in the yacht's hold.

He dared not speak to the icy form. He even looked out toward the ocean when she passed by him without a word or glance.

Chapter 15

Harry Wyatt Sullivan watched the sinister form of Kari Vilano-Lobos pass through the stateroom door and cross the polished floor. To most men she was the definition of evil, enveloped in a shroud of greed and power. Wyatt was not one of these men. He leaned his massive bulk to the side and produced a thunderous wet fart. The length and volume of the gaseous excretion was impressive. He smiled a fat slobbery grin and licked his beefy lips. He inhaled with gusto, drawing the noxious gasses deep into his barrel chest. "Kari, darling, how very nice to see you again."

Vilano-Lobos knew the crude expulsion was meant to demean her, to make her seem trivial and unworthy of manners. She ignored the smell and the fart altogether. Leaning across the desk she extended her hand toward Wyatt. He knew she meant for him to shake it, instead he took the small hand in his own damp palm and slurped a kiss.

Kari suppressed a shutter of utter revulsion and took her seat. She knew men like Wyatt needed to be stroked, to be feared, and to be flattered. At the same time, she was aware of the fact that all men find danger and the dark side attractive. She crossed one stockinged leg over the other with panther grace. "Mr. Sullivan…"

"I told you, when we're alone, call me Harry Wyatt."

"Alright, Harry Wyatt. You know I thought this meeting to be dangerous. But I see you have made ample preparations for concealing our rendezvous from prying eyes."

"Yes, well, Kari darling, wealth does have its privileges and foremost among them is privacy. What do you have for me?" He smacked his lips.

From the leather briefcase, Vilano-Lobos pulled a small video camera and a single zippered file folder. As she raked open the zipper, the captain entered the room. Wyatt spoke to him with great eagerness.

"Deke, it appears I am going to watch a movie. Would you get me a bag of popcorn, some hot dogs, nachos, and maybe an assortment of Milk Duds, Goobers, and Raisinets? Kari, what would you like to drink?"

"Mr. Sullivan... I mean Harry Wyatt, it's really not a movie, more like a series of slides, and it will only run maybe five minutes."

"I don't see your point, Kari darling. Again, what would you like to drink?"

Realizing her snafu and understanding that to decline would shout to the heavens what an immensely fat tub of shit he was, she said. "A Diet Coke maybe."

"Make that two Coca Cola's. I'll have one as well," Wyatt said, ignoring the "diet" as he always did.

Chapter 16

As quickly as Kari could assemble her equipment, Deke Joyner spread the array of junk food out on the desk. Wyatt grabbed a box of Milk Duds, and leaning his head back, he dumped the entire box into his mouth. Kari turned to ask where the light switch was so she could dim them for the slide presentation. What she saw was a man disguised as a rock crusher, mechanically slamming his jaws together. A thick, fecal-looking drool trailed down the corners of his mouth. Was he doing this to intentionally disgust her? *No*, she thought to herself, *it has always been this way for Harry Wyatt Sullivan.* She was sure at even five or six years of age, Wyatt had no need for self-restraint. He was not a little boy who would beg mom for a candy bar at the check-out lane. He was a lad who sneaked behind the maid and the cook into the pantry and gorged himself on boxes of sweets and whole packages of cookies. His gluttonous nature didn't only extend to food and drink, but to every facet of his life. He needed more money, more power, more toys. *He's the perfect American*, she thought to herself. *He doesn't understand the word "or." His world is entirely populated with "and."*

Now, owning the vast sugar cane fields of South Florida wasn't enough. He wanted what was on the surface *and* what was underneath.

This didn't bother her at all, because she was an "and" person as well. A taker, in the strictest definition of the word. She and Harry Wyatt Sullivan would take as much as they possibly could and leave the carcass of a hollowed-out peninsula for others to deal with.

She finally located the switch and dimmed the lights. She inserted a jump-drive and a series of pictures of the cane fields and surrounding South Florida landscape ticked across the screen. With each, she narrated the precise location and seismic numbers that painted a picture of the earth below the surface. Charts of sonar resonance followed, backing up the findings.

Behind her, Wyatt gargled a child-like chuckle. Each picture followed with a display of glee from the fat man. She could see through the shadows his rapid-fire hands grabbing fists full of candy, popcorn, and a hot dog here and there. The only pause in the feast was the intermittent long sucking sound he made as he pulled what seemed like gallons of Coca-Cola through a beaten straw.

The presentation was short, and minutes later, she turned the lights back to normal. Wyatt sat behind his desk like a fat-happy puppy. He lapped chocolate from between his meaty fingers. His entire face was covered in a dark brown smear. He looked to her as if he had been giving CPR to the south end of a northbound rhinoceros.

"So, as you can plainly see, Harry Wyatt, your suspicions have been confirmed. The oil is there, perhaps in quantities only rivaled in the Middle East. But our problem remains. The government will never issue permits for drilling so close to the Everglades and the beaches. They won't risk the tourist trade. They know seepage will undoubtedly occur."

"Kari dear, while you've been finding our black gold, I've been hard at work finding answers to those very problems. Indeed, oil drilling will not be permitted on the Florida mainland within our lifetimes, but it has already been permitted here in the Gulf for many years. And we are days away from the realization of a pipeline running from my sugar cane fields to this very location, this seemingly normal derrick."

Kari Vilano-Lobos was rarely surprised by what men could do when they had no conscience. But she truly was astounded at what Harry Wyatt was telling her—that it had already been accomplished.

He said, "As to the matter of seepage, which would alert the authorities as well as the geriatric land owners of South Florida to the windfall possible if oil was discovered in large quantities, I have recently made a new friend.

"A bright young man up at the University of Florida recently discovered, or rather engineered, a bacterium—a microscopic little bug, which as a matter of its respiration devours crude oil that has settled into either salt or fresh water."

Kari stared at Wyatt with true awe. She watched as he grabbed four Oreo cookies and put all of them in his mouth at once. Could such a slob of a man also be brilliant enough to pull this off? She said, "Then I would say the young man from the university is going to be richer than all of us. When he makes the bug available, the oil companies and governments from around the world will beat a path to his door and throw countless billions at him."

"Yes well, that's exactly what could have happened, but he was the kind of young man who would have given it away for the better good—a true socialist. I relieved the dear lad of his discovery, and, in addition to using it to mine the oil and natural gas from South Florida, I will patent the bug and sell it myself."

"If he is a man of conscience, surely he will cry foul and bring the authorities straight to our doorstep?"

"Again, that is precisely what *would've* happened. You're quite the visionary, Kari darling. Alas, the natural order of evolution ran its course. Survival of the fittest, if you will. I didn't just relieve the bright boy of his valuable bug. I relieved him of his life as well."

Kari Vilano-Lobos was impressed. She saw past the immense bulk and gaggle of chins. She felt a steamy dampness down below. It was surely the desire for the dollar sign.

"So my dear, shall we have dessert to toast our coming success?"

He groaned with effort as he lifted his nearly five hundred pounds of blubber. He fairly waddled, huffing and sweating to an immense couch against the wall of the stateroom. Kari was surprised to see Wyatt was nude from the waist down. His flabby legs jiggled as he collapsed on the couch. A small turtlehead of a penis showed below the shadow of the fat man's stomach.

Kari knew this was part of the "and" philosophy of life. She rose and pulled the black dress over her head. With her acne-ravaged face, she'd never seen sex as a pleasure, but simply a tool to get what she wanted. She pushed the stockings down her legs as seductively as she knew how. Wyatt's face lit up with the coming delight. She smiled a wicked smile, thinking of the possibilities if the fat man had a heart attack from exertion. Licking her finger, she circled a large plump nipple and prepared to climb Mount Sullivan.

Chapter 17

Back in Cable County

Mame Blake was Paul Washington's apprentice. He said she was quite a character. This was something of a compliment coming from Paul. It was late on Thursday evening when I called her. The phone didn't even ring before a gruff voice with no female resonance answered. "Mame."

"Mrs. Blake, my name is Cloud, and I got your name from Paul Washington."

"Yeah, he told me you might come a callin'."

"So you know I'm working on the missing trophy case."

"Yep."

I could tell right away, Mame was not one for small talk. "I was wondering if I might meet with you tomorrow morning and ask a few questions."

"Honey child, tomorrow is Friday. For me that means fishin'."

"Maybe I could meet you for breakfast before you go?"

"No, we'll be heading out a might early, a'fore five."

Great, I thought to myself, *she's obviously the next link in the chain and now I'm going to have to wait.* Putting a little pleading in my voice I said, "It's very important, Mrs. Blake, and I would really appreciate a little of your time."

During the following pause, I could sense she had cupped her hand over the phone and was probably talking to someone else.

"Cloud, you a fisherman?" She said.

Feeling a common bond, I said, "Go every chance I get."

"Well I'm not gonna change my plans, so if you want some of my time tomorrow, I reckon you'll just have to go fishin' with me."

Doo-wah-diddly fuck. Now I have to waste a whole day sitting on some muddy bank or worse yet an overpass bridge, hoping for a bite from a Bream or Catfish. I stifled the thought. "That would be just fine. Where should I meet you?"

"Do you know the Lawless Diner... Molly's?"

I felt a slim relief wash over. Maybe I could get my information without wasting the entire day. "I know the Lawless. I eat there just about every day."

"Well, Molly is a good friend a mine. We'll stop there in the morning a'fore we go for ice. You be there at quarter to five, ready to fish, and that'll give us plenty of time to talk about whatever you want."

I grimaced at the trap I'd walked into. Trying to fake a pleasant tone I said, "That would be fine. I'll see you there."

Chapter 18

I'm a night person, so when the alarm went off at four a.m. I didn't even hear it. The noise was plenty enough to wake Emma and Blue though. They alternately shook me and demanded I silence the damn thing and get my ass out of bed. I rolled over in a sleep coma and slapped the snooze. Nine minutes later, the same siren-like wail screeched from the clock. I was already back in the dusty fingers of the sand man. A cold talon of a toenail raked the back of my leg. This was Blue's way of warning me—another alarm might result in even more serious pain.

The ladies usually exit the bed prior to me. So I fumbled and cursed as I flailed the bed covers. I grudgingly slid myself out from between them and sat on the end of the bed. How in the hell could I have agreed to meet someone before the sun came up? Maybe I would just crawl back between the warm bodies and fake forgetfulness.

I looked over my shoulder and met four slightly open eyes. The message from those eyes pronounced, "WARNING, ENTER AT YOUR OWN RISK."

I left the bedroom and went to the condo where prince Jake, rules. He bounded from the open door as if the world was on day one. I thought to myself how nice it would be if I could wake up with such fire in my belly.

Fifteen minutes later, I was in my truck and sullenly driving the old country road leading back into town. I'd packed my fishing gear, but was sure it was far too sophisticated for where I'd be today. I punched the radio button on the steering wheel and The Wood Brothers explained life for the "Luckiest Man."

When I reached Molly's, I was fifteen minutes late. The fish were waiting, and my tardiness was evident by the scorn I saw on the faintly lined face of a fiftyish, beautiful woman.

She stood beside a four-door Ford F-250 pickup hitched to an enormous boat gleaming with the early morning dew. I hurried to park the truck and grab my gear. She saw me coming and walked toward me with her head shaking and her hands waving.

"Boy, you auta' know better than be late for fishin'. Put that puny shit back in your truck. Wha'd you think, we gonna go fish off a bridge or somethin'?"

Shame and surprise reddened me. I truly had acted as if we would be fishing with cane poles and wigglers. This woman was loaded for bear. I ducked back to the bed of the truck and put my rod and reel in.

One of the doors of the Ford opened and Paul Washington turned to face me with all of his white grillwork. "Hustle up, boy. The fish ain't patient, and if I miss one by a minute, I'll skin you alive."

The window on the back door of the cab slide down and the athletic director, Jack Malloy hung his head out. "Yeah, Cloud, get a move on."

I had completely underestimated this fishing trip. This woman was packing a boat big enough for marlin and she had the athletic director of a large southern university as a deck hand.

I struggled, tucking my tail between my legs and trying not to trip over my self-superior ego. As I hurried toward the truck, I thought to myself how I'd always hated it when someone who was obviously racist said, "Hey, I'm not racist or anything. Hell some of my best friends are black." Now I thought, "Suck on that white boy."

In the cab of the truck, the conversation was lively. These people were obviously old friends. I was the outsider. My opinion was not asked for.

Twenty minutes later, we passed through Palatka, a redneck hive in the mid-eastern edge of the Cable counties. We pulled into an ancient corner gas station. Jack jumped from the cab and began filling the tanks of the boat.

Mame and Paul entered the store. They bought all manner of cold cuts, two loafs of white Wonder Bread, and two cases of Sam Adams Summer Ale.

Before I could figure my role in all of this, the trio were back in the cab of the truck. Mame passed a bag of beef jerky around. I grabbed a piece and began to gnaw at what seemed like a boot heel.

***

An hour later, we were on the rough Atlantic. The boat jumped and slammed back into the surf with teeth-jarring intensity. Mame was at the wheel. Paul and Jack were rigging poles with new monofilament line. Then Paul went to the wheelhouse and began talking to Mame. I approached Jack. "You seem like an old hand. How often you do this?"

"Hey buddy, if Mame Blake asks you to go fishing with her, you *go*. She may be a custodian back on campus, but in the world of fishing, she is the damn master of the universe. They usually ask me out around once a month."

I looked up and Paul Washington was coming back. I met him halfway between the transom and the aft of the cabin. "Paul, what the hell have you gotten me into?"

"Boy, I'm seventy-four years old. One of my most favorite things in all the world is to see surprise on a confident young man like yourself. You should'a seen the look on old Jack's face the first time we brought him out."

"Who the hell is Mame?" I said.

A glimmer shone from Paul's eyes as he said, "For starters, she's Mrs. Paul Washington."

I looked at Paul with sincere awe. "She must be twenty years younger than you."

"Twenty-one to be exact. But what the hell does that have to do with anything?"

"Well nothing, I guess." I said regretting my comment.

I was no longer groggy from sleep. I'd had too many surprises for it to be only seven in the morning.

Chapter 19

It was noon before I had a chance to get close to the tornado that was Mame Blake. We'd caught our limit of dolphin and Wahoo, seven keeper grouper, and a mess of red snapper. I can't even remember how many other fish we threw back.

She had passed the captain duties onto Paul. He steered the boat back to shore with Jack Malloy at his side gleaning seafaring hints. It was to be an hour ride home.

Mame sat in a reclining captain's chair on the stern. She alternately sipped a beer and gazed at the receding horizon. I tentatively sat on the large white Igloo cooler filled with our day's catch. She smoked a slim, ratty cigar.

I raised my voice above the engines and the sea. "I was wondering if we could talk about what you saw the other night?"

"Well, I was wondering when you'd get around to it." Her dialect had shifted like Paul's the day before, from ghetto country to something much more educated.

"What did you see?"

"I was working in the Biotechnology Building late that night. It's part of my normal rounds, and I knew the boy who got himself killed. He was always in there way after all the rest had gone home, except sometimes he had a buddy who worked with him."

"Was the other fella there as well?"

"No, he was by himself. We'd already cleaned the floor where he was working, so normally I would've had no reason to go back up there. Thing was, when I went to leave, I noticed the door was unlocked, which was strange. Every once in a while, one of my people will leave it open by mistake. I'm always having to get on their behinds for the simple things."

"Who else has a key?"

"Whole lotta people got keys. All the professors that work in the building, the rest of the research crew, and of course my staff."

"So anyone might have left the door unlocked?"

"No, I locked the door myself, and when I checked the log on who might've already left, there wasn't single name unaccounted for."

"How can you be so sure?"

She looked at me with a little frustration. "On a count I been cleanin' that damn building for going on eighteen years now, and I always make sure everyone has left their stations so we won't disturb them."

I backpedaled, trying to cover my suspicious affront. "I didn't mean to imply you don't know your job."

"Course ya did. I understand you have your job to do, but don't go and try acting like you is one of us."

I felt stunned. I'm not a racist, some of my best friends are black.

She continued, "What'd you expect when I asked you to go fishin' with me? I'll tell ya what ya expected—ya thought you'd pull inta Molly's and find a broken down seventy's model Cadillac, probably some gaudy shade a maroon or pink. Ya thought there a'd be cane poles stickin' out the rear window and a coupl'a rusty cans of red wigglers sittin' in the floorboard. Ya figured we'd be sittin' on the bank of some public creek, or better yet, we'd be hangin' our lines from a concrete overpass bridge. Ya expected an old black cleaning woman, who probably can't see for shit, who'd be excited when a fancy-assed private investigator, a white one to boot, took some notice of some phantom she says she saw. And now that I called ya on it, you probably gonna tell me you ain't like other white folk, why some of your best friends are niggers. Cept'n you'll call'em black whiles you in front of me."

And down the stretch they come, it's Embarrassment, and Rage running neck and neck. Embarrassment takes a half body lead with only two furlongs to go, now

Rage raises his head, and what is this? Oh my. Ladies and gentlemen, the jockeys for both horses are whipping each other with a rabid focus. It's Embarrassment, no it's Rage, no Embarrassment, no it's Rage, oh for Christ's sake, it's too close to call at the line. It's a photo finish. The only thing we can say for sure, ladies and gentlemen, is that the overwhelming loser here is Cloud. Cloud the hypocrite, Cloud the damned, Cloud the closet racist.

"Listen here, you self-righteous…" I caught myself. "You listen to me. I'm damn sure not perfect, but don't go holding a mirror to my face that you yourself can't look in. It damn well wouldn't a mattered if I was pure of thought, mind, body, and spirit. I look white, so you had your little speech ready from the start." I stood from the cooler and turned toward the rear of the boat. *Fuck her*, I thought. *I'll figure this damn thing out without her.*

"Cloud!"

I turned with as much contempt on my face as possible. If she wanted to play persecutor/victim, then I would rise to the role. A bottle of beer sailed through the air from an underhand toss. I almost backed out of the boat before I caught myself and then the cold beer. The woman released a coal-black cloud from her cigar and smiled, revealing unbelievable even, white teeth.

"Now that we got that shit out'a the way, let's get down to business."

I was charmed. Despite my earlier feelings, this woman was wise, and she had pushed buttons I didn't know I had. I smiled, popped the top of the beer, and raised it to her.

"Now sit your big ass down and don't interrupt me."

"Yes, ma'am."

"That's better. Now as I was saying, I went back up to the floor where that boy was working. When I walked into the room, I seen two men dressed all in black with hoods over their heads, like Ninjas or sompthin'. I ducked behind a desk, and right then I saw one of 'em cut the poor boy's head clean off."

I looked adequately startled.

"Didn't know that did ya? They cut his head off and then packed everything on his desk in a big black bag. They wasn't there another minute, just took the stuff off the desk and ran out the door, not ten feet from where I was crouched down. Scared me ten years older. I can tell ya old Paul had his hands full of some comfort lovin' that night. I grabbed the phone and called 911 for the campus *po*leece. They came and asked all the same questions you have, but they were a might more condescending. When I told Paul about it, he shared his story, and we figured the men were in cahoots. Things like that just don't happen on the university campus, especially all in the same night."

I waited to make sure I wasn't interrupting. She threw the ragged stump of the cigar into the ocean and lit another.

I had what I came for. Time to become the brilliant conversationalist. "How did you come to know Paul?"

"A'fore you was born, Paul there was *the* bull *Rattler*. He was the tastiest piece of eye-candy any black woman ever laid eyes on. Did ya know he still holds the record for tackles in a season for Florida A&M University?"

I searched my memory, and a beam of light showed through. "You mean Paul is "The Butcher" Washington?"

The old woman just grinned back at me with satisfaction. "Sides, Washington comes to fish with a mighty long pole."

That was surely a little more than I needed to know. I turned with some crimson on my cheeks, but also with a manly congratulating smile.

Chapter 20

It was Saturday. I realized this as the first strands of sunlight edged through the curtains of our bedroom. I rolled to my right and noticed the alarm clock beaming fourth with a solid digital 10:15. With my early entry into the land of the living the day before, I felt obligated to rest at least this late. And now my only thought was food.

I got up and made my way to the kitchen, where there were instructions from the ladies on heating up a very nutritious omelet they'd prepared earlier. I got the omelet from the refrigerator and set it on the counter. I poked at it with a sullen fork. No meat… typical. I opened all of the cupboards and the refrigerator at least five times before I was satisfied there truly was no better option. I shoved the limp vegetarian omelet into the microwave, slammed the door, and set the time.

As the omelet underwent its nuclear transformation, I scratched my way to the bathroom where I unloaded and washed my face. There were two things on the day's agenda. One was talking to Larry Red, the research partner for the dead student. The other was an outing with the ladies that we'd planned some weeks prior.

In addition to reheating instructions for the omelet, the note on the counter reminded me of our date to pick up a new puppy that afternoon. Our little family had suffered a tragic loss a few months before, and I felt it was mostly my fault.

If I got going, I could find Larry Red before noon, question him, and be back in time for our date to pick up the new puppy. I inhaled the omelet, showered, and headed into town.

***

Larry lived in the married student-housing unit on the west side of campus. Student housing was made up of large dorm rooms stacked three high and seven wide, making "L" shapes. I had gotten his address from a friend of Emma's, who worked in the admissions department.

I approached his ground-floor apartment and noticed a child's bicycle, still bearing training wheels. I knocked on the door even though there was a bell. People always seem to respond to knocking with more efficiency than bells. An attractive, although unkempt, hippie-looking woman answered the door. "Yes?"

"Hello, my name is Cloud, and I'm looking for Larry Red." I could hear a small girl singing in the background.

"May I ask what you would like to see him about?"

"I have some questions about his research partner, Amul Instad Facon."

"Are you with the police?"

"No, I'm a private detective."

"Do you have some sort of identification?"

I took out my State of Florida license. She cracked the screen door a millimeter, and I passed the card through. She stood there for a full minute reading every line of the license. This was obviously one very cautious, skeptical lady. After satisfying herself of my authenticity, she passed the card back through and then pulled the door completely closed.

"Do you carry a gun?"

"Yes."

"Then you cannot come into my home. I do not believe in firearms of any kind, or people who carry them."

I was growing tired of this game. "You don't believe people carry guns, or you don't believe guns exist?"

She gave me her best "I pity you" expression and said, "That's just the type of adolescent response I would expect from a man who feels the need to carry a gun. Larry is not here, so would you please leave."

I stood there looking at her through the screen door. I must have cracked a slight smile.

"And don't think you can charm me. I am an educated, independent, free-thinking woman. I'm not interested in your testosterone."

Perhaps the smile conveyed more than I intended. Before I could offer a snappy comeback, which I'm sure would have won her over, a small lanky man walked up behind me. He was carrying two sacks of groceries and peered between them. "Can I help you?"

In the time I turned around, the inner door slammed shut. "Are you Larry Red?"

"Who are you?"

"My name is Cloud. I'm a looking into the circumstances surrounding the death of Amul Instad Facon."

"Do you have some sort of identification?"

This was fun. I was hoping we could keep this up for hours. Had these people been living in the Soviet Union or something? I stifled a sigh and handed over the same license. He took the same long minute she had, inspecting each and every line, then handed it back to me.

"I'm sorry. I can't help you."

"Well, if I could just ask a few questions…"

"No. Maybe I misspoke. I *won't* help you."

There was a carton of eggs on top of one of the bags. I remembered a time when me and my friends from high school thought the most unbelievably fun thing in the world was playing war—with raw eggs as ammunition. I considered introducing Larry Red to this game. He probably wouldn't appreciate it, but I would feel a whole lot better.

"May I ask why?"

"You may, but I feel no obligation to comment."

"You were a friend of Amul Instad Facon, weren't you?"

"This conversation is completed. Please remove yourself, or I will be forced to call the campus police."

Maybe if I took the eggs and gave one to him and let him have first shot.

I would close my eyes and give him a freebee. "Larry, please don't scare me. I'm liable to shrivel up with fear."

"Listen… Mr. Jeremiah St. Cloud. You don't know what you are getting into, so please leave me and my family alone."

"Have threats been made to you or yours?"

He pushed past me and fumbled the door open. He leaned his head inside and spoke to his wife. "Free, honey would you call the campus police and tell them some solicitor is aggravating us?"

I considered his statement, and then I saw the funny part. "Your wife's name is Free?"

He looked back at me with hatred and defiance. "Yes, and just so you know, I am a fourth degree black belt in the oblique doctrine of jiu jitsu."

"Your wife's name is Free… Red?"

"That does it, Mr. St. Cloud. I can tell from your tone, you are just one rude Neanderthal. Prepare to defend yourself." He said this as he set the two bags of groceries on the ground.

I don't step on small bugs. Even when a stray spider or cricket enters my home, I'm a catch-and-release man. I held my hands up in a conciliatory fashion. Taking a business card from my jeans pocket, I tossed it into one of the grocery bags. Larry Red was going through some preliminary stretching exercise that I'm sure he'd learned in *class*. I turned and walked back to the truck.

Chapter 21

On my way home, I stopped off at Pet Smart, the local doggy Disney World. I can remember not too many years ago, before I met Blue and Emma, I thought dogs were animals—pets. But the ladies have impressed upon me the true nature of dogs. I try to act tough at times, but I do love Jake. And I surely did love his partner Jack before he went on to the happy hunting-ground. I looked at the shopping baskets racked by the door. I passed them and got a full-size grocery cart. We were, after all, going to get a new puppy.

When I was a kid growing up, we had dogs. Dogs, plural. We had many. I still remember most of them, but from the first day we got them, I knew they were temporary. Dogs lived outside in my youth. When they did something wrong, you kicked them, or at least my old man did. And by god… a doggy bath was something they did on their own with their tongue.

Oh my, have things changed. I bathe Jake at least once a week, and he has a condo inside the house and plush digs in the yard.

I pushed the cart down one isle then another, only choosing the most mandatory items for bringing a new puppy home. And, of course, I couldn't let Jake get jealous. He needed some comfort items as well.

Do dogs give a damn what shape or form their treats come in? Do you think a dog likes bacon-shaped snaps or biscuits? I don't think the dog gives one hoot. This store was made for people—people who love animals. We impose our interests on them. When I buy food or treats for Jake at the grocery store, I feel I'm giving him second-class treatment. And what of that?

I noticed there's a whole row of pet supplies at the local grocery, and when I compared it to the items for human babies, it came up half-short.

I thought all of this as I wheeled my overflowing cart to the counter complete with gum-smacking cashier. She was probably seventeen and thought I was Dr. Doolittle. "Wow, you must really love your dog. What kind do you have?"

I blushed, "Jack Russell."

"No kidding. They're my favorite. I'm saving up to get one myself."

I was as much embarrassed by my overindulgence as my conversation with this nymph. "I also need to buy a collar tag."

She punched in the numbers while going on about her love affair with Jack Russell terriers. "The total comes to $159. 97. Will that be cash, check, or charge?"

I looked over my shoulder to make sure no one heard what an unbelievably huge ass I was making of myself. "Cash."

"Holly-shmolly, you're a frequent buyer. You've spent over one thousand dollars with Pet Smart this year. You get an additional five percent discount."

The annihilation of my pride was complete. I was being congratulated by a teenager with braces on her teeth, for being the number one pet-chump in all of the Cable Counties. I tried to hurry her along by passing her two hundred-dollar bills and telling her to keep the change.

No furry-assed chance!

"Oh no, I couldn't, Mr. St. Cloud, but I will apply your change to our Save the Felines fund. Do you know how to work the engraving machine?"

I pushed my heavy cart over to the self-engraving machine and made a nametag for the new puppy. On the name line I considered my conversations with Emma and Blue. They had pretty much dictated the puppy's name would be Sebastian. I summoned all of my machismo and settled for "Seb." No dog of mine would walk around with some sissy name.

Chapter 22

When I returned home, the ladies were waiting for me on the porch. I pulled up close and they both jumped in, filled with anticipation. I got a couple of greeting smooches and pointed to the back seat and the sacks of new puppy supplies. Blue jumped in the rear and poured the sacks out. There were many oo's and aww's as they tore the prizes and toys from their packaging. Then there came a silence, and I knew they'd discovered the collar with the name tag attached.

Emma looked at me with some expectation and I could feel Blue's eyes on the back of my neck. Emma spoke first, "What is this?"

I faked concentration on my driving. "What?"

Blue chimed in, "What does this name tag say?"

"Well I don't know, let's take a look." I took the collar from Blue and looked at it with great focus. "Says, the new puppy's name is... Seb."

There was a chorus of, "No, the puppy's name is not Seb. His name is Sebastian."

"Right, Sebastian. I just thought we could call him Seb for short."

Emma said, "If we call him Seb, he'll be confused about his true name and might develop some kind of a complex. We should all agree to call him the same thing, and I think his name should be Sebastian."

"Well, speaking of complexes, I think a country-boy-dog might develop much *more* of an identity crisis if he were saddled with a sissy name."

The air in the cab got thin as both women gasped. Blue shot a jagged comment my way. "Sebastian, is not a *sissy* name. It is a regal, cultured name."

"No, it's a *sissy* name, and our puppy might grow up to be a wuss if he has to bear it."

I could see the ladies begin to pass each other some code in female pheromone speak. I was truly enjoying the banter, but I was also determined to give the puppy a semblance of a male moniker.

They'd chosen their next weapon—seduction. Simultaneously, Emma grabbed my thigh, very high up, and Blue enveloped her arms around my neck from behind. Blue breathed lightly in my ear, then she licked the lobe. Normally that would have done it. I would have given in to whatever they wanted, but the boy's name was at stake, by God. I held firm. "You can offer any sexual treats you choose, but he will be named Seb."

The affectionate rubbings immediately ceased, and there came a sullen sigh from both the back and passenger seats.

***

H.T. Bradford was the man who sold me insurance. He was a lifelong friend of my family, and he bred Jack Russell terriers. He was the man who had furnished us with Jack. Hearing of Jack's demise some months back, he had told me to look him up. We had been to visit him the night the new litter was born and had picked what would become the newest member of our family.

Bradford lived in Levy County, the interior heart of the Cable Counties. His house was nearly a mile off County Road 232, through a forest of ten-year-old pines. As we drove into his yard, three older Jack Russells, a stout male and two younger, very fat bitches bounded up to the truck. We all left the vehicle, and the ladies began to make friends with the doggy parents of their new child.

Wearing baggy khaki pants and a weathered, tan chambray shirt, H.T. ambled down the steps of his barn. I shook hands with the man. Bradford is one to flirt at any chance. He's a permanent bachelor and likes women only slightly better than Coors Light and practical jokes. The ladies know him, but don't have the history with him that I do.

The ladies finished making acquaintances of the parent dogs, and with flowing anticipation turned to Harry. H.T. approached them and gave a little more than a fatherly hug to each. "Emma, Blue, I'm just so damn glad to see the two of you. I don't get nearly enough female company out here. An old man like me needs young females to visit. Reminds him why he keeps on breathing."

The compliments done, the ladies looked at Harry with wide eyes. I went into the house to get H.T. and myself a Coors Light, but I kept my eye and ear on the situation. As I was walking from the house, I could see a tearful expression on both female faces. They were doing a good job of holding back.

Blue took a step in my direction and said, "H.T. says he gave the puppy to someone else—a little blind, crippled girl."

I couldn't suppress a smile. Blue's face became as red as her dark hair. She stepped closer and through clinched teeth said, "Cloud, this isn't funny, this isn't funny at all. We've been waiting for that puppy for seven weeks now. I… Me and Emma had our hearts set."

I tossed a Silver-Bullet to Bradford and looked back into Blue's eyes. "Bradford's a horny old devil, but I reckon even he, on his most eager night, couldn't produce an erection the size of that bulge in his pocket."

Blue looked to Emma. Emma looked at me then back to H.T. Bradford did a half squat, a little wiggle of his hips and reached into his pocket. "Well, what the hell… what's this?"

In his cupped hand was a tiny ball of tan and white fur. He looked at Emma and Blue, then smiled as only a father can. He reached out and put the tiny puppy in Emma's hands.

Blue looked at me for a severe instant, smacked me on the shoulder, then ran to Emma. The ladies collapsed to the ground and began to make all manner of cooing sounds.

I reached out and toasted H.T.—one cold silver can to another. One satisfied smile to another. I reached in my pocket and produced a check. Bradford shook his head. "Not necessary, I just want him to have a good home."

I tucked the check in his shirt pocket, "I appreciate this, old man. If you don't want the money, then buy some dog food."

Chapter 23

Qatar

The slight dark form of Jamil Rancon Facon had aged forty years. He lay naked on a cold marble table with a sheet underneath him. His eyes were puffed, red, and haggard. As broken and ripped as his back was, his heart was worse. He'd tried to get rid of the anguish by adhering to the custom. He'd stood in the courtyard of his palatial home and flogged himself for twenty-four hours. When the pain in his chest didn't ease, he continued for an additional eight hours. At that point he collapsed. His servants, worrying for his life, removed him to a makeshift operating room and began to stitch the gashes. They tended his wounds with natural antibiotics and washed most of the blood away with healing salve.

He considered taking his own life. But unlike what most suicide bombers believe, the Quran forbade this. If it were not for the slim thread of faith he clung to, he would have cursed Allah, and he would have excommunicated himself from the ancient religion. *No*, he thought, *this has nothing to do with Allah. This has nothing to do with the Quran or with Islam. I am a devout Muslim; this has to do with revenge. Allah forgive me. This is a vendetta.*

The two women shrouded in white leapt back when he suddenly sat up. Women in the Muslim religion were not asked for their opinions, but they certainly thought this man, this great man, should lay still for many days.

A small man wearing a crisp blue suit hurried to the side of Jamil Rancon

Facon. He spoke in thick Arabic. "Your imminence, you must rest. You must let the doctors work to heal your wounds."

Facon gazed through unholy bloodshot eyes into those of the waiting lawyer. "Hevy, you are a good and loyal man even though you are a lawyer. I appreciate your concern, but if I do not get to the next order of business, I fear I will forsake my religion."

Hevy took a step back and tried to fathom what Facon had said. "My king, you do not mean that. You could never turn your back on Allah."

"Allah… had nothing to do with this. Allah would never have let Amul die at the hands of some barbarian in America."

"Perhaps you should rest. You speak words which you do not mean."

"Get me Ahmad."

"Oh… my king, you do not want him. He is not one of us. He's an animal, a savage."

"Hevy, I will say this but once. You are a loyal subject, and I appreciate your deep convictions, but over the next days I will ask for things you are unaccustomed to bringing me. If you question me again, if you hesitate or falter in any way, I will replace you. Do you understand?"

"Yes, my imminence, but let me at least remind you that Ahmad is a Sikh, a descendant of the Arabian Knights, a man with very little conscience."

"That is precisely why I have asked for him. Get me the Sikh."

Chapter 24

Silasteck Ahmad grew up in India, the son of wealthy fisherman. At the age of seventeen, his father sent him to London to study at Oxford. In India, his religion had made him a minority, in England his dark skin, silver-bangle bracelets, and high woven turban made him an outsider. In life, he was nearly seven feet tall, this above all other things made him a near-outcast, a freak even among his countrymen.

Returning to India, he discovered that his aged and dying father hadn't been able to retain his fishing empire. When Ahmad tried to regain control of his father's business, he met the forces of an Indian mafia. A sect of Hindu nationalists had taken over his father's company and meant to keep it.

Having no other family in India, Ahmad fled the country to the safe confines of Qatar, a more hospitable place, which was growing in affluence with the foundation of oil money and technology.

An educated man, Ahmad, attempted to copy the successful systems that had led his family to wealth in India. The political climate was tough, and he found the need to raise money by offering himself as a strong-arm man for local businessmen. He gained a reputation for ruthlessness and results.

On several occasions, the Sultan of Qatar, Jamil Rancon Facon, hired Ahmad to take care of some state business.

Silasteck Ahmad intended to make for himself the life his father had wished for him. Disciplined and driven, he worked within the fish shipping business. His only foray outside of this was to lead hunting expeditions into the jungles of Africa, South America, and the subcontinent of his home, India. He was schooled from youth to track and understand the nature of the wild beasts of the planet.

He'd been expecting a visit from the Sultan's consigliore. When Hevy walked into his harbor-side office, Ahmad smiled beneath a long beard.

"Hevy, it has been some time. Let me get you something to drink."

Above all things, Hevy despised delivering messages, commands, and actions to the Sikh. He spoke in his native Arabic. "The Sultan requires your services."

Ahmad peered at the man, nearly half his stature. "Please speak English."

Hevy felt a warm fullness of satisfaction. "I said, the Sultan needs your services."

"Yes, well, I have fulfilled my obligation to him. I have repaid my debt for the loans he afforded me for my business."

The lawyer glowed in his power. After all, he was sent by the Sultan. "You are in no position to deny him, my friend. The Sultan lets you build your business at his pleasure. He could just as easily send you back to the jackals of your home country."

Ahmad rose and stood directly in front of Hevy. The big man grasped the lawyer by his starched jacket and picked him up so they were on eye level. "Hevy, you are not my friend, but one fine day I will explain the meaning of life to you. In the meantime, take me to the Sultan. At least he is a man I still respect."

Chapter 25

The Mercedes sedan arrived at the rear entrance to the Sultan's home. Hevy was prudent in that he wanted no one to witness the Sikh entering. Normally the Sultan did all of his correspondence with Ahmad through his lawyer.

A palace guard approached Ahmad and asked him to raise his arms so he could be searched for weapons. Ahmad stood firm and looked contemptuously at Hevy, who breathed a sigh of consternation then told the guard to let him pass. He knew Ahmad was armed with a large blade, one of the seven indicators a man was of the Sikh religion. He also knew Silasteck Ahmad would never let another man separate him from his blade.

In a rather bland room, Ahmad awaited the Sultan's arrival. He was aware of the fact that the Sultan's only son, Amul, had been killed at his university in America. Ahmad guessed this was reason the Sultan sought his services. He'd never shunned any request of the Sultan, but this might be the time. Ahmad had no desire to travel to America. He'd seen enough of western culture when he attended Oxford. He thought the Americans to be of a disposable mentality when it came to the earth, matters of a more global nature, and the human spirit. He also regarded them as the most arrogant creatures on the planet.

Jamil Rancon Facon, the Sultan of Qatar, slowly crossed the marble floor. Ahmad had great affection for this man. He was the only person who had treated him like anything but a thug, the only one who had given him any respect.

Ahmad noticed the crippled condition of the Sultan. He rushed to his side only to be warned off by the trailing Hevy. The Sultan looked at the lawyer and said, "Hevy, thank you very much, but I wish to speak with Ahmad alone."

Hevy was taken aback. He was not accustomed to being excluded from anything the Sultan did. He looked to the Sultan for a moment to make sure he understood. The Sultan nodded, and Hevy grudgingly took his leave.

The Sultan waved for Ahmad to bend down and brush-kissed him on both cheeks. Then Ahmad helped the stumbling Sultan to a backless couch. His understanding of the Sultan's pain, both physical and emotional, now humbled him. He'd been prepared to rebuff whatever requests the Sultan made. Now, he realized that wasn't an option.

"Sir, what do you require of me?"

"I know that being a Sikh you do not honor any man, especially a Muslim like myself. Please, when we are alone, call me Jamil."

Ahmad felt the name around his gums. It seemed like so many rough stones. "How did you become so injured? Tell me who did this, and I will bring an unholy wrath on their entire home."

"That is not why I have summoned you. I'm sure you already know my son has been killed."

"Yes. Let me offer my most sincere condolences."

"Yes, well thank you, but as you might imagine, I will not be consoled. What you probably do not know is that he was decapitated. This was not the work of some amateur. I would like to believe it was the work of an American, but alas I think it might be because of me."

Ahmad gathered a breath to reassure the Sultan, but he was waved off. "I have many enemies. I am not sure if they are responsible or if it was truly an act of some savage from America, and I do not care. My body is a shambles because I have followed the Muslim custom. I have tried to purge the rage from my mind and soul. I cannot. You must go and find the men responsible and bring them to me. I want for them to still be breathing. I would go myself, but I am old, and I fear I would cause an international incident."

Ahmad got to his feet. "I will do as you wish."

"You will have whatever you need. Money, access to other human resources, weapons, anything. I only require that you bring them to me alive. I will be the one to take their last breath. Do you understand?"

"Yes."

"When you return successfully, you will have no further worries that relate to wealth. I will make you a very rich man."

"I will do as you wish."

Chapter 26

Back in Cable

The confines of our bedroom was a sanctuary as far as I was concerned. No matter how lovable and sweet a dog could be, he wasn't allowed inside the bedroom. That first night with Seb, I learned this was a rule of one. After a very short debate, I understood that the smallest, newest member of our family was indeed going to be allowed inside the bedroom, not just the room, but also the bed itself.

I attempted to raise an argument, to get some kind of an intelligent conversation going on the merits of letting a dog, no matter how cute and small, sleep in the bed. I was loudly ignored. No counter argument was offered; it would just be so.

After an hour of trying to find myself in the right position on the bed, I conceded and softly closed the door behind me. I found Jake the loyal laying in his condo, even though the door was open. I empathized with his plight. We were old news. The puppy was the new king of the castle, at least for a time.

I called Jake to the kitchen. There, I cut up a sirloin into bite-sized pieces and cracked two raw eggs over it. Setting it on the floor, I thought myself the champion of the underclass. At least I still danced with the one who brought me.

I made a nice bed of several quilts on the leather couch. I settled the pillows into just the right degree of arc and took deeply of the distinct aroma a large piece of furniture covered in cowhide can produce. Of the many things Jake and I had in common, we did not tarry over food. He came licking and wiggling to the couch. I scratched his ears the way I would like my feet rubbed. He seemed to understand and thanked me with a lick, then found a nice little piece of cowhide for himself at the end of the couch. Sleeping on a couch with a dog is far, far different from letting them sleep in the bed—at least for Jake and me.

**

Sundays were our days to do our own thing. I was sure this meant for the ladies ravishing affection and squalor on our new puppy. Seb, as he would henceforth be known, had never in his little doggy mind imagined the life he would have.

When I awoke, the ladies were already well into their day. Jake, I realized, had also jumped ship. I walked to the porch and saw the two beautiful female humans and the handsome male canines playing some made-up game of tag and hide the ball.

I put on my running gear and walked into the yard. I was hardly noticed. I snapped my fingers, the usual command for Jake to join me in a run, the normal delight of his doggy life. He also ignored me.

As I ran, I put together the facts of what I learned so far. There wasn't a lot to go on, but my conversation with Mame Blake had sealed in my mind the connection between the heist of the trophy and the death of the college student. Since I wasn't getting any help for the time being from Larry Red, I felt the next best thing was for me to find out as much as I could about Amul Instad Facon.

Maybe this issue didn't completely revolve around his research. Maybe this had something to do with who he was or what he might have done.

For a former military operative, most people would think, a five-mile run would be physically natural. This wasn't the case. I could make about half of that before I began to wheeze and wonder why the hell I did this to myself.

On the way back to the house, I stopped off at the paper box and got the

Sunday edition. Back in the yard, I found the trusty hammock and laid down, paper in hand. In the Local and State section there was an article about the college student being killed. It rehashed the dramatic details of the murder, then went on to tell a little about the boy's background and family.

Amul Instad Facon was someone of great significance. He was the only son of Jamil Rancon Facon, the Sultan of Qatar. I couldn't gather from the article the exact station within his country's government the Sultan held, but I understood him to be a very important and powerful man. Even in our rag of a newspaper he was labeled first and foremost a Muslim—this seemed to be his overall distinction, as far as the paper was concerned. We Americans are very fond of labels and categorizing people.

I took my paper and headed into the house. The ladies and the dogs were missing. I found a note on the kitchen counter. "Gone to show off Sebastian, will be back in time for supper, Love B and E."

Sunday dinner was a custom, and it usually came around five in the evening. This gave me about three or four hours to research Jamil Rancon Facon, his son, and anything that might be relevant to the case. I grabbed my laptop, powered up, and began searching the net for information.

Two hours later, I hadn't had any flash of brilliance, but I had learned some things. The Sultan of Qatar was truly a very powerful man, and not just in his country. Qatar, like Florida, was a peninsula. It laid within the Persian Gulf on the eastern side of Saudi Arabia. Qatar had some very note-worthy neighbors. Iran was due east across the Gulf, The United Arab Emirates was to the south, and Kuwait was up the coast to the north. Even though I'd spent time in all of these countries during my service to the United States, and I'd been out of government employ for some time, I could make the connection. Oil. All of these countries were rich in oil money.

The Sultan was the chief executive. He therefore had much of the control over the oil resources of Qatar. An interesting fact was that the Sultan had been educated abroad. In the United States, as a matter of fact. He was an alumnus of Harvard University.

Amul Instad Facon didn't receive much copy. There was a story about his birth, then nothing until he decided to pursue his higher education at our own southern university. An Arabic newspaper reported that the younger Facon had gone against his father's wishes wishes and enrolled at the University of Florida to broaden his understanding of the world.

During his Master's Degree studies, the *Alligator*, the campus newspaper, had done a story on Amul Facon. It detailed some extraordinary finds in the field of biotechnology as it related to petroleum-consuming bacteria. *This all makes perfect sense*. Coming from an oil-rich country, there are bound to be some spills. Develop bacteria that could erase the spill, become a national hero.

What I didn't find was a connect-the-dot diagram leading me from petroleum-consuming bacteria to the theft of a national championship trophy. I hate it when I get such good information and can't understand what it means.

Larry Red knew something, and he was scared. I needed to know what he was keeping to himself and who was trying to scare him. Since Larry was less than cooperative, I needed something to hold over his head, or I needed to hold his head to a hot stove until he told me what I wanted to know. The memory of the small bike with training wheels in front of his apartment door made me reconsider the stove. I decided to ask Blue if she knew anything unlawful that Larry was accused of. This was a much more civilized approach.

Chapter 27

After a steak dinner, during which Seb ate more than any human except myself, I persuaded Blue to help me look into Larry Red. She made a few calls and a fax emerged from the printer. Larry Red had a record, and not an insignificant one. He had been arrested on three separate drug offenses, no distribution, all possession and use issues. He had mainly run afoul of the law while attending seventeen different demonstrations. Larry was obviously a passionate lad. He'd let the situation get the best of him during these demonstrations and had been arrested for indecent exposure in all seventeen cases.

Apparently Larry reasoned that taking all his clothes off at the public demonstrations was the best way to call attention to his cause of the month. He didn't discriminate when it came to cause. He stripped equally for women's, animal, and foreign human rights.

I found out that Larry was the son of a rich South Florida man. He was also attending the university courtesy of a public fellowship. Larry didn't need scholarship money, so he was rebelling. He and his old man must not have seen eye to eye.

This all came together as very powerful information. Tomorrow I would visit Larry Red again, and this time it wouldn't be at his home.

***

The next day, I found Larry's lime-green scooter parked illegally in the Biotechnology parking lot. I'd gotten his plate number courtesy of Blue through the DMV.

I called Chili Holcomb, a friend from cases past, who worked for the university police department. He came to the Biotech lot and put a bright yellow boot on the scooter. I thanked him and sat in my truck listening to Chris Rea sing "Auberge."

When Larry saw his booted scooter, he fairly threw a fit. After throwing his book bag much farther than I thought him capable, he kicked the scooter several times until it toppled and fell on its side. Then he sat down on the curb, his head in hand.

I didn't think Larry was a bad guy, but I needed him to soften up, not only to help me, but also to get some justice for his dead research partner. I walked up to him. I could hear he was crying. Great, just what I needed. A cry-baby as a witness.

"Hey pardner, you alright?"

Larry looked up through tear-streaked eyes. When he recognized me, his demeanor became a little more defensive. "What the hell do you want?"

"Same thing I wanted the other day, some information regarding Amul Instad Facon."

"I told you already. I won't help you."

"Yes, but I thought maybe you might have reconsidered after thinking on it a little deeper. Why don't you let me give you a ride home?"

"Hell no man, they see me with you, I might join Amul on the most-dead list."

"Who is 'They'?"

"That's the whole point man. I can't tell you."

I was not proud of what I was going to do. "Larry, you're going to have to tell me. I'm the only one who's going to put all of this together, the only one who can help you. When the threat subsides, *they* won't need you anymore, but *they* will still fear the knowledge you have, and *they* will probably come after you."

"No way man. As far as I know, *you* might be one of *them*."

"Well, I tried this the easy, straight forward way, now we'll have to get *mean*. How'd you think your neighbors and the university faculty would feel about a guy with a drug record—and a history of showing his dangling uglies in public—living on campus and doing research in the Biotech lab?"

Larry's face grew flush with anger. "How do you know about all that?"

"That's really not the point. What I need is information."

"You're a real bastard. You're the kinda man who kicks a fellow when he's way down, aren't you?"

"Let me give you a ride home."

"No way. I guess I have to talk to you, but we damn sure can't do it at my home. Let's go somewhere public and anonymous."

We sat at an off-campus bagel bar. I'm not a big bagel fan, but Larry ate only vegetarian cuisine. He was edgy and nervous and seemed more interested in preparing his bagel than eating it. I sipped a Coke.

"What was Amul Instad Facon working on?"

"Did you know that his dad is the king of Saudi Arabia?"

"No. I know his old man is the Sultan of Qatar though."

Larry looked up, surprised. He had a smear of cream cheese at the corner of his mouth. "Whatever. The main industry over there is oil, and they're constantly having big spills in the lakes and oceans when they're transporting the oil. Amul was working on developing a bacterium that actually eats the spilled oil whether it's in salt or fresh water."

"Was he successful?"

"He's dead isn't he? I'm sure they didn't kill him on account of failure."

I gave him that one. "*When* was he successful?"

"The truth is… I'm not sure. I knew he was getting close, but so far all of the experiments had come up a little short. The night he was killed, he told me he felt the answer was inevitable and imminent."

"So he might have figured it out that night?"

"Yeah, and the sorry bastards killed him for it."

"You keep referring to this 'they'."

Larry looked around the room. He seemed to be trying to identify the enemy. He looked back at me, then his gaze wandered right and upward, the sure sign of manufacturing. "The big American oil companies. They're the ones who wanted his bacterium."

"Larry, that is a lie. I'm not a patient man."

He measured my intent and resolve. "Okay, man. I'm going to tell you, but if I end up dead, I swear, my ghost will come back to haunt you every day of your life."

"I carry a few silver bullets with me wherever I go. Tell me."

"I don't know his name. Amul would never tell me, but some big South Florida sugar tycoon had been hassling him for months. He was always offering to hire Amul, wanting to make contributions to his research. Amul always blew him off. He wanted to develop the bug and bring it home to Qatar—to his father as a gift."

"What else do you know about the sugar man?"

"Nothing really, only that he is a big man in the industry, has family going way back in big sugar. He also always made calls to Amul ship-to-shore."

"He was calling from a boat?"

"Yeah. I don't know what that means, but yeah."

I paid the bill and took Larry home. He had me stop a block away from his house so his wife wouldn't know he'd been talking to me.

"Your scooter will be at your house in the morning."

"You did that? You may be trying to help, but you are one cold bastard."

Chapter 28

I liked living and working in the Cable Counties. It was peaceful and predictable for the most part. That was the reason I came back after government service. Now it appeared I was going to have to go to South Florida. As far as I'm concerned, it was a foreign country, a noxious mix of New York wannabes, crabby looky-loos, and tourists, tourists, tourists. A country boy can survive, but not for long in that group.

I decided I would give Carter Wells an update the next morning and then head off to Miami. I had a few contacts down that way, and hopefully they could tune me onto a wayward sugar baron who lived on a boat.

Blue was decidedly independent. She never wanted help or protection of any kind. That was precisely why I called my good friends Earl and Bean to make sure they would keep an eye on the homestead while I was away.

I hit the speed dial, and after about nine rings a booming voice casually answered. "Get-A-Head Taxidermy, you snuff 'em, we stuff 'em."

It was Earl. I enjoyed giving my old friend hell at every corner in the road. I did my best impression of a dainty scientist. "Yes, this is Mr. Erogenous Zone, and I'm calling from the Smithsonian Museum in Washington, D.C. One of our fellow scientists, an explorer, has uncovered parts of a frozen mammoth near the thirty-eighth parallel, the North Pole. We were wondering if you might offer your services in the way of taxidermy to preserve the specimen?"

I could never tell whether Earl understood my tricks or if he just played along. "What parts you want preserved?"

"Well, sir, this is the unusual part. It is the reproductive organs of the mammoth."

Earl yelled to his brother so that he was sure I could hear. "Hey Bean, a man from the Smithsonian Museum wants to know if you'll stuff a big ole mammoth's dick."

Evidently Earl understood the joke and was passing it off on his brother. I almost felt Bean scratch his big, bald dome of a head. I heard him talking in hushed tones to Earl in the background. "Hell, I don't know nothing 'bout mammoths, brother."

"Just talk to the man, ya big sissy."

Bean fumbled the phone to his ear. "This's Bean, what can I do for ya?"

"Mr. Bean, this is a very delicate matter, are you capable of preserving the sex organs of a prehistoric beast?"

Bean hesitated. He surely wouldn't want to disappoint. "Well, I'm not rightly sure. What kinda animal... I'm sorry, what kinda sex organ you talking 'bout?"

"A prehistoric mammoth's penis."

Again, Bean fumbled. "Well, I don't.... how big is the, ah, penis?"

"Why does that make any difference?"

"Well, I'm not sure, I don't rightly know how to get my hands around this."

"Mr. Bean, I get the distinct impression you may be too involved in your work. Do you often fondle and caress the penises of the animals you stuff?"

Bean hesitated and then the light shone in. "Fuck you, Cloud, and you too, Earl."

I could hardly continue my driving. "Hey, Bean, put Earl back on."

"Yeah, well fuck you, Cloud *and* your big mammoth dick."

Earl secured the phone, but he was laughing as hard as I was. "What'cha need old buddy?"

"I'm heading down south for a few days, and I was wondering if you could check in with Emma and Blue on the sly while I'm gone?"

Earl's tone became immediately serious. "Emma and Blue in danger?"

"No, not really, but I'm working something that could be trouble."

"Yeah, no problem. We'll visit one day and call on a few others."

"Just be casual though. I don't want Blue thinking I don't believe she can take care of the family."

"No problemo."

"Hey, put Bean back on."

I heard Earl stifle a laugh. He knew I was getting ready to needle Bean a little more. "Hey brother, Cloud wants to talk to you."

I took in a full lung of air, and when Bean said, "Yeah?" I bellowed my best elephant trumpeting sound and hung up the phone.

Chapter 29

The Florida Straits

The *Big Thunder* cruised through the Florida Straits. On board were five new passengers, all moneyed old cronies of Harry Wyatt Sullivan. In addition to the five potential clients there were also an equal number of high-priced call girls recruited into service from the Mons Venus strip club in Tampa. The men were presented with all manner of fine foods, and their drinks were never dry. The call girls were hopping from lap to lap and eagerly filling glasses.

Harry Wyatt sat on a full futon couch, sampling the contents of every tray which passed his way. He slurped an oyster Rockefeller here and speared a morsel of Peking duck finger there. He washed it all down with Cristal champagne.

Wyatt was in his element. Kari Vilano-Lobos canvassed him for needs. She could smell the money within the confines of the yacht's cabin. There was a lottery windfall on the forefront, a bidding war of epic proportions in the making. Kari knew this was not the big payoff, but a cool million couldn't hurt her personal account. She, at times, still shuddered at the thought of snuggling into the warm, sweaty clasp of Wyatt, but she reminded herself that money—enough of it—was worth any short pain.

A loud foghorn signaled the witching hour of midnight. Wyatt waved to Zan, who had served as steward for the evening. The lights came bright, and all the unwanted occupants of the vast cabin were herded on deck. The only remaining members of the party were the five moneyed men.

Zan brought Wyatt a large figure covered in satin black material, then stood beside Wyatt holding the treasure. The auction was at hand. Harry Wyatt pulled the black sheath from the treasure and all five men gasped in unison. Before them was the National Championship Trophy, the tangible evidence of the state university's triumph over all gridiron opponents.

Wyatt uttered a statement he had waited for some time to say. "Let the games begin. Do I hear three hundred thousand?"

Chapter 30

Miami, Florida

Trying to avoid attention as much as possible, Silasteck Ahmad emerged from the cramped plane. This was not an easy task for a nearly seven-foot tall Arab dressed in the traditional Sikh garb. Mothers pulled their young from his path and whispered admonitions against staring. Flight attendants tended his needs before he could utter a sound. The melting pot was in full swing, but Ahmad was an outsider of great magnitude once again.

Hunched over, he strode through the air bridge and into Miami International Airport. In the departure lounge, he stood to his full height and stretched his back muscles without raising his hands. He looked around the wealth that was America. Just hours ago, he'd left Qatar, a nation rich in oil but lacking the infrastructure to make sure the wealth trickled down to the middle class. Here, he saw men and women of a very average position in life move freely and with impunity.

At the gate, he was directed by a heavyset woman to the customs area. She didn't even ask whether he was a citizen or not. In order to fit in as much as possible and avoid prying eyes, he had prepared himself for the unwanted stares and subtle racism.

At the customs desk, a handsome young black man asked him a series of questions, to which he answered all the appropriate non-answers. Politely, but with obvious skepticism, the young man stamped his passport and told him to have a nice stay. Ahmad thought for a moment to say to the customs officer, "Brother it is I, don't you recognize me?"

He passed on the sarcasm and continued to the baggage area.

As the carousel made its rounds, he felt eyes on him. He wondered how many studied him because he was freakishly tall, how many were uncomfortable with his native clothes, and how many were frightened by his Arabic heritage.

With a nondescript leather suitcase in hand, he stood in front of the rental car counter. The receptionist was obviously intimidated when he took his turn at the desk. She asked him to wait a moment, and within seconds, an older round man with a red complexion took her place. "How may I help you?"

Ahmad learned his English at Oxford. He had the smooth vowels and aristocratic air in his language. "Yes, my good man, I wish to rent an automobile."

"May I see your passport?" The red-faced man wore a forced, customer-service smile.

Ahmad produced the worn passport and stood patiently and compliantly. After the red-faced man inspected the passport and was convinced he had no choice but to offer a rental, he said, "We will need two forms of identification besides the passport and a major credit card for security."

Ahmad could see that the man was hoping he would come up short. Predicting just such a situation, the Sultan's staff supplied Ahmad with several forms of identification and a dozen credit cards with a combined credit limit reaching nearly a million dollars.

First, the red-faced man said he only had economy cars. When Ahmad pleasantly smiled back, the man altered his original offer and said they had one full-size vehicle left, a Ford Explorer. Red-face added with bent eyebrows that this was a rather expensive vehicle. Ahmad nodded and after several minutes was finally given a single key with a paper tag. He could tell Red-face predicted the Explorer would never return.

As he left the rental company office and walked towards the parking area, a man he'd never met handed him a leather shoulder-bag and continued ambling in the opposite direction without a word.

In the vehicle, Ahmad fumbled with the panel controls until there was cold air flowing at high volume from everywhere. He'd heard of the Americans' fanaticism for air conditioning and for comfort. If he had to endure their stares and slight insults, at least he would enjoy their cool air.

From the shoulder-bag he extracted a series of maps all laminated and packed in a waterproof folder. He also unzipped a hidden false bottom and gathered a half-saber and an electronic stun gun.

With the maps on the passenger seat and the hardware tucked into his billowing robes, he approached Interstate Highway seventy-five and headed north.

Chapter 31

The Cable Counties

I loaded a small gym bag and an Army duffel into my toolbox and snapped it shut. Jake was sitting in the driver's seat and the small ball of fur that was Seb sat on the ground by the door longingly looking up at the superior position Jake had attained. I picked up the small dog and sat him inside the truck on the seat beside Jake. Jake looked at him as if to say, "You can come, but this is *my* truck."

Emma and Blue bounded down the railroad tie stairway and began smothering me with exaggerated kisses and farewell comments. I could tell they were secretly glad to have the home front to themselves for a few days. This is as it should be, but I was pretty sure the furniture would be rearranged when I came home and at least one of my high-comfort items would be missing.

I entered the cab and pushed Jake and Seb to the passenger seat. Both of the ladies looked shocked. They hadn't considered I would be taking the boys with me. They looked at each other and gathered momentum. "Cloud… you are *not* taking our new puppy with you."

Oh, the little pleasures. "Why not?"

Emma drew on Blue's contempt. "He's just a baby. You can't take a baby off to do some dangerous business."

"So what you're saying is that you're not worried about my safety, but you don't want the baby to get hurt."

Blue wasn't sure if I was shinning her on or not. "You're damn well right. The *baby* stays with us."

I smiled and opened the door of the truck. The boys sat there, ready to get on with the trip. I scratched Jake furiously and then popped my fingers. He knew the signal and with sad eyes exited the truck. I handed the ball of fluff to Emma. The ladies erupted with the stroking and cooing.

Blue looked up from the small dog. "Are you flying down?"

"No. I figure I'll need to get around quite a bit while I'm down there, so might as well drive the truck. Besides, I like the drive."

There was a twinkle of guilt in their eyes. I got out of the truck and hugged them both with intensity.

Two hours later I passed through the land of the Mouse, listening to the fourteenth installment of *Bag of Bones*.

Chapter 32

The Florida Straits

Kari Vilano-Lobos sat sunning herself on the aft deck of the *Big Thunder*. The yacht sliced through the warm waters of the Florida Straits heading back into the Gulf of Mexico. The rough waters of the Atlantic had almost completely subsided.

Harry Wyatt Sullivan sat under a huge canopy on the far side of the deck. He was in no danger from skin cancer, but the modesty police would have made their biggest bust ever. He lounged naked on an air pillow the proportions of king-size bed. A compact yet noisy generator supplied power to a deck air conditioner blowing frigid air over the vast expanse of his fatness.

Kari watched Zan sitting at Wyatt's feet, intermittently using an assortment of large hedge trimmer-sized clippers and a horse hoof rasp to pedicure the toenails of the fat man.

Zan seemed pleasantly unaware he was executing such a grotesque task. The young man bobbed with the sea and rocked to the beat of something playing in the headphones he was wearing.

In a surprising instant, Wyatt bellowed, raised one fat foot and smashed it into Zan's face. The headphones yanked from his head, and he tumbled over backwards into a piled coil of hemp rope.

As Wyatt attempted to look past his vast bulk at his mangled foot, Zan rose with filed, pointed teeth bared. Kari reached into the vinyl bag at her side and rested her hand on the cold steel of the Beretta M9. She was not a woman accustomed to waiting for men to solve problems.

As Zan was leaning forward into a crouch, Wyatt grabbed at his thick wrist and held up an electronic key ring-sized device. Zan froze momentarily and considered the situation with his primitive mind, his expression still distorted with rage at having been kicked in the face. A decision flashed through his eyes. Kari Vilano-Lobos raised the Beretta at the same moment Wyatt pressed a button on the key ring.

A sickening sizzle ensued, and Zan collapsed to the deck and clawed at the silver collar around his neck. Wyatt leaned all of his immense bulk forward and watched as the young man used both hands and feet to try and pry the collar from his neck. Just when the action was waning, Wyatt clapped his hands twice to get Zan's attention. Then, with a fat-happy smile on his face, he pressed the button again. Kari joined Wyatt in a long, exaggerated laugh.

Chapter 33

The Florida Turnpike

Just south of Orlando, I punched in the number for one of my former classmates at West Point. Captain Jesse J. Kirk and I had been plebes—freshmen—together at the Military Academy and had served in separate units during Operation Desert Storm. Jesse stayed in the Army just long enough after the war to acquire the rank of captain. He'd always wanted the moniker, "Captain Kirk."

Now he was in the FBI. He was the Special Agent in Charge or SAC of the South Florida arm of the Bureau. He operated undercover as the owner and, yes—captain—of a salvage and treasure rescue business.

After a couple of rings, a young woman with a pleasant and eager voice answered the phone. "Captain Kirk's Salvage & Rescue, how may I help you?"

Remembering my wild young friend from years before, I was amused to hear such a professional voice representing him. "Yes, is the captain in?"

"Why yes he is," she answered cheerily. "May I tell him who is calling?"

"Yes, tell him it's Cloud."

The mannered young woman wasn't accustomed to hearing a name without some sort of title attached. She floundered for a moment then said, "I'm sorry, did you say Cloud?"

Her air of politeness was contagious. "Why yes, I did."

She may have detected the mocking tone in my voice. "One moment, please."

While I was waiting, a sleek, new-model SUV full of gelled and blow-dried young men passed me. A back passenger window lowered and a full bag of McDonald's waste products was thrown from the window. The bag skipped once against the shoulder and came to a rest, intact. I quickly pulled to the side of the road and reversed the truck. I picked up the trash and got back in the truck and proceeded at a little faster pace than before.

Kirk came on the phone. "Heeeey there, needle dick, injun bastard. Bout time ya gave me a call."

Of course, this was how it would be. Let the games begin. "Being a graduate of West Point, I would think you could summon the brain cells to remember *injun* is an ugly insult."

"Damn, I'm glad to hear a man's voice. Ya can't possibly imagine how many male pussies I talk to every day."

"Maybe they're recruiting."

He laughed a grated, cackling sound into the phone. "I got a joke for ya…"

"Tell me tonight. I'm coming to your home, the Sodom of the South."

"Fuck that… what? You're coming here? Well, I'll be a crippled bitch in heat. When?"

"Tonight. I'll be there in two, maybe two-five."

"That is outstanding, Lieutenant, but I'm still gonna tell ya the joke." Even the formal address of lieutenant was meant as an insult. Kirk knew what came after and where I'd probably ended my rank, which was several notches above captain.

"Kirk, listen. I'll be there and then you can tell me."

"So… the Lone Ranger gets captured by some hell raisin' injuns… *you* know the type."

"Kirk…"

"Shut it, limp dick."

Better to let him tell the joke and get it over with.

"Anyway, the Lone Ranger gets captured by some Indians and they have him all tied up. They're gonna burn him at the stake, ya follow?"

I grunted.

"Lone Ranger says, 'Hey chief, I want a coupl'a last requests.' The injun chief, he says, 'Lone Ranger you have been a worthy adversary for many years. We will grant you two last requests.' Are ya listening now, Cloud? This is the funny part."

Another grunt.

"Lone Ranger says, 'I want to talk to my horse, Silver, and I want one hour to make my peace.' So they bring the horse around and the Lone Ranger whispers something into Silver's ear. The damn horse takes off like his ass is on fire. 'Bout an hour later, the Chief pipes up, 'Okay, Lone Ranger. We've given you your last requests, and now we're gonna burn ya.'"

"Just at that moment, Silver comes over the horizon, galloping with all his equine might. On his back is the most beautiful woman ya ever saw, and she's buck-ass-naked. Silver wheels on his hind legs right up in front of the Lone Ranger, very proud of his delivery. Ya listening, Cloud? This is the knee slapper."

Grunt.

"The Lone Ranger says, 'Silver, ya dumb mother fucker, I said, *posse*."

I couldn't help myself. It was very funny and I gave Kirk his desired pay—a big belly laugh.

"That's a good one, huh?"

"Yeah, that's one for the books. Listen, I'm working a case and I need a little help. Can you meet me tonight?"

"Course. Why don't ya meet me at the Alligator Farm on the corner of East 110 and Dale Mabry, at what, eight?"

"I know the intersection, but what's the Alligator Farm?"

"It's a restaurant. Hell of a place. Kind of a tourist attraction and eats place all wrapped up in one."

This didn't sound like some out-of-the-way dive. "Kirk, why don't we just…"

"So I'll see ya there at eight," he said, and then hung up the phone. Captain Kirk hadn't changed one bit. In fact, FBI life might have given him broader boundaries.

Chapter 34

The Cable Counties

Silasteck Ahmad wheeled the Ford Explorer into the parking lot of the married housing units on the University of Florida campus. He marveled at the toys and playground equipment sitting in the plush yard. In India, this could be a city park. Here, it was a playground meant for the youth of only the married students who couldn't afford off-campus housing.

At the door of the unit, he moved aside a child's bicycle with colorful ribbons dangling from its handlebars. He pressed the doorbell.

A young woman dressed surprisingly similar to him answered the door. "Yes?"

With all of the cultured and practiced grace Oxford taught him, Ahmad said, "Thank you, I am looking for the man known as Larry Red."

This was the first American he'd encountered who didn't stare at him immediately with distain or suspicion. She warmed with a broad smile. "Won't you come in?"

Ahmad thought this to be far too easy. But, when given beans, you make curry. "Thank you."

The apartment was surprisingly sparse. The outer walls and vast playground made one think the inhabitants must have lived very well. Contrary to this, the apartment itself was furnished with very few pieces of furniture. What there was had obviously come second and third-hand from middle-class homes. An energetic young girl bounced on some inflated balloon toy with the head of what should be the American national symbol, Mickey Mouse.

The young woman said, "Please take a seat, and I'll get my husband. Could I get you something to drink?"

Ahmad was overwhelmed by her courtesy. He'd hardly expected this kind of greeting and fumbled with the offer. "Yes, that would be most appreciated. Maybe some water?"

The young woman fairly skipped with excitement to fulfill his need. A minute later she gave him a large mason jar full of ice water. "I'm sorry, we don't have proper glassware for a visitor. My husband will be right out." With that, she retreated with her daughter to another room.

A moment later, a disheveled-looking young man came in. He looked as if he had been sleeping despite the late hour of the day. A shock of dirty dishwater hair stood on end from his scalp. He wore what appeared to be some sort of loose, brightly colored pants and a well-used T-shirt sporting psychedelic flowers. "I'm Larry Red. How can I help you?"

Ever aware of his manners, Ahmad rose to his full height and offered his mitt-sized hand. The student took his hand limply and sat across from him on a mushy beanbag chair.

"You are Larry Red?"

"Yes."

"I've been sent by the father of Amul Instad Facon. He is the Sultan of Qatar and he is very eager to find out who might have caused his son's death."

Larry rolled his eyes and gained a very self-important countenance. He virtually chuckled. Ahmad produced an eager face, but he was put aback by the display of ego. Larry took in a large amount of air and said, "Well, the circumstances behind Amul's death are sketchy, but a man came to see me just few days ago, and I think he might have something to do with it."

"Who was this man?"

"His name was Cloud. He *said* he was a private detective trying to solve Amul's murder, but he was very rude, and I believe he might have something to do with Amul's death."

"What makes you think he might have had something to do with the Sultan's son's death?"

Larry looked exasperated, "Well, to start with, why the hell should he care? And second, he was a slick-looking American, someone we should all be aware of. *And* he tried to force his way into my house, like he was hunting some clue, no matter what."

"What did you tell him?"

"Nothing. I didn't tell him anything. Oh, he tried to be real smooth and trap me into telling him some hidden information."

"I want to thank you, Mr. Red, on behalf of the Sultan. I appreciate this, and I hope you will forward any further information which comes your way."

Larry became weepy. "Oh, you can bet I will. I'm not one of those ridiculous Americans who believe the rest of the world is made of second-class citizens."

Ahmad felt he needed to bathe after speaking with this man and his wife. But so was the life of a foreigner trying to make good in America.

Chapter 35

The Gulf of Mexico

Deep in the Gulf of Mexico, the *Big Thunder* idled to a halt, and its rubber buoys chaffed the docking station of *Wyatt One*, the largest oil derrick in the Gulf. Several men lived and worked on *Wyatt One*, and none of them had ever had a conversation with the owner.

The lower level, the one below the surface of the tranquil Gulf, was lavishly furnished. It was a virtual penthouse apartment, albeit beneath the sea.

Harry Wyatt Sullivan, perched aboard a customized all-terrain vehicle, drove his immense blubbery bulk into an elevator that ran between the highest level of the oil derrick and the submersed penthouse. On board the elevator, Kari Vilano-Lobos pressed a button that took them down.

In the penthouse, Wyatt moved onto an expansive couch. The effort was evident, as thick tendrils of sweat erupted on his forehead. He clapped his hands twice. Zan appeared from a dark corner and made every effort to comfort the big man. There was much tucking of pillows and shoe-horning of fat to get Wyatt into a comfortable position.

"Zan, refill," Wyatt said as he tinkled an empty glass.

Kari Vilano-Lobos read a series of charts. She brought the rolled papers to the table in front of him. "Everything seems in order. The pumping will begin tonight. By morning more oil will have been excavated from the Florida peninsula in one night than has been mined in the state's history."

Wyatt rolled toward the table, and a wet, ripping sound emerged. Kari couldn't decide whether the sound was from the stretching of the leather's fabric under duress or from one of Wyatt's orifices. A deep cheesy odor filled the room. Her nostrils answered her question.

"Are the tankers in place?"

"Yes, the shallow waters presented some problems, but that has all been worked out."

Zan approached bearing a large glass, miniature glaciers bobbing on the surface. Wyatt took the glass and said, "Zan, bring food."

He hurried off to do the master's bidding.

"Kari darling, all seems to be on track. Let us celebrate."

Kari Vilano-Lobos turned from her charts and graphs. She hid an inner shudder, smiled, and began removing her dress. Wyatt's hungry eyes took in every move just as his palate might.

"Kari darling, I was thinking of an oral delight. Let's experience the talent those luscious lips hold."

Chapter 36

The Cable Counties

This rural outpost wasn't a place where Silasteck Ahmad thought it would be easy to fit in. Besides the university campus, there weren't many places where he thought he could camouflage his enormous height and traditional robes. Of course, he needed to follow up on the information that Larry Red supplied, but this small outback city would have a network that would definitely inform the man he was hunting of his presence.

Ahmad circled the married housing units and headed back toward the interstate highway. He thought he might have passed one building where he might find some information and still keep his operation covert. Tucked between a fried chicken restaurant and an outlet named Bob's Discount Beds, he saw what he was looking for. The sign was green with a white backing and a large number seven prominently displayed. He figured he might find someone of Arabic descent working the counter in the small store.

Ahmad ducked as he entered the store and immediately drew stares from the two men behind the counter. No one else was in the building. He turned and locked the double doors. One of the clerks that wore a scraggly thin beard punched his counterpart in the ribs and motioned with his head to the big man coming through the doors. The other clerk, inflicted with a goat face, looked first to his friend with irritation at having been poked and then to the huge shadow in front of the counter. Goat-face fairly squealed a slight prayer to Allah.

Ahmad glared at the two clerks. He thought them to be of Saudi descent. He wrapped his lips around a rapid-fire order in Farsi. "I'm looking for an American who lives nearby. His name is Cloud."

The two clerks trembled. The one with the scraggly beard squeaked in a prepubescent voice, "Oh great one, you are a Sikh, no?"

Ahmad nodded.

"I know of this one, Cloud. He has friends who frequent our humble establishment for the vices of tobacco and alcohol."

The intimidation was working. Ahmad boomed, "Tell me of the infidels. Where do they live?"

The beard began to shake his head and at the same time, tears of fear ran down his cheeks. Goat-face spoke for the first time, "He is in the bed with one of the police women."

Ahmad brought his huge hand down onto the counter with the sound of a thunderclap. "I did not ask you about his woman. I asked where his friends live."

"We do not mean to anger you, oh great one. Just one moment. He was with his friends the other day when they bought a money order. Please forgive me while I search the records."

Ahmad reached across the counter and grabbed the other clerk by his goat face. "I will wait, but not for long."

The beard fell to floor with a cardboard box in his hands. He rapidly shuffled through the cards. Even as he searched he heard his friend whimpering. A small yellow puddle began to form at the feet of his goat-faced friend.

The beard praised Allah as he held a card above his head. "Here… here it is, oh mighty Sikh. The card registers his friend's address as 16303 Lawless Road. It is a business address, called Get-A-Head Taxidermy."

Ahmad pushed goat-face back and the man collapsed into his own yellow puddle. "Of course, my friends. You will remember… I was never here."

The scraggly bearded man nodded and knelt to the floor. He prayed the hulking Sikh would never return.

Chapter 37

Silasteck Ahmad drove along Lawless Road until he saw a large sign in the shape of an enormous deer head, complete with antlers. The deer was smiling as he smoked a fat cigar. Below read, "Get-A-Head Taxidermy. You snuff 'em, we stuff 'em."

Ahmad smiled to himself. Of all the things the Americans did well, nothing compared to their skill in marketing and advertising. If they could turn their high-powered marketing intellect toward shaping their image to the rest of the world instead of their military might, they would have far fewer problems.

He parked the Explorer under the canopy of a huge oak tree. On a distant limb of the tree, a bench swing lazily moved in the dense breeze. As he crunched along the gravel drive, Ahmad felt the unbelievable humidity. His robes mopped up the light coat of sweat his body quickly produced. No wonder these Americans loved their air conditioning. He'd endured much hotter conditions in his native India and in Qatar, and he'd felt the stifling humidity of England, but never the combined forces of sweltering heat *and* claustrophobic humidity.

The building was made of cinder block, but the front was covered with ragged pieces of old driftwood. It gave the building a haunted look, as if it should have been in a dark, tangled forest with a troll guarding the front door. He'd read of the *other* America, the one very far and distant from the much-heralded cities of New York, Chicago, and Los Angeles. The men who lived in these rural outposts were more of a breed he felt he could identify with. Life moved much slower in these country towns and villages. It was similar to the way time had forgotten the deserts of the Middle East.

The door of the building was built high and very broad. For once, he didn't need to duck his head. What could that mean? As he passed through the door, an overhead bell announced his entry. He saw two large men working behind a circular wooden bench in the middle of the building. One of them, an intensely black man, was pushing his whole arm down the gullet of an anaconda snake. The other man was white and even bigger. The big white man pushed fake eyeball marbles into the fierce face of a wild boar. Both men wore denim overalls and no shirt. Despite the dank, frigid nature of the room, both men were soaked in sweat.

He overheard the white man say to the black man, "All's I'm saying, brother, is if the woman didn't have no arms or legs, it was a damned evil thing for the sorry bastard to throw her in the middle of a lake."

The black man retorted with a significant sigh. "Bean, why the hell can't you understand that it's just a joke? There really isn't no crippled-up woman and no evil bastard man. It's just a damn joke."

Ahmad had intended to use a very cautious and pleasant approach, but this room with animal heads hanging in staggering numbers from every wall and the sight of the two sweaty men didn't seem to leave much room for subtlety.

Earl noticed the stranger first. He struggled to free his arm from the mouth of the snake. Bean stood to his full height a second later, still holding the marble eyes of the wild boar.

Ahmad noticed the black man was probably six-four or so and very heavily muscled. The white one was even bigger, maybe six foot six, lean but powerfully built. Ahmad hoped he could mentally out-maneuver these men. He had no interest in trying to get his information the hard way. Still, he fingered the inner pocket of his robes for the blade and stun gun.

Earl, finally free of the snake's mouth, began to wipe his arm with a towel. He smiled and approached the counter. "Howdy there stranger. What can we do for you?"

Before he could answer Bean whistled and said, "Earl, holy-good-god, it's the Jolly Green Giant."

"Shut it Bean, that's not a very neighborly thing to say." Bean lowered his head, properly chastised.

"I wish to employ the services of a friend of yours. I believe his name is Cloud."

Earl's eyes shifted in a suspicious nature. "What do you want to see Cloud for?"

Ahmad stretched his patience. "It is a private matter. Do you know where I may find him?"

Bean, in his typical country-boy hospitality said, "Cloud's a real good friend of ours."

Earl immediately looked back at Bean, severe scorn on his face. Bean again looked chastened. "What's your name big Fella?" Earl asked.

Ahmad spoke a little too quickly. "That's hardly important, but if you must know, my name is Silasteck Ahmad."

Earl felt the rebuke. "And why is it you're looking for Cloud?"

"As I said, it is a rather personal matter which I would like to speak with Mr. Cloud about in person."

Earl didn't know what it was. He'd referred many a man to Cloud over the years, but this didn't seem right. It was a little itchy. "Well I'll tell ya there, Silas, me and my brother Bean here are pretty good friends with old Cloud. Almost like family. I don't reckon he'd mind much if you told us what'cha want him for."

Ahmad realized he would not break through this pair of firewalls without some force. Both of the big sweaty men now stood directly in front of him, only the wooden counter separating them. He needed a distraction. Ahmad pointed at the fierce features of the boar's head. "That is excellent work. How many kilos was the boar?"

As Bean turned to comment on his handiwork, Ahmad, with lightning fast speed, produced the stun gun and pressed it to Bean's armpit. A sickening, flesh-burning sizzle erupted, and Bean collapsed to the concrete floor. Earl jumped the counter with surprising speed and grace. He wore a hungry, primitive look of vengeance on his face. "All right there, Silas. You just gone and done hurt my brother. Now I'm gonna take a pound and half of ass meat off ya."

Silasteck fumbled with his robes to bring the blade to bear. Before he could free it from its sheath, Earl rumbled forward and slammed into him with bone-crunching force. The two men fairly tore out the innards of the building down. They slammed their fists into each other's bloody faces and used elbows and knees to soften the body of one another. Earl was rocked by an overhand, contacting his temple. He staggered back and tried to regain focus.

As the world became clear, Earl saw the towering man, now wearing bloody robes, holding Bean by the foot. A short beveled saber was resting between Bean's big toe and the second toe of his right foot. Ahmad said, "I need to find this man named Cloud. If you do not tell me where I can find him I will begin cutting the toes from your brother."

Earl stood up straight, tears of rage ran down his face. "I don't know where Cloud is. He went down to South Florida. Miami or something."

"That is very unfortunate for your brother. I fear he will walk with a limp."

Earl threw his hands up. "No… don't hurt him. I… I can make a call. I… can find out where Cloud is… just don't hurt Bean."

Ahmad nodded. "Make your call."

Chapter 38

Blue

The Cable Department of Law Enforcement SUV hummed along the backstretch of County Road 346. At the wheel, Blue drummed her fingers on the steering wheel to the beat of a distant tune in her head. The ring of her cell phone interrupted the pop opera only she could hear. She looked at the digital display on the phone.

"Earl, in all the years I've known you, the only time you call me directly is when Cloud is out of town. Now, that either means you're sweet on me, or, and I mean this as a question, that Cloud has requested you check up on Emma and me in his absence. Now which is it? I actually hope you are going sweet on me."

"Well, Blue, you finally caught on. Of course I'm sweet on you. But that's not the reason I'm callin'. I need to get in touch with Cloud right away."

"Do you have me on speaker phone?"

"Yeah, honey. Me and Bean are just as busy as we can be, so I'm talking to you while at the same time I'm stuffin' this here big-assed snake."

Earl and Bean were childhood friends of Cloud. The three of them had teased and tortured each other their entire lives. She figured this was just one more in a long line of practical jokes. "He went down to South Florida. He's working a case and was going to get some help from that FBI friend of his down there."

"Kirk? Is he down there to visit with Captain Kirk?"

Blue gave a small superior laugh. "Yeah, that's him. What the hell, is that his real name?"

Earl actually sighed a little in relief. If he was turning this Arabian madman loose on his friend, at least Cloud would have one ally in Captain Jesse Kirk. "'Fraid so, honey. We were all in Desert Storm together before Kirk went on to the FBI."

Blue turned slightly green with envy. She desperately wanted to own a Federal Badge herself. "Well, that's where he is, so ya need anything else?"

"No honey, just wanted to see where he was and I confess, I was checking up on ya. Cloud wanted me to make sure you, Emma and the boys were all right, while he was away. By the way, how is your puppy, Jack?" Before Blue could give away her surprise Earl continued, "Sorry honey… gotta go, gotta customer." The line went dead.

Blue looked at the phone, shocked. She pulled to the side of the road as tears began to form in her eyes. How could Earl be so insensitive? He knew Jack was dead. He'd died nearly six months earlier in a violent gun battle. She was tempted to call the calloused son of bitch right back and cuss the wallpaper off his walls. She hesitated, and the cop instinct took over. Earl *never* called her directly in the past, and he mentioned the dead dog, *and* he seemed in an awful hurry to get off of the phone. Something was going on here. She made a call to dispatch and then flipped on her lights and sirens. It would take her nearly forty minutes to cross the counties and reach Get-A-Head Taxidermy. She hoped she would be in time.

***

Ahmad nodded at the sweat-slickened face of the black man. "I assume you know this Kirk and can give me his address."

Earl trembled with nervous rage. "I can tell ya, but then what? You just gonna kill my brother anyway and probably try to kill me as well."

"You have no reason to believe me, but I give you my word that if you give me the address, I will release your brother. I am a man of honor. I will have to detain you, but I will cause you no further permanent harm."

"Well, Silas, you're right. I don't believe you, but I don't rightly have a choice do I?"

"No, I fear. You do not."

Earl began rifling the cards on an ancient Rolodex. When he paused, Ahmad released Bean's foot and approached the counter. He still wielded the short saber in Earl's direction. Upon looking at the Rolodex, Ahmad ripped the front card from the roll and placed it in an unseen pocket. Before he could allow Earl to fight back, Ahmad pulled the stun gun from his robe and pressed the device to the big man's neck. Earl fell into a heap on the floor.

Chapter 39

Miami, Florida

Towering Royal Palms surrounded the parking lot and grounds of *Alligator Farm*. As I walked up the worn, river-rock path leading to the entrance to the building, I read a lighted sign.

Alligator Farm
Restaurant and Bar

In 1936, Wild Billy Barker established The Alligator Farm. It was and has remained a tourist attraction for visitors from every country of the world. The Alligator Farm, as always, is dedicated to the preservation of the state's indigenous reptiles. In 1985, William Barker the III, the heir of the founder, evolved the foundering tourist establishment into both a scenic landscape for native reptiles and a restaurant that serves the very finest in reptilian cuisine.

Enjoy your visit to
Alligator Farm

I smugly chuckled to myself. I wondered what Wild Bill would think of his offspring's idea. I imagined the elder Barker would turn rapidly in his grave if he knew what Wild William was doing with his creation.

The lobby was an ode to the alligator and his reptilian friends. Every manner of plastic had been formed into the likeness of the only surviving dinosaur. Hats, banners, rubber replicas, handbags, shoes, shirts, drink cozies, place mats, all bore the insignia of Alligator Farm. The alligator was being celebrated right out of existence. It was all for sale. A spoiled bunch of young tourists wearing shirts decrying their lust for Wisconsin Cheese chased each other up one isle and down another, making their version of gator growls while wearing plastic headpieces in the form of the vicious beasts.

I approached the hostess and asked for a table as far away from the souvenir shop as possible. She looked mildly offended as she slapped a big gator-head sticker on my chest.

There were no tables suitably far enough from the souvenir shop, so I settled for a seat at the bar. I told her I was expecting a rather loud obnoxious fellow named Kirk. She warmed to me immediately. "Are you a friend of the captain's?"

I felt I should get some alcohol into my system immediately before I started shooting these fools as fast as possible. "Yes I am acquainted with the sorry son of a bitch. When he gets here, kick him as hard as you possibly can in the testicles and then usher him to this seat beside me."

Her brilliant smile dimmed a few watts and she backed away.

***

Despite its showy souvenir shop entrance, the Alligator Farm's bar was a much more old-school environment. A long mahogany bar fronted a huge back mirror with an intricately carved border of wooden reptiles. The lighting was furnished by oil lanterns and was appropriately dark.

I was practicing an old bar room trick with a book of matches when I saw the lean, tall figure of Captain Jesse Kirk walk through the swinging doors. His cover was good. He looked nothing like an FBI agent, much less the agent in charge of all South Florida, but then again, he never did give a damn. He was wearing tattered khaki cargo pants, a blue short-sleeve button up, Birkenstocks, and a weathered fly-fishing cap complete with hooks and flies.

An experienced agent, Kirk located me through the dusky light right away.

It still took him almost ten minutes to reach me as he made small talk with every waitress in the bar. There were half a dozen fanny pats and kisses on the cheek during his trek. To the room, Kirk was loud and typical. To the women he nuzzled, he was all charm.

I stood as he approached and offered my hand in a gentlemen's greeting. He scowled, slapped my hand away, and engulfed me in a huge bear hug, completely lifting me off the ground. He did this because he was genuinely glad to see me, but also because he knew I despised dramatic greetings.

Pushing me back toward my stool, he said, "Nuclear-Mushroom-Cloud, how the hell are you my friend?"

Kirk did have a way with words. "Fine, I'm doing right fine."

"Well I'm not. Ain't been laid in almost..." he looked searchingly at his bare wrist, "nearly eighteen hours. Just about to burst with testosterone poisoning."

And so it would be. Some friends you made in life were high maintenance. They required constant watering, feeding, and pruning. Kirk was a cactus, one of those people I could neglect for years and the moment we saw each other, we would pick up right where we left off.

"Goddamn, you done shrunk down since the military. Looks like you should be the water girl instead of a pro-commando. And what the hell is this?" he said, while skinning the side of my head. "Holy head of gray, are you getting old, motherfucker?"

"Not old, ya slinky ass. I'm worn from all the sex and having to beat the fair maidens back at an alarming pace."

"That's my man, the old lieutenant who come from the country and could troll for pussy like a rock star. Tell me 'bout your life."

"I live up in the Cable Counties now. Have a little private detecting business, two women, two dogs, and a few million in the bank."

"Gaawwd damn, son. Those could be the lyrics to the next hit single."

"What's up with the life and times of the infamous Captain Kirk?"

Kirk hadn't been just any normal cadet at the Military Academy. He had been Captain of Cadets, the highest-ranking student during his senior year. He'd been responsible for the care and welfare of nearly a thousand cadets and had managed to make straight A's the entirety of his tenure at West Point.

He almost got serious. "Well, my friend, I'm just one year away from completing my ten-year plan. I've served my country as both a soldier and an FBI agent for my whole adult life, and about one year from now, I'm gonna cut the cord and start a business of my own. I've got it all worked out. I've made the contacts I'll need, and I'm going to be the highest-paid bounty hunter in the history of the world. I'm only gonna go after men on the FBI's most-wanted list—men who have at least a million dollars on their head. I've been hunting them for years and finding them. Now I'm gonna get paid for it."

I wouldn't have expected anything less than the most outrageous from my old friend.

Chapter 40

Kirk threw his head back, finishing the second of two shots of Fortaleza, a very smooth, hundred-year-old tequila. He washed it down with a loud slurp of beer and a belch. "Tell me 'bout old Earl and Bean. What are my favorite ex-sergeant's up to?"

I couldn't resist teasing my old friend. "Joined the priesthood."

Kirk's face turned a severe shade of black. "The fuck you say?"

I smiled.

Kirk understood and smiled back. "Good one, old buddy. I thought you was serious for a minute there."

"I got a couple problems. Well, to put it more accurately, a case that has grown two heads, and I was hoping you could help me out."

"Do what I can. What'cha got?"

"You heard about the National Championship Trophy being stolen?"

"Aww. My flattened tail feathers. You got *that* on your plate."

"That's how it all started, but now it seems the trophy heist might have been cover for something with a little more substance. I figure if I keep after the trophy, I might roll one into the other."

"What's the other?"

"Same night the trophy was stolen, a kid was killed on campus. I've been following a trail that could lead me to the asshole who stole the trophy, but it just might lead me to the same asshole who killed the boy."

"Got anything strong?"

In our vocabulary, when something was "strong," or a person was "strong," it was righteous, real, hard-fast and could be counted on. I looked back toward the bar mirror. "No, not yet."

Kirk raised two fingers, signaling for two more shots. He was in the game now. "What do you need from me?"

"I need to know who does business, this kind of business, from a boat."

He looked at me like I was just as unsophisticated as I truly was. "Hell man, there are just about two hundred thousand boats in South Florida, and every one of 'em has an owner who would give away the kids' inheritance to get one notch up on the ladder."

"This one probably lives on the boat, is a little more on the fringe than a tax evader, and doesn't mind killin' to get what he wants."

"That does narrow the scope of things, but not as much as you might hope. Who was the boy got killed?"

"His name was Amul Instad Facon. He was working on some kind of bacteria that could digest spilled petroleum."

Kirk looked stricken. He glanced around the room, then gestured for the bartender to bring the check. His dialect changed from its country origins to the professional he was. "Let's go out back. I might be able to help you, and you might just be able to help me."

Chapter 41

"Out back" was a walk of nearly a football field's length from the rear of the Alligator Farm Bar to an urban oasis. After we walked through at least a half-dozen check points, all completely camouflaged, but manned, we came to, as far as I know, the only out-door strip club in the entire world.

At each security checkpoint, Kirk gave a burly safari-dressed young man a twenty-dollar bill. When we reached the inner sanctum, a tribal-looking fellow took a hundred from Kirk.

"Best kept secret in South Florida. The Belly of the Beast is the hottest and most exclusive strip club in the world. Horny bastards from all over the planet come here to wish upon a bearded clam. We passed cheap 'cos I'm the captain, as far as these folks know. Usually the wicked would have spent a thousand just to get a glimpse."

***

The Belly of the Beast was much less populated than the tourist-laden bar and souvenir shop. There were scarcely twenty people in attendance, all male and heavily moneyed. The staff was all female, the waitresses, the bartenders, and, of course, the dancers. The dancing platform was made of rock and had several waterfalls cascading in between women in every stage of undress.

On the big jutting center rock was a very tall and full woman. She began her dance cloaked in the tattered remnants of a maiden who has been captured by cannibals. Two shorter but equally buxom lasses danced on either side of her. Each had a large python wrapped around her neck.

Kirk smiled at me while I indulged my eyes. He was obviously a veteran. "Hard to believe these lovelies are people just like us. They have to shower, shave, wear deodorant, and even though they wouldn't admit it, I'm pretty sure they fart from time to time."

I frowned. "Leave it to you to desecrate such a lovely vision."

We took a seat at a bamboo table that stretched the believability that woody vines could be shaped into anything so ornate. We didn't order, but just about the time my behind sunk into the leather seat, the same drink I had ordered inside was refreshed with a brand new one. The scantily clad waitress dipped bunny-style and set a full bottle of Fortaleza and two clean shot glasses in front of Kirk.

"You don't come here very much, do you?"

Kirk chuckled. "The life of an FBI man is fraught with danger and uncertainty. We seek small islands of comfort to keep sane. This is also the gathering place for more lords of crime than hell itself."

"Give me an example."

"When I was a little boy growing up in Hastings, my family was in the potato growing business. My dad was the king of our family, and as me and my brother grew into teenagers, he felt it necessary to make sure we understood he was the 'He Coon.' Several times during my youth, I remember the wondrous event that was dinnertime. This was always a silent affair, except for my father asking questions meant to shame us into admitting we weren't giving our all in some aspect of life. On a few occasions, when he wasn't satisfied that we were paying proper homage to the king, he would tell my mother to clear the table, and then would ask us if we trusted him. I was the oldest and was bent on pleasing the old man, so I would answer for both Rex and myself. 'Of course, we trust, with all of our hearts and souls.' He would pull out the end of the table, where the extra leaves were supposed to go, leaving a five-inch gap. He would say, 'Put your hand in the slot, and don't move it no matter what. If you do move it, I'll beat your sorry little asses.'

"As young lads, we were far too afraid of the old bastard to do anything but put our pencil-sized fingers into harm's way. Then the old man would look at us, deep into each of our eyes, and when he was satisfied, he would act like he was going to shove the leave gap shut. In all of the time I lived at home, I never could keep my hand there. He never went through with his threat to beat my ass, but the disappointment on his face was more crushing to my spirit than a broken hand would've been. Also it didn't help that Rex never moved his."

I listened intently to the story, but couldn't see how it fit in with our present situation. "Kirk, I wasn't asking for an example of your battle with fear and freedom. I was asking for an example of evil crime lords."

"Oh, well… just keep that story to yourself then."

"Yeah."

Kirk pointed to the center of the large stone bar. Sitting on a velvet pedestal was the National Championship Trophy. I'm afraid I truly gasped. "Is that what I think it is?"

Kirk threw back a shot. "If you think it's your missing trophy, then yeah."

"How'd you know? How did get here?"

"The owner of the Farm, young master Barker, is something of an eccentric. He runs with the real criminals to bolster his reputation. Word is he bought it off a man for a little under a million."

"Who?"

"Well that's what we have to figure out now, don't we?"

Chapter 42

Kirk looked around the outdoor pre-bordello. "Every one of the men sitting here is capable of paying for and pulling off a stunt like swiping the trophy. But several of them—hell, *most* of them—have cornered one little market or another, some legit, most not."

"Well goddamn Kirk, why don't you start busting them?"

"For starters, my country friend, evidence. These fellas didn't get rich because they were sloppy or failed to cover their tracks. This is the big league of crime. Second, let's take your trophy, for example. I don't give one tiny rat's ass about that trophy. I only care where it can lead me. Hopefully it leads me to crimes of significance, something that could really hurt people."

"Alright, alright, point made. Who would be your best guess for the trophy heist?"

"I got two in mind. And guess what, you lucky dog? They're both here this splendid evening."

I looked around the room. I guess I was looking for a drooping Black-Bart mustache or a sinister-masked villain. "Who are they?"

"See the really drunk guy up at that front table, the one who keeps trying to tuck hundred dollar bills into 'our lady of the snakes' panties? That's J.D. Re`bel. He runs the guns and a little prostitution in South Florida. He's a big football fan and definitely feels invincible, probably 'cos he's slipped us a dozen times or so. He fits real nice with everything you've been telling me. The only problem is, I hear he's been having some internal management problems, some of his lieutenants trying to take over aspects of his organization, so he's probably a little too busy to worry about something like the trophy."

"Who's the other one?"

"Before I answer you, I want to remind you not to stare. Besides being rude, it's a damn good giveaway."

I peeled back my hawking of the patrons and said with more than a little irritation, "Yes, Obi-Wan, I'm sure I'm not up to your standards of stealth, but I do know a little about surveillance."

Kirk smirked broadly, thrilled his little dart had hit its intended target—my ego. "Behind you, over in the shadows under an immense palm is one of the fattest tubs of shit you've ever seen. His name is Harry Wyatt Sullivan, but he prefers to go by just Harry Wyatt, and he has absolutely no record, and no crimes that we can attribute to him. But he's dirty, just as dirty as he is wide, only we haven't caught him yet."

"What's he suspected of?"

"You name it. We've gone after him for everything from tax evasion to multiple murders to international espionage. He always slides through on his bloated belly. He comes from money, big money provided by generations of big sugar."

Ding. Still, I needed to know more of what Kirk knew. "What makes you think he might be in on this?"

"I'll give you one guess?"

I was in no mood to play games, but I tried to assemble the facts as I knew them. "Fatso lives on a boat."

Kirk threw back another shot and looked very satisfied. "Absolutely fucking bingo."

Chapter 43

We decided to split up. I would take Harry Wyatt Sullivan and Kirk would take J.D. Re`bel. Kirk said he would put a team on each of the men first thing in the morning, but for tonight maybe we could just gather a little more information.

Within twenty minutes, Re`bel was so drunk, a couple of the men in his employ came to his aid and helped him make as gallant an exit as possible. They took him out through a hidden gate where I could see a stretch limousine waiting. Kirk nonchalantly got up and made his way from the bar.

Harry Wyatt wasn't nearly such a lightweight as J.D. It was about two hours later before the fat man motioned for a waiter to move the table away. Wyatt didn't walk. He came from the shadows perched on a modified ATV. He went through the camouflaged gate the same as J.D. Re`bel. I left a fifty on the table and hurried as fast as possible without making a scene toward the entrance door. I hoped Wyatt would leave the way I'd come in, as my vehicle was surely in the opposite parking lot as his. No such luck.

By the time I reached my truck, I knew Wyatt had a ten-minute head start. I circled the block where the Alligator Farm sat. I pounded the steering wheel in frustration. I was sure he must have had something to do with the death of Amul Instad Facon, but I'd lost him.

I assured myself, since now that Kirk and the FBI were on the case, I would have very little trouble picking him up tomorrow. I headed in the direction of Kirk's home. I tried to forget the missed opportunity by tuning to a soothing album the ladies had put in my player for just such occasions. Sister Hazel belted forth with "Change Your Mind."

What the hell was I doing anyway? I was being paid to retrieve the trophy, not to follow up on the death of some student. Why should I care about some foreign exchange student being killed. He was somebody I didn't know, *and* I wasn't being paid to care about him. I caught myself thinking of something I had recently read in a National Geographic Magazine. The author began with the old cliché, "When a tree falls in the forest and no one is there to hear it, does it make a noise?" He followed by saying, "Americans are oh so insulated against trees falling on other shores, they believe themselves to be over and above the crashing branches and rot which will surely come. When a tree falls, is cut in the rain forest, is burned or incinerated by napalm in a distant country, a little less oxygen is produced that day. And a little more pollution and trash is created."

We may not be our brother's keepers… or were we?

Chapter 44

The Florida Turnpike

Silasteck Ahmad drove almost too fast. He didn't remember when he'd last gotten a full night's sleep. That was of little consequence. He'd spent many a night in his life lying sleepless and for more mortal reasons than this. He was a few hours ahead of the big black man and his white brother. The effects of the stun gun would linger, and they would feel some tingling for a month or so, but they would surely be on his tail by morning. A quick phone call to Cloud would alert the prey to his pursuit.

Following the address the black man provided him, which he expected to be false, he arrived at a nondescript neighborhood on the outskirts of Miami. He was surprised to find a big black truck parked in front of the house. His friends from the 7-Eleven back in Cable had said that Cloud drove just such a truck.

He fumbled with the radio tuner as he sipped at the watery excuse for coffee he'd bought at a corner store. Perhaps when the job was done, he would patronize one of the Cuban coffee stands so prevalent in the area of Miami known as Little Havana. He searched the radio until he found a morning show that was all talk. The DJ was professing the downward spiral the United States would take if they continued to let every rag-head and sand-nigger set up shop at the corner of USA, one and main. Oxford educated or not, he wondered, was he a rag-head to these people? Or a sand-nigger? What the hell was a *real* nigger anyway?

At about six-fifteen, a tall man with disheveled hair left the house and got into a plain blue Buick sedan. Ahmad thought this to be the man who owned the house, not Cloud. He considered following this man to see what was what, but then concluded that his primary target was most likely in the house.

Ahmad didn't remember falling asleep, but he awoke and immediately looked at the dashboard clock. He shifted his eyes in a light panic and saw the truck was still there. He rubbed his eyes furiously and yawned in the dank cheese of the slept-in vehicle. A big man was not for surveillance, he was for action.

Twenty minutes later, Ahmad figured this as good an opportunity as he would get. Now dressed much like every common American in jeans and a white cotton shirt, he left the Explorer. He approached the door with some degree of trepidation. What if Cloud was a warrior, such as himself? To hell with that. Cloud had seen his final American sunrise.

Ahmad knocked on the door and waited. Within a minute, a man as dark as he was, wearing only boxer shorts, answered the door. "Yes? What can I do for you?"

The man appeared still sleep-weary. This was good. "I'm looking for the man named Cloud."

Ahmad saw recognition and alarm in the man's eyes. He pulled out the stun gun and stuck it to the man's neck. The man stumbled backwards and reached for a shoulder holster drooped over the back of a chair. Ahmad wasn't accustomed to anyone withstanding the shock of the stun gun. He looked left and right and then followed the falling man, pressing the gun to his ankle and hitting the button again.

Chapter 45

The Cable Counties

Cable Department of Law Enforcement cruiser number 168 backed down from its one hundred and ten mile-an-hour hustle across the counties. Blue had tried repeatedly to raise Earl or Bean on her mobile phone, but she'd received no answer. She wouldn't let herself panic. She knew Earl and Bean could take care of themselves, but this business included Cloud, and her nerves got a little more ragged with each unanswered phone call.

Dust and gravel spewed from her tires as she slid to a halt in front of Get-A-Head Taxidermy. Nothing seemed out of the ordinary, but she called the address into dispatch and told them she was going in.

Blue reached back into the cruiser and grabbed the shotgun. She checked the load and jacked a round into the chamber. The air was eerily tranquil. The life-like eyes of the big buck on the sign peered down at her. What would she find on the other side of that door? Her heart pounded against the bulletproof vest. Blue knew if anyone had hurt Cloud, she would kill them. She would forsake her training, her usual calm demeanor, and she would pump the scattergun and shoot until there were as many holes in the bastard as she could make.

She wanted to call out, but perhaps she would need the element of surprise. Maybe she should call for backup? That was what she was trained to do. No time for that—and dispatch would surely expect her to wait for the backup to arrive. There was no way in hell she was waiting for a goddamn thing.

In one swift move, Blue slung the screen door open and stepped inside, the shotgun at her cheek making a wall-to-wall survey of the interior of building. She shuffled into the room continuing to canvass the floor, ceiling and walls. Her breath was catchy and the adrenaline made her mouth feel as if she'd been eating sand.

Seeing no one, she made her way toward the circular workbench. "Earl, Bean, this is Cable Agent Sara Tableau," she called out. There was no answer.

There was a scratching sound to her left. Blue wheeled and almost shot Reuben, Earl and Bean's cur-hound pup. She eased the pressure back from the trigger, but kept the gun rock-steady at her cheek. She looked over the edge of the workbench and saw both Earl and Bean lying motionless. She felt her cheeks go hot. The rage was working itself into her veins. She wanted to jump the counter and tend to Earl and Bean, but if there was still someone here, that's exactly what they would expect her to do. Instead, she continued her canvass of the building. Blue took a moment to call dispatch on her mobile radio. "Dispatch, this is Agent 168. I am at previous ten-twenty with multiple ten-fifty three's. Am requesting backup and eleven forty-one, rapid emergency rescue."

Blue kicked open the back screen door and was momentarily startled when a bell tinkled overhead. She knew there was an old cook shed out back. As she approached the building, she noticed a faint plume of smoke rifting from a brick chimney. There was someone in there. She could feel ice-cold sweat rain down her back under the bulletproof vest. The door was propped open and she swung the barrel of the shotgun inside and into the wide, loving eyes of a large motherly black woman. Blue recoiled as she realized she'd almost emptied the 00 buck shot into the eye of Mama Bean.

Mama Bean spoke calmly despite the wild look in her eyes. "Blue, child? What in heaven's sake are you doing?"

Blue lowered the shotgun. "Mama Bean, are you alright?"

"Of course, child. What in the world is going on?"

"I guess you didn't hear anything. Earl and Bean are down in the shop."

"I know where they are. They been down there all morning whilst I been cooking up these here chitlins."

"No, Mama. They're *down*, lying on the floor. I'm not sure they're okay. Come with me."

The old woman's face fell, and her eyes took on the look only a mother with a child in danger could reveal. As big as she was, Mama Bean nearly ran over Blue as both women hurried back to the shop. Blue hurdled the counter as Mama Bean came around the outside. Blue lay her shotgun down beside Bean's body and began checking his vital signs. Bean was completely out, but all of his vitals seemed normal, and he was breathing. Mama Bean was soundless as she rolled Earl face-up and began rubbing his face with her calloused hands. "Oh my lord, baby child, wake up. What's wrong, sweet love? Please God, don't let him be dead."

Blue ran over to where Mama Bean cradled Earl's head and checked his vitals as well. They were the same as Bean's. Mama Bean looked through tear-riddled eyes, "Blue, tell me—tell me my babies are alive."

Blue gave her a faint smile, "They're alright Mama. They're just unconscious. I've already called for an ambulance. Let's see if we can bring them around."

Blue ran to a sink, grabbed two rags and soaked them. She returned to Mama Bean and handed her one. Both women were swabbing sweaty heads when the EMS crew burst through the door.

Thirty minutes later, both Earl and Bean were sitting on a wooden bench. They both had wet wraps on their heads and seemed to be almost functioning normally. Overcome in the moment, Mama Bean retreated to the cook shed with Blue. The old woman was still shaking, and she could only find relief in the familiar task of tending a boiling kettle.

Two burly emergency service technicians escorted Earl and Bean into the cook shed and helped them sit down at the picnic table. Mama Bean seemed not to notice.

Blue walked the two techs back out and stood in the yard talking to them. "What happened?"

"Somebody hit them with a stun gun. I'd reckon about twenty thousand volts. Not enough to do any permanent damage, but they'll feel like they got thirty-six loose teeth for a while."

"What now?"

"Well, they need rest. Their nervous systems have taken a hell of jolt, and they just need to take it easy."

"These boys won't take this easy, if I know 'em. They'll be moving hard, pretty damn quick. Will that cause any permanent damage?"

"No, but they'll crash once the adrenaline seeps out."

"Thanks, guys. I really appreciate what you did."

"It's what we do, you know that, Blue. As good as any."

As the EMS guys retreated, Blue turned back to the cook shed. When she passed through the door, she saw Earl and Bean's huge shoulders shuddering with convulsions as they both wrapped Mama Bean in a gigantic hug.

Chapter 46

Blue sat across the picnic table from Earl and Bean, as Mama Bean did her best to dote on both her boys. The boys were slurping and wrestling with bowls of something resembling gray, dead-snake soup. Blue suppressed a gag reflex as Mama Bean put a bowl of the same in front of her. Never one for subtlety, Blue asked, "What *is* this?"

Earl, Bean and Mama Bean all looked at her with sincere confusion. Mama Bean finally said, "Child, them's chitlins. Haven't you never had chitlins?"

Blue gathered as much grace as possible as she poked at the putrid-smelling bowl of worm guts. "No, I don't think so."

The boys looked surprised, but quickly resumed the revolting task of raking the gray tubes of flesh over their waiting teeth.

With a stunned look on her face, Mama Bean sat beside Blue. "You mean to tell me child, you done gone and grown up here in the South, and you ain't never had chitlins?"

"I'm sure I would've remembered. What are chitlins, anyway?"

Mama Bean heaved a heavy sigh. "They're only the tastiest morsel God ever let a good human eat. Them's hog guts, the intestines. I can't hardly believe you ain't never had'em."

Only because she didn't want to hurt the old lady's feelings, Blue took in a big sock of wind. "I'm sure they're just as good as you say, but I just don't think I could..."

Mama Bean reached over and patted Blue's hand. "That's alright, honey child. You just keep comin' round, and we'll make a real country gal of you yet."

The boys simultaneously pushed empty bowls toward the center of the table. Mama Bean noticed and shot from her seat as if propelled by mortar to get seconds for them both.

Blue took the moment. "Earl, what happened? What's up with this shit, and what does Cloud have to do with it?"

Earl unrolled a span of paper towels and mopped the gap in his face. "Blue, we gotta get in touch with Cloud, and I mean right now. That motherfucker…"

Mama Bean shot Earl a look to curl his toenails.

"Sorry, Mama. That bastard, son-of-a-bitch, big-assed sack of shit… is after Cloud, and you seen what he done to Bean and me."

Earl looked to Mama Bean. She turned to her boiling pot with a faint approving smile on her face.

"Is he really with Kirk?"

Earl nodded.

Blue looked at her phone, low bars, "Mama Bean, could I use your phone?"

***

Frustrated, Blue slammed the phone receiver back into its cradle. "Nothing Earl, do you have another number for Kirk?"

"No, but he's the big cheese for the FBI in South Florida. I reckon we could call information and get him through his office."

After ten minutes and just as many channel switches, Blue was on the line with Captain Jesse James Kirk. "Blue, I left him at my house this morning. We had dinner last night and were following up on some leads. Did you try his truck?"

Blue let out an exasperated sigh. "Of course I tried the truck and your house sixteen times so far."

"Well, let me get off with you and I'll call in some boys to check out the house. I'll be on my way right now."

Blue was at her terminal end of patience. "Listen Kirk, I don't really know you well. We only met that one time. But let me tell you, if Cloud is hurt in any way, I'm holding you personally responsible, and I'm the meanest bitch you ever imagined. You find him, and I mean right this minute. You call in every favor, snitch, and low-belly criminal you know and get my man in touch with me."

Kirk thought to himself, if any woman could possibly care about my ass like that, I'd damn well think myself to be in the warm glow of heaven. Still he couldn't resist a sermon, "Listen, bitch, I'll do my damndest. Where can I reach you?"

Blue knew he wasn't the enemy, but he was still playing games, even at such a time. "I'm on my way down there. I'm bringing Earl and Bean, and somebody else who'll be even more intent on cutting your balls off. If Cloud is—"

"Give me the number. And Blue? I'm on your side, so cut the shit."

Blue trembled with rage. She looked over each digit of her mobile phone with a barb. "However this works out, Kirk, I want a chance to teach you some manners when it's all said and done."

Kirk smiled. "It'll be my pleasure... Bitch."

Chapter 47

Miami

Shasta pulled at the G-string riding up her sculpted ass as she hurried along the path connecting the Alligator Farm to the Belly of the Beast. She was late just about every day, but she figured she made up for her tardiness with effort and intensity on the stage. She smiled at Gordon, the bouncer in his tribal costume, as she passed through the sweeping palm frond entrance.

Her music was already playing, and she was sure Marcus, the dickhead manager, had already put somebody else in her place on the rotation. The only way to keep her job was to do what she always did, explode on the stage and make every crotch in the male-infested place bulge with lust. Just as the music reached the point where someone was supposed to emerge from the dark background shadows, she did a cartwheel, four back somersaults, and landed, licking her fingers, on the jagged outcropping of the main stage. A huge plume of propane fire lit up the running waterfalls. It was magic, and she looked through heavy mascara at the boned-up men in the front seats. With three well-timed bats of her dark lashes, she said to those waiting hard-ons, "Want some?"

***

Harry Wyatt Sullivan dropped another oyster shell and his jaw at the same time. Sex-on-a-stick, this nymph was just the dessert he craved.

Just at that moment a staggering, sloshed J.D. Re'bel sat down heavily at Wyatt's table. Wyatt was incensed at the interruption. J.D. mouthed carefully, but the words still came out slurred. "Harry Wyatt Sullivan, you old bastard, how the hell are you?"

Wyatt hoped to keep the conversation short by saying just what he was thinking. "J.D., you drunk retard, I was just fine until you sat your sorry ass down at my table and ruined the eye-contact I was making with the fine young lady doing the dancing."

J.D. was too drunk to register Wyatt's irritation. "Well that's spectacular. Thinking you might bone her, huh?"

What the hell was a man to do? This moron was messing up his infrequent shore leave. "J.D., where're your goons? That pack of well-dressed pimps you travel around with?"

Re'bel laughed as if this was the funniest thing he'd ever heard. He leaned into the table and made an ineffective whisper. "I snuck out on 'em. They been fuckin' up my social life, if you know what I mean."

Wyatt was a man of short temper when it came to dealing with most people. He had an idea, it might mess up business here in The Belly for a while, but what the hell, he didn't get around much anyway. "Don't look now, but I think one of your boys just ducked into the shadows beyond the bar. Probably trying to follow you without your knowing it."

Re'bel tried unsuccessfully to look with nonchalance towards the bar. Wyatt saw the man take the bait. "If I were you, J.D., I'd go right on over there and give that boy an ass-chewing."

The drunken man tried a look of intensity on for size. "You know, Harry Wyatt, I think I'll do just that." Re'bel leaned out of his seat and kept the perpetual motion of the drunk with him all the way to the shadows.

Wyatt turned his many chins slightly to the left and spoke into the fictional jungle behind him. "Zan, dinner time."

Zan moved stealthily after J.D. Re'bel.

Wyatt enjoyed nearly three more hours eating and watching the ladies as they made quite a show of losing their clothes.

J.D. Re'bel never enjoyed anything ever again.

Chapter 48

Blue, Emma, Earl, and Bean made the six-hour drive from Cable to Miami in a little over four. With all that had happened, the mood was frenzied. Earl and Bean had enough rage for everyone, but they were amazed at Blue's determination and almost frightened by Emma's intensity.

Emma was normally the calm one, the matriarch of Cloud's unusual little family. The placid, polished English professor was now on red alert. She oozed fear, but at the same time, she smelled of violence. Earl and Bean kept mostly quiet.

As the foursome pulled into Captain Kirk's drive, the already thick air in the vehicle became stifling. There were four nondescript sedans parked in front of the house. Blue drove around them and jumped from the vehicle just as it stopped moving.

Kirk met her at the doorway. He didn't need an introduction. Blue met his eyes from five feet away and never broke stride. Just as she blew right past him, a tall dark woman he'd never met wheeled and punched him nicely in his haughty teeth.

More from surprise than from pain, he reached to his mouth. He licked his gums and tasted blood. He followed them inside. Earl and Bean were just managing to extricate their vast bulk from the Dodge Durango.

Kirk motioned to the men in the doorway and spoke into a hidden microphone. "These ladies are with me. Do not interfere."

Earl and Bean, somber, but managing a half-smile stood in front of him.

Bean offered his hand, and Kirk slid past it to hug the big man. He backed from the embrace and did the same to Earl.

Earl said, "Captain."

"Sergeants, how the hell are you all?"

Bean mostly tried to let Earl do all of the talking when they were approached. Earl said, "We've been right fine, up until now. What have you found out?"

"Somebody came in here after I left and looks like they took him. I can hardly believe I'm saying that, 'cos I can't imagine anyone, present company included, who would be *man* enough."

Bean looked over at Earl. Kirk could see a look of hesitation and shame on their faces. Earl sighed. "Well, Captain, I reckon *we* could imagine someone man enough." Earl gave the story of their brief but lasting encounter with the Arab.

Kirk took it all in with some degree of frustration and fear. "You say the man was dressed funny. What do you mean?"

Bean knew when he spoke, he revealed to the world his lack of sophistication. Still, he could resist the urge no longer. "Like in Aladdin and the Magic Lamp, only he was huge—and I mean *big*, too."

Kirk looked at Bean—all six foot six inches and nearly three hundred pounds of him. If Bean was saying the man was big... "A man that big and dressed like Aladdin, somebody would've had to see something."

Emma and Blue came in for the last of Kirk's statement. They seemed none too pleased with this elementary deduction. Kirk thought it best to extend the olive branch. He didn't need wild-assed women out there making his life even harder. "Sorry if I was crass when we spoke on the phone," he said to Blue.

Blue nodded. It would be as much of an apology as he would get from her.

Earl dipped into the conversation and formally introduced Emma to Kirk. Kirk hadn't been able to see what a beauty she was when she punched him in the mouth. The raven black hair, dark skin and features—and she was very tall. Kirk wasn't sure what he'd done to her, but he apologized anyway.

Emma spoke with a raspy sandpaper voice, one that cuts your eardrums but feels oh so nice. "I didn't hit you because you were insensitive with regard to Cloud. I hit you because you called my girlfriend a bitch."

Chapter 49

Forty thousand feet over the Atlantic Ocean

When I woke up, I felt like I would rather continue to be unconscious. I tried to take inventory, but even that hurt. I certainly didn't want to move, which was a good thing because I quickly realized I was bound with some expertise to my seat. Several thick rounds of duct tape held my wrists firm to the arms of the chair and my feet felt the same glue of rough tape.

I managed to shrug my shoulders a little and shift my rear in the seat. I felt the rip as several hairs on my wrists and ankles gave way to the sticky tape. A thick swatch was holding my mouth shut, making breathing possible only through my nose. I licked at the bitter glue, trying to free my lips a little. It tasted of sulfur.

As I looked around my surroundings, I felt my seat fall out from under me momentarily. I was on a plane. A window provided a monotonous view of clouds and blue sky.

There was one other person in the cabin—the man who had surprised me in the doorway of Kirk's home. He was absolutely enormous even while sitting down. He looked at me with indifference through coal-black eyes. If I had found myself under water staring at those eyes, I was sure the crushing jaws of a Great White shark would have followed them.

My traveling companion noticed I was awake. He shifted his eyes to my bindings, then back to my face. I kept my look neutral, trying not to let him

sense the discomfort of my body and the duress in my chest.
 I feigned sleep.

Chapter 50

Miami

FBI Special Agent Brian Bellows hated working for Captain Jesse Kirk. In Brian's mind, the captain was barely one notch better than the criminals they pursued. The captain kept the men who worked for him on a very short leash. But the rules simply didn't apply to the captain himself. Special Agent Bellows had been with the Bureau for barely three years, but even in that short time, he could recognize a prima donna.

Compound his arrogance with his southern dialect, and you could only assume that Kirk had done favors for the dark side during his career. But even Brian couldn't discount the victories. Kirk always got his man. As a team member of the Special Agent in Charge, at least some of the captain's success rubbed off on him.

Brian had been given the dog duty of being in charge of incoming communications. This was another reason to hate the old man. If Kirk would only see his ability and give him a chance, then he could catch the right clue that could break a big case.

Brian walked into the entrance area of the home and saw the captain speaking to two very attractive women and two Neanderthals. He put on his best ass-kissing face and approached the Kirk. "Sir, a communiqué from headquarters. Could I speak to you in private?"

Kirk rolled his eyes at the overly-proper language. "Brian... just tell me— and listen boy... Never mind. What is it?"

Bellows felt his face go hot with anger and embarrassment. He thought to himself, *One day, one day…* "Sir, there is a problem over at that strip bar, the Belly of the Beast. They think somebody has been killed."

Kirk tried to mute his impatience. "Brian, it's nearly noon. The damn bar ain't even open. Do they have a dead body or not?"

Brian looked around the group standing with the Captain. "Sir, I really think I should tell you in private."

Kirk slapped at the back of a chair several times. "Brian, tell me right this goddamn minute."

The young agent made up his mind right there to request a transfer just as fast and as far away as possible. "The opening cleaning crew found some parts—some ah… body parts near the bar. There's a whole lotta blood but not much to determine whether there is a… body or not."

The redhead chimed in. "Are you saying there're no bones or teeth, or anything?"

Brian looked at the intruder. He didn't answer to friends of the SAC; he didn't even want to answer to the SAC himself.

Kirk saw the impending explosion coming and tried to cut it off. "Brian, that's all. Could you run out front and ask one of the uniformed officers to give you a can of Squelch?"

Brian looked at the woman with abject distain and left to do his important task while maintaining a sideways glance at her.

When the young man was through the doorway, Earl and Bean both busted out with uncontrolled laughter. Emma looked at the two brothers as if they had lost their minds.

Blue shifted her eyes back to Kirk. The FBI man was smiling. She could imagine what was so funny. "Agent Kirk, I'm sure this is a once-a-day laugh riot for you, but don't you think we should behave as if the situation were a little graver?"

"What's Squelch?" Emma asked.

Earl jumped in to save the situation. "It's radio frequency. It's in the air waves."

Emma looked confused.

"The Captain was just getting rid of that boy. Squelch don't come in a can, it's… it's damn, it's just a way to get fellas who are in the way, *out* of the way," Bean said.

Chapter 51

South Florida Sugar Country

The back gate of a customized Land Rover touched down softly onto the loose black sand. In every direction, crisp long leaves of sugar cane hung limply beside the stalks. Harry Wyatt Sullivan maneuvered his retrofitted ATV from the vehicle and down the ramp. This area of the sugar plantation was known as Scrug Quarter Parrish. No one, not even Wyatt himself, could remember why the desolate area had been named so.

Kari Vilano-Lobos waited for Wyatt to get his wheels on the earth, then closed the gate of the Land Rover.

Cal Taylor, the foreman of Scrug Quarter Parrish, looked on as his boss, a man he'd never met, drove his ATV in close. He saw a very slim brown boy dressed completely in white. He reckoned this was a nurse of some sort. In the background, several harvesting machines mowed through the cane field, pitching up a black dusty cloud.

Taylor kept his arms at his side in a humble posture. He'd heard rumors of the rage Wyatt could exact when things were not up to his expectations. Wyatt locked onto Cal Taylor with eyes ensconced in desert-wear sunglasses. "Cal, we've not had a very intimate working relationship over the years, but I hear you're an A-Number One straw boss."

Cal loosened a bit with the praise. "Mr. Sullivan, we're bringing nearly forty-three tons per acre this season, and that's a conservative estimate."

Wyatt couldn't care less. Sugar had brought him this far, but from now on, it would merely be a diversion. "Cal, I would like for you to leave a three or four row buffer out near the road, kind of a moat made of sugar cane stalks."

Taylor scrunched up his face in misunderstanding. "Mr. Sullivan, the perimeter of SQP along the road amounts to nearly fifty acres. That's more than two thousand tons of sugar at our present rate."

Wyatt had anticipated just such an answer from a competent farmer like Cal Taylor. "Cal, I appreciate your diligence. Just so you can rest easy, you need to know I'm prepared to pay a double bonus on the sugar you would have harvested. I got my reasons, and I know a smart fellow like yourself can understand that."

Cal *didn't* understand. Why in the name of God would you leave good sugar in the field to rot? His lips parted to make just such a statement, then he thought better of it. He looked over his shoulder at the new barn and wondered. No one had been allowed to get within fifty yards of the place. It had been built since last season, but to his knowledge had nothing to do with the sugar growing business.

Taylor just nodded and asked, "Will there be anything else, Mr. Sullivan?"

Wyatt shifted his gaze to Kari Vilano-Lobos. She reluctantly moved forward and produced a brown bag. She handed it to Cal Taylor without a word.

Cal accepted the bag and looked quizzically at the fat man.

"I'm paying the annual bonus now, up front. There's fifty-thousand dollars cash in that bag. You take your share and then distribute it any way you see fit to your crew. I trust your judgment." Wyatt gave as much of a smile as he could muster.

Chapter 52

Wyatt rolled into the enormous barn and breathed deeply. It was the rotten stench of crude oil being mined, but to Wyatt, it smelled delicious. Kari walked just to his side, an intimidating presence in her black leather outfit. She kept her sunglasses on despite the gloom. Zan seemed overwhelmed with the gadgetry.

A middle-aged Asian man, fumbling with a clipboard, ran to Kari. He spoke in broken English. "Ms. Boss, pumps are functioning at high capacity and with extreme efficiency."

Kari looked at him as if he were a bug. She snatched the clipboard from his hands, and he cowered. After she examined the paperwork, she slammed the clipboard back into the man's chest.

Wyatt was wrestling with his sunglasses. The cord around his fat neck was pinched in the deep folds. "Kari darling, do tell what our production rate might be."

A wet, red tip of tongue slipped from between black lips and dampened one corner of her mouth. "It's huge, more than we ever expected. I estimate that we will rival the Alaskan oil fields."

Wyatt wiggled an index finger at Zan, who produced a cigar nearly as wide as it was long. He clipped the end of the fat stogie with a practiced mark. Just as Zan was putting the cigar to his mouth, Kari snatched it from him. He almost pounced, but a stare with tangible awareness from Wyatt gave him pause.

Kari Vilano-Lobos licked the tip of the phallic cigar and then held it firmly in her lips. She turned and with both hands began to search the pockets of Zan's pants. He could only slink as her knuckles grazed the expanding space between his legs. After a zealous search, she took her hands out but kept her shaded eyes directly on Zan. She rolled the cigar between fingers glossed with black nail polish. With the other hand, she flicked the blue flame of the lighter and carefully lit every cinder.

Kari inhaled deeply. A small crack of porcelain tooth was evident at the corner of her mouth as she tossed the lighter just out of Zan's reach. She turned the cigar from her mouth and offered it to the jowly face of Wyatt. He accepted the moist end and looked severely at Zan, who dipped his head with shame and knelt to retrieve the lighter.

"Kari darling, let us visit the spill scenario."

In front of a bubbling tub resembling a toilet with back flow problems, Wyatt and Kari met another Asian man. This one spoke perfect English. "Ms. Boss, the spill scenario has been underway for nearly three weeks. Just yesterday we applied the bacteria to this outer tub."

All eyes turned to the clean-flowing tub to the right of the boiling septic waste of the original tub. "Are you saying that twenty-four hours ago, this clean water was just as polluted as the original?" Kari asked.

The man beamed with pride, as if he'd enacted the miracle himself. "That is precisely what I am saying. Yesterday at this exact time, this clean water held twenty-two parts per million unrefined crude oil. In less than a day, the water is eighty-percent cleaner than ordinary drinking water. At this point it could be bottled as Evian."

Harry Wyatt Sullivan pressed a pedal on his ATV and headed for the exit. Kari followed with a lightness to her step.

Wyatt tossed the half-smoked cigar towards Zan, who caught it in mid-air and extinguished the flame against his tongue. "Well my dear, it appears our dear, departed college student was quite the visionary, don't you think? If he had survived, he might well have been awarded some Nobel Prize. Let us get in touch with the big oil companies and start a bidding war for the bug."

Chapter 53

The airspace over Doha, Qatar

I stretched against the tape; it didn't yield. Through fluffy eyelids I saw the big man. He never seemed to tire or falter. I recognized in him a professionalism that, though he was my captor, I admired.

I felt my balls seize as the plane touched down. I could only wonder where on God's green earth this suppository had landed me. As a world traveler, I was very aware, as a kidnap victim, I had some learning to do.

When the plane finally came to a complete stop, I heard the voices of several eager men speaking in Arabic. A man with a stringy beard poked his head into the cabin. My captor rose to his full height but had to bend his head forward to miss the top of the capsule.

The man who had put his head into the cabin was obviously trying to take control of the situation. My captor would have none of it. After a barrage of spitting Arabic, my captor slapped the head-in-the-cabin with such a severity as to eject him from the plane. I didn't know whether to see this as a positive sign or not.

The plan I had formulated was weak. It depended on an indifference to detail the big man had not shown so far. But, I just couldn't think of anything else, and I reckoned the next move was going to be a bit more severe, so what did I have to lose?

I continued to act groggy as he bent to cut the tape from my legs and wrists. He roughly pulled me to my feet and slapped me twice to get my attention. I cowered at being struck. He was aggravated with my clumsiness and pushed me toward the door of the aircraft.

In the doorway, I latched onto the inner railing and let loose a soft moan. He moved to pull my hands loose and then I had him right where I wanted him. I crouched low. As he bent over me, I exploded into him with my shoulder. He was caught off balance and fell backwards with the force, tumbling down the ramp.

I pulled a lever beside the door and the stairway began to retract. I quickly moved toward the cabin and kicked the door with everything I had. Even though I had never flown a plane with jet engines, under the circumstances, I was prepared to give it a go.

The cockpit door flew inward and I lunged at the pilot. With my hands around the pilot's neck, the last thing I remembered seeing was the glint of a gold tooth as someone from behind cracked my skull and the light of the world evaporated as if the sun had exploded.

Chapter 54

I woke up briefly and looked through hooded eyes as I was unloaded from someone's shoulder. The damp floor came up to meet me and my chin make contact with rough stone. As I was fading out again, I had a strange thought. I had gotten out of the military because, among other things, I had already suffered five concussions. I thought a life outside the sport of covert intelligence would be a little safer on the old melon. For the second time in the last few hours, the haze of the day faded to gray.

In my dream, I was jogging around the lip of a small lake. As I ran, the earth tilted and I had to overcompensate so I could stay on the bank. With each step the degree of the tilting earth grew steeper until I was no longer jogging but crawling, trying to stay in sync with terra firma. I lunged to grab hold of a small stand of water grass at the edge of the lake. Even with the grass firmly in my grasp, the world continued to tilt on a spiral and I found myself holding on to mother earth so I wouldn't be flung out into the cosmos. Then, I was drowning—the water wasn't over my head, but being forced against my face continuously through some high-pressure pipe.

I rolled to my right and saw a small light, high above. I put my hands out and tried to kick toward the light. Another bolt of water crashed over my face as if wave upon wave were trying to force me down. A moment later I realized I wasn't drowning. I wasn't hanging upside down from the earth. I wasn't unconscious anymore.

I spat and felt the slime from a strand of saliva slink back towards me and rest against my bare chest. Getting to my knees and still feeling the moist stones, I looked between my shaking arms and realized I was naked.

I fell sideways onto my back and looked up into three very grim-faced men. One of them was the one who had captured me from Kirk's home. He wore a bloody bandage around his head.

I rubbed at my aching face as one of the other men yelled at me. He was spitting some unknown profanities and dousing me with buckets of water.

I struggled beneath the deluge. I held my breath for one bucket and then managed to speak. "I... don't know what you want. I... don't know what you're saying."

The third man, who was much smaller but seemed to be the one in charge, held up his hand toward the bucket brigade. He bent down close to my face, his features were blurry and I raised a hand to make sure he was really there. I was rewarded by the big man smashing his foot down onto my outstretched arm. The pain was sobering, and I was sure he had broken some bones in my forearm.

As I rolled into a fetal position to protect myself, I heard the smaller man say, "Do not kill him. Do anything else to find out if he had any accomplices, but do not kill him."

The bucket man bent into my range of vision and spoke English for the first time. "You killed my cousin, make no mistake you will die a long and painful death, but if you tell me what I want to know, I won't make you eat your own heart."

That was comforting. I struggled to speak again. "I haven't killed anyone; you have the wrong man."

The small man spoke again. "Asheen, forget these stupid measures, give him the shot."

Someone slipped a loaded syringe into my neck. The feeling which came over me was entirely pleasant. I felt warm and sloppy. I even smiled as I rolled onto my back and laughed at their upside-down faces.

The big man jerked me from the floor and slammed me into a rough wooden chair. I didn't care. I was seeing a warm glow around each of their faces and was feeling the comforting edges of the chair.

I only remember the first question they asked. I was confused as to why they would ask such a thing. "Why did you kill Amul Instad Facon?"

Chapter 55

The following blackness was the end of sanity. I was carried away by the devils from hell astride horned white horses and a limbless woman. Several times I called out for Blue or Emma, but each time I received no response. I saw the hazy face of my father as he ranked on me through a drunken stupor. I saw Earl and Bean, but they were always running away from me. Then I saw the ragged hole in the Earth as I threw the corpse of my little dog Jack into its bowels.

When I next achieved consciousness, I was alone. I was naked, shivering, and hedged against the wall of some dungeon. Cramps of hunger stabbed at my gut and my mouth felt like I'd been eating glue.

I recalled a book I'd read about a man who'd been a prisoner of war during World War II. He realized his captors could take everything from him but his mind. He would not give that to them, he decided. He played golf, drank and joked with friends, made love to his wife, and sent his kids to good schools, all within the confines of his mind.

I decided this was my model. I constructed a pleasant evening at my home in Cable. I was tending a fire in the back yard, getting ready to grill some fat steaks. Emma and Blue were sitting on lawn chairs in the shallows of Lake Santa Fe. Their giggles and shrieks of glee were tempting, but we had company. Earl and Bean sat at the edge of the fire and ate boiled peanuts and laughed at all of my jokes.

Just as I was feeling the shivers and shudders began to stall, the room was bathed in ferocious light. I rolled onto my belly and held my hands against my face to protect my eyes from the invading light.

When I could stand the light, I saw the same three men were again in my little corner of hell. The thought came not from my brain, but from my spine. I jumped up and ran yelling, naked and full of fear and hate at the small man. Before I could reach him, the big man slammed a concrete fist into my eye. I felt my face crush and envelope his hand. Amazingly, more to me than anyone else, I kept my feet and backed away. I was laughing. I felt the madness growing hair on the back of my neck. Treat me like an animal, and an animal you shall deal with.

I backed off and heard myself cackling like the mad man I had become. I dug my toenails into the grit of the stone floor and ran at the small man again. Again the big man slammed his fist into the side of my face. This time it had a little more bite, and as I backed away my legs went limp. My knees buckled, and once again I became intimate with the wet, sticky stone floor.

The same man bent over me and stuck the same syringe into my neck and the same initial feelings of warmth overcame me. I fought the winged devils from hell again that night.

As far as I can remember, this happened four more times.

Chapter 56

Miami

Blue slammed her hand down on the desk, scattering several top-secret documents. "I'm coming with you, and that's all there is to it."

She, Emma, Earl, and Bean had just come from the gory scene at the Belly of the Beast and were sitting in Kirk's office. While Kirk and company surveyed the scene at the top-notch strip club, he'd sent several agents to investigate what little information they had collected.

It didn't take long for the agents to make a connection between the dead college student and the hulking figure who kidnapped Cloud. It seemed everyone involved had a common connection with the Middle Eastern country of Qatar.

The dead kid was the son of the Sultan of Qatar. The kidnapper didn't have a name as far as they knew, but from what the agency could figure, he was a frequent weapon for the Sultan.

Kirk knew dealing with anyone in the Middle East was dicey. Normal diplomatic relations would force a bureaucracy into action, which would move forward at less than a sloth's pace. Kirk decided swift action must be taken. He would use every card in the deck to make a deal, but an extraction was probably the only way to get Cloud back.

Blue didn't think she had gotten the bastard's attention. She raked every paper, phone, and pencil from the SAC's desk. "Did you hear me, you incredibly insensitive bastard?"

"I heard you, Blue, and I'm telling you, it just ain't gonna happen. Now calm your ass and let me tell you how it's gonna go down."

Blue's chest was heaving. Emma came to her side and tried to comfort her. Earl and Bean fidgeted.

"You don't have to take my word for it, Blue. Ask Earl and Bean. Women don't rate much in the Muslim world. You come with us, and you'd just be baggage. The kind we'd have to watch out for instead of getting Cloud back."

Blue looked into Earl's hollow eyes. He nodded.

"I've called in every marker I have. I will have to resign when I get back, 'cos I tell ya, I'm probably gonna have to break every international law there is to get him back. But let me tell ya something else, lady, I don't have many friends on this whole goddamn earth, but Cloud is just that, and I ain't letting him die over there."

Blue was moved by the SAC. She backed it down a little. "What can we do?"

Kirk knew he had to give her something to do or she would find a way to follow. "These people think Cloud did something he didn't do. While we're over there trying to convince them of that, you need to stay here and figure out who really did it. Somebody killed that kid and tried to cover it by stealing the trophy. Find out who killed the kid, and when we get back, we'll all go and cut their balls off."

"Earl and Bean…"

"…are experienced operators. We've all fought over there before. Earl and Bean know the people, their customs, and the terrain. I can't do it alone, and I can't take any agents with me without causing an international uproar."

Emma saw the pain on Blue's face, and she could hardly stand it. She bent toward Kirk and took his face in both of her hands. "You go and bring our man back, understand?"

Kirk nodded.

Chapter 57

Within twenty-four hours, Kirk, Earl, and Bean were airborne aboard a small jet that Kirk blackmailed the use of from a South Florida drug lord. He *had* used every marker he'd collected during his career with the FBI to get the equipment and supplies they would need.

This wasn't exactly how Kirk envisioned his exit strategy from the Bureau, but then he hadn't known his friend would be caught in such dire straits. Kirk sat in the dim light of the jet's cabin scratching out his plan on a yellow legal pad. He'd drawn up many a battle plan, but never with so few human resources and in such a hostile environment.

An encrypted satellite phone beeped every few minutes, and another friend of the SAC would ante up information or supplies. Kirk knew his superiors would begin to miss him after only forty-eight hours. He framed the mission into this time limit. Once he was found out, his ability to call in favors would diminish quickly.

It was really for the best anyway. After forty-eight hours, if they hadn't found Cloud and had him back in the air, well… that would probably mean they'd all be dead anyway.

The flight should take just under twelve hours. They'd land them in Qatar on a private airstrip owned by a wealthy Saudi businessman who Kirk had helped out some years ago. He encouraged Earl and Bean to rest and sleep as much as possible during the first part of the flight. He told them the second half would be for reviewing the game plan and setting up a few contingencies.

Just as Kirk settled in for a couple of winks himself, the sat-phone rang. He listened for a moment and then began to make notes. It took only two minutes for Kirk to receive the best bit of intelligence he'd gathered so far. He disconnected, thanking his friend for the information, probably for the last time.

He finished up his plan, napped for about an hour, then woke Earl and Bean. "Gentlemen, I received a tip from a friend of mine who I consider a very reliable source. There was a minor disturbance at the Qatar International Airport a couple of days ago. Some witnesses said a man fitting Cloud's description was unloaded from a private jet after a bit of a scuffle. My source says he looked unconscious. The source was able to provide me with the aeronautical identifier numbers on the tail of the plane. I traced them and found out the plane is registered to a dummy corporation, but it's really owned by the Sultan of Qatar himself. From this, I think we can positively conclude the Sultan or someone working for him has our man."

The two ex-Army men listened with rapt attention. "Captain, you have any intelligence detailing the location of the Sultan?" Earl asked.

Even after years of being civilians, Earl and Bean slipped back into the language and customs of the military with ease. Since this was an extraction and had every semblance of a military operation, Kirk spoke to the two men in military dialect. "I have mapped out the exact location of the palace, as I guess you'd call it, where the Sultan lives. However, getting in there and getting Cloud out will be very difficult. The Sultan has a state security force guarding the palace grounds. I'm expecting one more favor from one of my friends. If it comes through, then we should have the layout for the whole palace and the grounds surrounding it. I have considered a more diplomatic approach—just going in and trying to reason with the Sultan, tell him Cloud had nothing to do with his son's death. The problem with this approach is that I don't think the Sultan will believe me, and we will've put them on alert to the fact we know he's there."

Earl spoke again. "Captain, if we did it that way, they might just go ahead and kill Cloud, and then probably us as well. Then send out some news release saying we were a rogue element trying to terrorize the Sultan."

"Exactly, so we're going in covert and with the surprise. I hope to find out exactly where Cloud is and get to him before they can consider that option."

"So how're we going in?"

"When we arrive, it will be the middle of the night, roughly 0200 hours Qatari time. A black-ops chopper will meet us at the private airstrip where the jet lands. It will take us directly to the home of the Sultan. The problem is that I couldn't get them to come back for us after we extract Cloud. We'll have to find some other means of transportation to get us back to the airstrip."

Bean was focused. He was trying to take in every word so he wouldn't make any mistakes. Bean, a man who many would consider slow in the civilian world, had been a brilliant soldier. Give him a map, directions, and an order, and the man followed it to perfection.

"Captain, that doesn't seem a very optimistic exit strategy on our part. Shouldn't we try to get some transportation arranged before we land?" Earl asked.

"Point well taken, Sergeant, but time is not on our side, so we'll take the ingoing transportation and make do on the way out."

All three men thought about the gravity of the plan. It was far from perfect, but no one could suggest any practical changes. Earl thought to himself how odd it was that he still didn't feel any fear for himself. He could only focus on the danger to Cloud.

Kirk continued with the plan. "When we reach the target, we will go after the Sultan himself. If we have him as a hostage, we can be reasonably sure of getting out. Besides, I assume the palace is substantial and we'll need him to get us to the exact location where they're holding Cloud."

Kirk pointed to pile of duffel bags. "I know both of you were Army Rangers. I hope you haven't forgotten what you learned in Air Assault School."

Both of the boys looked at the captain with more than a little dread in their eyes.

Kirk ignored that. "The chopper won't land; we'll be making a dynamic air entry from the helicopter. What I'm saying is, those black bags over there contain the rigging for repelling onto the roof. Tell me right now if either of you don't think you can do it."

The military bearing took over Bean's mind. "I'm ready, Captain."

Earl was just a second slower, but he said the same. Kirk knew this would be the men's conclusion. He spoke with a smile. "Good, then let's suit up."

Chapter 58

Barely ten minutes after the screech of the jet's wheels, Kirk, Earl, and Bean were in the cargo area of a helicopter. The chopper lifted off, and with the upward motion, Earl felt his stomach rise into his throat. Kirk and Bean were feeling the effects of adrenaline as the moment of danger approached.

The sky outside was deathly dark and very few lights reflected on the horizon as they entered the airspace of Qatar's capital city. Moments later a red shadow of a light blinked twice, signaling the men they were almost in position. With a series of hand signals, the men checked each other's equipment and communicated that they were ready to go.

The light in the cargo area changed from red to yellow. The chopper was in position and maneuvering for target. Kirk slid the door open and stepped one foot out onto the railing. Earl and Bean followed and stood in the doorway. All eyes were on the yellow light.

With one blink, the light turned from yellow to green, and Kirk instantly pushed away from the chopper, stepping out into the blackness. With no hesitancy, Earl and Bean followed. Twenty feet down the slithering rope, the men landed on the roof of the Sultan's palace.

The black ops chopper was nearly silent. The three men took up positions and secured the roof. The chopper moved noiselessly off into the darkness.

The layout map of the house seemed to be up to date. Kirk only hoped his contact who had supplied the map was as keen as he'd been a few years prior. They found a doorway and moved down a long spiral set of stairs, covering each other with every step.

The layout map indicated the Sultan's bedroom was on the top floor of the palace, a kind of penthouse. Cautiously and without a sound, the three men moved down a short corridor and came to the door of the Sultan's bedroom. It was unlocked, but creaked slightly as Kirk pushed inwards.

They were armed—MP-5 machine guns with laser sighting. Red, thin shafts of light moved from floor to ceiling to walls. A snuffled snore came from a large bed with a canopy. Kirk gave Earl and Bean a hand signal telling them to cover, while he went to the side of the bed.

The Sultan was sleeping soundly. Kirk wondered what he'd expected—a harem, at least a wife or two—but the Sultan was alone. He had come prepared with several rags dipped in chloroform. He'd been prepared to wrestle a few women and put them into a deep sleep. This wasn't necessary, and Kirk breathed a sigh of relief.

Earl looked over his shoulder at the captain, just as Kirk drew a serrated knife. Earl knew the captain was a righteous man, and he trusted Kirk wouldn't kill unless necessary.

Kirk tilted the knife blade to the dull side and pressed it against the Sultan's neck. The snoring stopped and the Sultan opened his eyes. He didn't make a sound.

Kirk bent close and said, "Do you speak English?"

The Sultan nodded. His eyes were wide with surprise now.

"We are here to get our friend. His name is Cloud, and I believe you are holding him here against his will."

The emotionally exhausted Sultan considered his options. He would not let these men take from him the man who had killed his son. He spoke softly and tried to lower his eyelids. "He killed Amul. He killed my son. I would rather you go ahead and use your knife than let you take him from me."

The clock was ticking, but Kirk reasoned if he could make some kind of trust connection with the Sultan, then he might just avoid an international incident. "He did *not* kill your son. In fact, he's a private law man and has been working round the clock to filter out the person who did. You have no reason to believe me, especially since I came into your home this way. But I'm telling you, and I think you probably already know, Cloud isn't your man."

The Sultan felt the pain in his heart. It felt almost the same as the moment he had found out Amul had been killed. He wanted to believe this *Cloud* was the bastard who killed his son. He wanted to exact revenge and then try to heal his soul. Yet he knew the man holding a knife to his throat spoke the truth. A tear trickled from his eye.

Kirk realized the pain the Sultan was in. He hadn't considered the man had lost his only son. He relaxed the blade and pulled on the loose robe the man wore, sitting him up in the bed. "We're taking Cloud with us. There is nothing you can do to stop us, but I give you my word, if you help us, with Cloud's help I will find the man who really did kill your son."

The Sultan didn't trust him. But the memory of Amul wouldn't be served if he himself were killed. He decided to help the man—at least to the point when his own security staff could make their move.

The Sultan nodded. Kirk let him rise from the bed and put on a robe which hung over one of the bedposts.

"Where is Cloud?"

The Sultan was confident these men couldn't escape the palace grounds. "There is a small room in the basement."

Kirk had been in many hostage situations. The first rule was to deflect the first offering. "And I guess you're going to tell me there isn't any way to reach him except to go through the interior of the palace?"

That is exactly what the Sultan was preparing to say. He was amazed at his wily captor. "He's in the basement. It's an ancient dungeon built many years ago. I can take you there through a back entrance."

When things go this smooth, be very suspicious, Kirk thought. "Alright, please take us to him."

Chapter 59

Moving with stealth, it took several long minutes to reach the basement. Kirk was surprised they didn't run into any ambushes. The basement was like something out of the Crusades. The dank stone walls wept slime, and the cries of past prisoners hung on every wall.

The Sultan pointed a shaking finger at a large wooden door. The timber could have been centuries old. One turbaned guard stood outside smoking a cigarette.

Kirk whispered to the Sultan, "I'm going to let you go. I want you to tell the guard you need to see the prisoner. Understand, if you do anything else, I will kill the guard, then you."

The Sultan did as he was asked. The young guard opened the door and stood to the side as the Sultan entered the room. When the guard looked in after the Sultan, Kirk crept up behind him and smashed the butt of the knife down against the base of his skull. The young guard fell into a heap.

As Kirk was taking care of the guard, Earl and Bean slid past him into the room. The Sultan stood aside with his head hung low. Earl passed the glint of red laser over the entire room and saw a naked skeletal form hugging one corner. Bean ran to the naked man and rolled him away from the wall. The captive went to cry out, but Bean slapped his enormous mitt over the man's mouth.

Earl stepped closer and saw the face of his childhood friend. He coughed once and then put his hand against the slime of the dungeon wall as he gagged.

Chapter 60

Cloud hardly looked like the man they had grown up with. His face was so severely bruised as to look like an over-ripe eggplant. Even in the pale light, his skin had a yellowish tint. He recoiled from even the slightest amount of light.

Kirk saw the shock on Earl and Bean's faces and immediately took a good look at Cloud. He wheeled abruptly and grabbed the Sultan by the front of his robe. Kirk slammed him against the stone wall repeatedly, silently cursing him the entirety of the time.

Bean, who normally wouldn't let such a thing happen, turned his back. Earl held Cloud's head and spoke softly. "Hey buddy, you probably already know this, but you look like shit."

Both of the boys were surprised as Cloud actually smiled with the dawn of recognition. Cloud lifted a blue-hued hand with black fingernails and touched Bean's face. "In my dreams, you were always running away. I just had to make sure you were really here."

Kirk released his grip on the Sultan, who sank to the floor, letting out a groan. He hurried over to Earl and handed him a canteen. "Give him some water."

Earl held the canteen to Cloud's lips. He coughed with the first few sips, but then was able to take a gulp. Kirk tapped Earl on the shoulder. "Don't let him drink too much. He'll cramp up after going so long without water."

Kirk wanted to let this little reunion go on, but he knew time was against them. "Bean, throw the piece of shit Sultan over your shoulder; we're taking him with us. If we get out of this cluster fuck, I'm gonna make sure he gets what's coming to him."

Earl took off his shirt and wrapped it around Cloud's thin shoulders. Then he hoisted Cloud over his own shoulder and followed Kirk and Bean from the dungeon.

Minutes later they were outside the building. They moved and covered each other along a grassy mall which circled the palace.

Kirk raised a clenched fist and everyone stopped. Kirk looked back at Earl and Bean with their duel loads. He used two fingers to point at his eyes and then motioned toward a Mercedes sedan sitting in the driveway. There was one guard standing beside the car. Kirk made another set of hand gestures and slipped off into the darkness toward the car.

Earl watched the guard. He blinked and the guard was no longer there. A faint night sound told him the coast was clear. Bean and Earl hustled to the car with their human baggage.

Kirk expertly drove through the streets of the capital city as if he had lived there his whole life. No one said a word until several moments later when Kirk pulled the car out of what appeared to be the city limits and leaned his head back. "Our ETA for the airstrip is nine minutes. How's Cloud?"

Earl held Cloud across his lap. "He don't look so good, Captain."

"I reckon those boys back at the palace will notice the missing car right about now. They'll check on the Sultan and find out that he is 'oops oh' as well. You know what happens next."

Kirk used his encrypted phone. "Pilot, this is Green Mosquito. We are on our way. ETA on your location is now… six minutes. Fire up the engines and get ready to take us the hell out of here."

"Roger, Green Mosquito. Fires are lit and burning. Can be in the air within two minutes of your arrival."

Kirk flipped the phone shut and put the accelerator to the floor.

Chapter 61

The Mercedes screeched to a halt on the boarding side of the jet. Kirk began firing off orders, telling Earl and Bean to get their passengers on board. He ran from the car and to the steps leading to the jet. His heart nearly stopped when the most monstrous-looking man he had ever seen ducked his head through the entryway.

Bean stopped abruptly, dropped Cloud, and bent to one knee in a firing stance. Several lights fired to life behind them and the aircraft's engines began to shut down. The man in the jet's doorway held up a hand, and at least twenty men with guns trained ran towards them from the darkness.

Earl fumbled with his weapon, dropped it, and then reached for the knife at his ankle. A single shot rang out, and the knife in Earl's hand clattered to the ground. Earl felt the sting in his hand. It felt as if a bullet had torn right through the fleshy part between his thumb and forefinger.

Animal instinct took over, and the normally docile Earl ripped the Sultan's head back exposing his neck. Earl opened his mouth and placed his large jowls over the pumping trachea of the Sultan.

Even Kirk's mouth fell open as he witnessed what Earl was doing. In all of the hostage situations he'd been involved in, he'd never seen somebody threaten to bite the throat out of one of the captives.

Kirk recovered and said to the man in the jet's doorway, "One signal from me, and my man will tear open your Sultan's windpipe."

Ahmad descended the gangway and stood looking down at Kirk. He spoke in perfect Oxford-born English. "We find ourselves in what you Americans would call a Catch 22. I will kill the Sultan myself before I let you take him, and I assume you feel the same way about your friend."

Kirk took a half step forward. There was barely an inch between their bodies. "Well big man, I guess we might as well start the dance. I figure you to be the first body to hit the ground." Unseen to all, Kirk pressed the barrel of his side-arm into Ahmad's belly.

No one had been watching the half-naked corpse. Cloud stumbled to his feet and clumsily removed the shirt that served as his only clothing. He took the long arms of the shirt and tied them around his waist into a makeshift skirt. As he staggered towards the two men at the base of the jet, all guns retrained their aim on his heart.

Kirk and Ahmad didn't falter with their gaze. Both men continued to look deep into the eyes of the other.

"Stop it… both of you, just stop it. This thing has gotten all outta hand, and even though nobody knows it, we're all on the same team."

Chapter 62

Cloud

Captain Jesse Kirk spoke to me, but he never took his eyes from the man in front of him. "Cloud, you're in bad shape. There's no way you're in any condition to handle this."

I was seeing double. The lack of food, the drugs, and darkness in a dungeon were taking their toll. I sank to one knee and scraped my hand along the dusty ground. I let a handful of sand pass through my fingers. I hadn't known whether I would ever touch real earth again. "Gentlemen, this sand feels remarkably similar to what I could touch if I were kneeling down in Cable instead of Qatar."

The big man was smart. He wasn't all brute strength, and let the devil be damned. He broke eye contact with Kirk and looked at me. There was no fear behind the dark eyes, but there was dread, a sense of continuing conflict, which made him itch for more peaceful times. "What do you propose?"

"You escort me onto the plane. Earl over there will bring the Sultan on board. Everyone else will stay outside. I'll need only a few minutes to tell the Sultan what is really going on. I don't know who killed his son, but I have some pretty good leads, and I know all of the circumstances behind the boy's death. The Sultan will want to hear what I have to say."

This move gave the upper hand to no one. Earl and I would be on the plane, but Kirk and Bean would be under the watchful eyes of twenty or so armed men.

He thought about the proposal, trying to figure out how I might be tricking him. I *wasn't* tricking him, so it took him some time to go mentally through possible scenarios. While he was thinking, I tried to gain a little good faith. "What's your name?"

"Silasteck Ahmad."

"What do you say, Silasteck? Can we give this a try?"

Ahmad took a while, but said, "Yes, we will give this a try. I am going to take one step back and give a signal to my men."

Kirk seemed to fidget. He didn't like losing ground. But I could tell he was going to put his trust, his life, in my hands.

Ahmad took a hesitant step backwards and raised his hand above his head. I yelled over in Earl's direction. "Earl, you, me, the Sultan, and Ahmad here are getting aboard the aircraft."

Earl stood, the Sultan in his arms. He never took his teeth from the Sultan's throat. A few minutes later, the four of us were sitting in the plush cabin of the jet. A nervous American poked his head from the cockpit door. I cautiously motioned to get his attention. He was very unsure, but he opened the door a fraction of an inch more. I said, "Do me a favor if you would. See if you can find me some pants."

The pilot looked to Ahmad for permission. He nodded. I reached over and put my hand on Earl's arm. "Thank you, buddy. I appreciate what you're doing. But let this be a normal conversation. Let the Sultan go."

Earl looked deep into my eyes. He was so caught up in the situation, he had a hard time removing his mouth from the Sultan's neck. When he finally did, I was amazed to see the Sultan come to life with such speed. He exploded from Earl's grip and ran to Ahmad's side. "Kill them. Kill them now, Sikh."

Ahmad looked at the Sultan. I have seen that look before when a white man commanded a black man. Ahmad blinked heavily and said, "Sir, I believe we should listen to what this man has to say."

The Sultan was unaccustomed to having his order's questioned. He looked at Ahmad with hatred and would have branded him a traitor had the situation not been so combustible. The Sultan gathered himself and seemed defeated. "Perhaps you are right. Let us hear what the wretch has to say."

With all the sincerity I could muster, I told the Sultan everything I had discovered. The National Championship Trophy, the men who killed his son at the Biotech Lab, the petroleum bug, and finally Larry Red. When I was halfway through my story, the Sultan began to weep. By the time I finished, his shoulders were shaking uncontrollably with sobs. As much as my body hurt from the torture this man had visited upon me, I still felt for him. I couldn't imagine losing my only son. And if someone had maliciously taken him from me, I would have done the same—probably worse.

Ahmad was so uncomfortable with the weeping I feared he would simply leave the plane and wash his hands of the whole situation. I was surprised when the big man leaned toward the Sultan and enveloped him with a huge arm. I let the sadness play out.

The pilot shuffled into the cabin and humbly held up a pair of enormous Bahama shorts with a gaudy flower pattern. I nodded and held out my hand. The pilot handed me the shorts. Knowing I couldn't leave, I shucked the make-do skirt and donned the shorts. I had a foot and a half of drawstring on either side when the shorts finally felt snug enough to stay up. I slid the soiled shirt back on and felt like a new man now that I didn't have my dangling uglies out for everyone to see.

The Sultan spoke, even though his head was still buried in Silasteck's armpit. "I am so sorry; I am shamed by the pain I inflicted upon you. I see now that you were trying to help me, help my son. Perhaps I always knew, but the pain was so great, I needed the violence. Allah will not forgive me for what I have done, but perhaps in time, you might."

I had already refocused the point of my vengeance. I was thinking of the time when I would get my hands around the neck of the bastard who had caused all of this. "Sir, I cannot imagine your pain. I am and will forever be sure I would have done the same were the tables turned. I do have one last request though."

The Sultan's mood changed and he looked at me with steely passion. "Ask anything. Whatever you need to find the man who killed my son will be yours. I would give away everything to have him back. Since that is not possible, I will pledge the same to his memory."

"I want Ahmad to go back to the States with us."

The big man lost composure for the first time. His eyes grew wide, and he looked at me with utter confusion.

"Ahmad is his own man. I have already asked too much of him. I have taken advantage of his true nature and his loyalty for the last time. If he chooses to go with you, then so be it. But I will not ask, even for the retribution I desire."

Ahmad looked at the Sultan. For the first time in his association with the sub-monarch, he saw the man as an equal. He wasn't being commanded; he wasn't even being asked. This changed everything. "I would consider it a great honor to represent you. I will go with these men, and as your Allah as my witness, I will bring justice to those who killed your son."

The Sultan reached up and touched Ahmad's face. "Thank you, my friend. Thank you."

Chapter 63

Miami

Nineteen hours later, I found myself staring at the ceiling in Kirk's home in South Florida. Emma lay to my right and Blue to my left. In those moments I didn't let myself do anything else but appreciate what station in life I'd achieved. No man I knew enjoyed the bounty of friends I could call mine. Of violence, I had learned something. I would reflect later on just what that was.

It was two o'clock in the morning. I'd been back in the U.S. for roughly ten hours. I was still feeling the effects of dehydration. I slipped from between the covers and the two women and headed for the kitchen. I stood with mouth agape in the doorway of the kitchen. Earl, Bean, and Kirk were sitting around the kitchen table playing poker. At the fourth side of the table sat Silasteck Ahmad.

Ahmad wore a baseball cap turned around backwards. His white robes had been replaced by a king-size pair of overalls. The bulky denim outfit still only stretched to his mid-calf. I leaned against the doorframe and watched.

Kirk was trying to control the game, but he had the smallest pile of chips in front of him. "Goddamit, Silas, I know your big ass is bluffing again. Here I sit with a rookie Arab, a sissy-assed black man, and... Bean, what the hell can I say about Bean, and I'm losing. I can't believe I'm losing to you sorry bastards."

Bean spoke up. "Yes, I am very happy you think I'm a sorry bastard." Bean had the biggest pile of chips in front of him.

Earl made the call, and all four men laid down their hands. Kirk pushed away from the table. He said in exasperated tone, "I'm telling ya, Silas, I don't believe for one minute you ain't played this game before."

Ahmad used one big claw to rake in the multi-colored chips. "And, if I remember properly, you must retrieve the next round of beer."

I stepped into the light of the kitchen. Earl noticed me first, but Bean shot from his seat and ran to my side as if I needed convalescence. I smiled and waved Bean off. "You gentlemen have room for one more?"

Kirk returned from the kitchen. "You damn well have to pay a late entry penalty."

I looked to a worn leather chair and spied my flight bag. All eyes followed as I rummaged inside the bag. I returned to the table and threw a hundred-dollar bill in the center of the table. "Will that cover?"

All of the men looked jealously at the single bill, then to their waiting pile of chips. I got nods and sat down.

Chapter 64

The Gulf of Mexico

Harry Wyatt Sullivan sat aboard the *Big Thunder*. The yacht cruised just off the southern tip of the Florida mainland. Wyatt was much more comfortable now since he was back on his boat and not wading through the humanity of South Florida. He was never one to socialize with the commoners. He always felt in charge when he was aboard his floating palace.

Dinner had been going on for him since the early afternoon. Piles of spent plates marked the destruction he had reckoned on many a crustacean and hoofed animal. Wyatt adhered to the alcoholic's mantra of never leaving a drop behind—except in his case it would be a crumb.

Kari Vilano-Lobos entered just as Zan was clearing dishes from the stateroom. She seemed in a very good mood, not because she wore a smile or any outward sign of happiness a normal human might, but because she had a sweep to her walk that spoke of power.

Wyatt noticed her and like a whale exploding a long-held breath, belched. He used the linen tablecloth to wipe his greasy face. "Kari my dear, by the way you wear that wicked little mouth of yours, I assume you have good news."

Kari sidestepped the loaded arms of Zan and the vicious look in his eyes. "You will be very happy to learn I've lined up four bidders for the bug. Each has posted a hundred-thousand-dollar negotiator's fee of good faith."

Wyatt continued to be fascinated with the expertise of the dark woman. "Do they know the fee is not refundable?"

"No, but they will be in no position to ask for the return of money. In fact, whoever of them leaves with the bug will probably count the others as clients."

"When do we meet with our group of bidders?"

"Tomorrow afternoon. We'll pick up all of the principles at an upscale dock and landing off Islamorada in the Florida Keys."

"What will be our agenda?"

"We will take them out to the reef and let them do some sport fishing. When the anglers have taken as many fish as we can feed them, they will clean up and prepare for a large banquet, complete with hostesses who will be shuttled here via charter. The following morning when they're all feeling hungover, and hopefully a little embarrassed or guilty for the night's activities, we will hold the bidding. We will have a one-hour time limit, so these men must come prepared to pay, not to negotiate."

"What makes you so sure the losers in the bidding won't call foul, or try and at least recoup their initial hundred thousand?"

"Some rather damning evidence, which will be collected during the night's festivities."

"What if you get one or more rather docile souls? A fellow loyal to his wife or a devout Christian?"

Kari slid the dark glasses down to the tip of her nose and peered out over the top with condescending eyes. "Harry Wyatt, there are no such men of that character. Not with what we'll be putting in front of them."

Harry Wyatt tilted his huge head back and bellowed with laughter. "Once again Kari darling, you have exceeded even my most grandiose imagination."

Chapter 65

At precisely noon the next day Kari stood on the gangplank connecting the *Big Thunder* with the dock at Islamorada. Several revelers from the Tiki Bar, sporting deep pink icy drinks passed her and made suggestive comments. The stare Kari gave them made all of the bravado fall into the water like so much unused bait.

Kari wore baggy black pants tied at the ankle and slit all the way up to her sculpted hip. Her top was a halter, tied between bulging, coffee-colored breasts. To her, the outfit wasn't a fashion statement, but just another negotiating tool.

As each of the four principle negotiators boarded the *Big Thunder*, they worked hard to keep the saliva from dripping down the front of their expensive suits. Not one man noticed her pitted, acne-scarred face. Their eyes were wandering other parts of her anatomy.

When all four men were on board, Kari signaled to Deke Joyner, and the *Big Thunder* headed out to open water.

When they were about a mile out to sea, Wyatt propelled his unusual little vehicle on deck. His air couch had been erected under a large canopy. He drove close, and with Zan's help, he tumbled his large bulk onto the mattress.

Kari, the perfect hostess, made sure all of the men had a refill of their drink of choice, then invited them to gather around Wyatt. Zan, wearing white knee shorts and an elaborate Asian coat buttoned to the neck, served the men rich crab cakes with spicy, citrus habanero sauce.

Wyatt began with a congenial greeting, but quickly turned to the business at hand. "Gentlemen, as I'm sure you're aware, we are here to deal on the price of a rather interesting bug. The bacterium, which my laboratories have developed, is capable of consuming raw crude oil spilled into either fresh or salt water. My associate, Ms. Lobos, will distribute a small packet of information detailing the process." Wyatt nodded, and Kari handed each of the men a slim envelope.

"I was sure you would require a practical demonstration, so I have prepared just such an experiment for your inspection."

Zan walked forward with a large glass container. He fastened it with rubber cords to the table in front of them. Wyatt pointed, and Zan grabbed a five-gallon bucket from the deck and removed the lid. He effortlessly hoisted the bucket and approached the glass container. Wyatt paused for drama. "Ordinary Everglades swamp water. Zan, if you would."

Zan poured the water from the bucket into the glass container. Everyone watched as Kari approached and poured a gallon and a half of black, chunky muck into the water, which all of the men were expert enough to accept was pure crude oil. The water instantly turned black-brown and took on a syrup-like consistency.

Kari Vilano-Lobos now stood at Harry Wyatt's side holding a wriggling rainbow fish, which seemed to accentuate her outfit but contrasted with her toffee-colored skin. "Gentlemen, in this glass container we have severely contaminated water. The spill, which we have produced, would be akin to seven large oil tankers spilling their entire cargo into the waters at Valdese, Alaska, instead of just one. You are welcome to make your own samplings."

All of the men rose and produced small packets of vials from breast pockets. Each dipped an eyedropper into the water and then squirted the contents into a test tube. The four men looked to each other and made quiet comments as to the authenticity of the tainted swamp water. When Wyatt was satisfied the men were certain of the contents of the glass container, he nodded at Zan.

Zan again approached with an identical glass container. This one however contained a dozen palm-sized fish that bumped the walls in aggravation within their confined environment.

"In this second container, we have a dozen Amazonian Red Piranha. These are the most vicious bastards on the whole planet. They are also highly tolerant of any poison known to man, including the spilling of crude oil into their environment. As I'm sure you're all aware, just two years ago a tanker spilled a load off the coast of Peru. Every plant, animal, and other form of life suffered a catastrophic demise. Except, that is, the Amazonian Red Piranha. They were virtually unaffected. Of course, they also died later because they had nothing to prey upon."

The four men murmured and nodded at each other.

"Just so you know, these are really authentic Piranha, I'm afraid we have another, rather distasteful, demonstration."

With that, Kari tossed the unsuspecting rainbow fish into the mouth of the glass container. Within thirty seconds there was no sign of the fish save a faint red glow to the water. One of the men rocked in his seat then bent over the side of the yacht and vomited.

When the man was back in his seat, still looking pale, Wyatt nodded at Zan. Without hesitation, Zan plunged his bare hand into the water and grabbed one of the angry fish. He tossed the wriggling barbarian into the tainted water of the other container. He repeated this five more times.

Before the last of the six fish were in the soiled water, one of them began to float to the top. His brethren in the container turned on him and began to feed. Before the first carcass could be consumed, all six fish were floating, belly-up in the dirty water.

"As you can see, this water is poisoned to a much more radical degree than could ever be expected from one normal oil spill." Wyatt leaned his immense bulk forward and dumped a small vial, maybe a half-inch long, into the water. "Tomorrow, just before we start the bidding process, we will dump the other six fish into this same container. At that time, I'm sure all doubts will then be relieved."

All of the men stared in fascination and horror. Wyatt continued, "Enough work for today. Let the fishing began."

The boat idled to a halt and Zan began handing out shiny fishing rods to each of the men. Within moments, the first man had landed a blue-silver dolphin. All memory of the demonstration was erased as the men hooked into a school and Zan busied himself with the task of unhooking and re-baiting.

Chapter 66

As the setting sun extinguished into the placid sea, the aft deck of the *Big Thunder* was transformed from fishing rig to a plush outdoor banquet flat. A charter boat approached and came alongside the *Big Thunder*. Temporary riggings were attached, and the two boats were tethered together as one. Six ladies teetered on high heels and attempted the crossing from one vessel to the other. Four men in tuxedos followed them. The ladies were the hostesses, and the men were waiters and servers.

When everyone was seated at the long table, Wyatt made his grand entrance aboard his custom ride. The lust in his eyes was evident to everyone as he approached the table full of food. At least one of the petroleum-bug negotiators thought that he had better get all he wanted from the first round of food. Wyatt didn't seem to be one for sharing seconds.

Wyatt addressed the group. "Let us all join hands and give thanks for the bounty we are about to receive."

Several in the group, both negotiators and hostesses, and even Kari herself, gazed quizzically at him. They all hesitantly joined hands, and when every head was bowed, an explosion of scraping sounds emerged from the head of the table. Every head raised and looked to Wyatt, who was furiously digging into the buttered, rump-meat of a large rock lobster.

Wyatt lowered the body of the crustacean, revealing a wide smile. "I just love doing that. Gives me a little head start." Then he plunged his thick jowls back into the lobster.

The dinner was long and drawn-out to seven courses. Wyatt virtually wept as the table was cleared each time. He saw the picked-over plates of the hostesses and wanted to ask for their remainders.

Wine and liquor flowed during the meal. There was much feigned laughter from the hostesses and more groping of thigh and higher by the negotiators. By the time the last dish of sorbet was cleared, each of the men had made dibs on the women, with one exception. A scholarly-looking gent at the far end of the table was making polite conversation, but really didn't seem interested in the women. Wyatt motioned to Kari, and she excused herself from a boring conversation.

"Kari my dear, for all of your talents, it seems Mr. White at the end of the table might have tastes that run to another gender."

Kari whispered into his ear. "Yes, an oversight on my part. He has a wife and four kids, so I assumed. But not to worry, I will come up with something."

The night proceeded just as predicted. All of the men, who each wore a gold band around the fourth finger of the left hand, indulged in drink and then in the company of the hostesses.

At around midnight, Wyatt excused himself but proclaimed the night young and encouraged his guests to make themselves at home. Three hours later, he lay in his oversized bed still listening to the grating music and laughter above. If everything went to plan, Wyatt would never have anyone else aboard his yacht again for business.

Chapter 67

At six-thirty the next morning, Wyatt woke to the vicious shaking of his captain. "Mr. Sullivan, Ms. Lobos requested I wake you and bring you to the forward stateroom."

Wyatt was rarely in a good mood, but he was a beast in the early morning. "What in hell's name is it, man? Can't the two of you solve whatever it is?"

Deke Joiner looked pale. "I... I'm really not sure, sir. Ms. Lobos just said there's been a situation and she needs you as soon as possible."

If the magnitude of the deal had not been what it was, Wyatt would have slapped Joiner and told him to bring Vilano-Lobos to him by force if necessary. As it was, he sat up on the bed and asked the captain for his robe.

Aboard his custom ATV, Wyatt switched a lever to run on batteries. It was soundless as he roughly bumped down the hallway to the forward cabin.

Deke Joiner pushed the door open, and Wyatt gaped in horror. Zan sat in the middle of a pile of blood-soaked sheets and bedding. He was furiously gnawing on a large bone. In a far corner of the room Kari stood pointing a compact shotgun at Zan. She had red droplets of blood on her face and neck. Larger patches of blood soaked her clothes.

She saw Wyatt and told the captain to close the door behind him. Zan continued to scrape the remaining meat from the bone. Wyatt was fumbling for words. Kari spoke, but never let her eyes stray from the bloody cannibal. "We have a rather fucked-up situation here, Harry Wyatt. It seems our concern over Mr. White's sexual preference was solved last night when he brought young Zan down to his room for a little slap and tickle. Wherever the hell you got this animal, I guess after-play includes eating your mate. When I heard some screeching, I came down to investigate. At that point, White was still alive, but just barely. I got the gun and have been watching more horror than I should ever have to see. He *ate* him, Harry. I mean he ate the whole damn man. What you see there on the bed is all that's left of Mr. White."

Even in the sight of the carnage, Wyatt was regaining his composure. "We will explain to our remaining bidders that Mr. White was called away during the night on a family emergency. In fact, we'll use this to our advantage. We will make a fake offer, seal it in an envelope, and tell our remaining guests that Mr. White made the opening bid."

Even Kari was aghast at the man's cold heart. "Harry Wyatt, what the hell are we going to do with this animal? What are we going to do about the condition of this room?"

"The room can be cleaned and renovated. As for Zan, I have just the thing." Wyatt dangled the electronic key ring attached to his wrist. For the first time, Zan stopped gnawing on the bone and looked at Wyatt. He growled a low guttural sound, which came from the jungle where he'd been born.

"Kari darling, go and compose Mr. White's offer for the bug. Where do you think we should start the bidding?"

Kari kept her back to the wall and shuffled her feet sideways until she was standing beside Wyatt. Even in her current situation she was all business. "Harry Wyatt, do you recall the information I gave you on the cost of the British Petroleum spill in the Gulf? BP settled for billions on that spill alone."

"Yes my dear, so what is White's bid?"

"I think he would have at least offered five."

"Say the whole number my dear. We haven't gone to all of this effort to make a mistake at this juncture."

Kari looked over the butt of the gun at Wyatt. "Five hundred million. At least that would be a good start."

Chapter 68

Kari left the room and went to her own. She stripped her clothes off on the way and threw them overboard. She propped the shotgun beside the shower stall and scalded her body in hot water.

She emerged from her steam-soaked room outfitted in business attire. At last she felt comfortable. The rough fabric rubbed against her skin—the shark was getting ready for the feeding frenzy.

A soft knock on each of the remaining negotiator's doors was enough to awaken the hostesses within. Six yawning and disheveled women emerged from the staterooms and stood on the aft deck of the *Big Thunder*. The four tuxedoed waiters were already there sharing a joint. The charter boat had arrived alongside, and everyone went on board. Minutes later they were gone.

At one thirty, Kari had assembled the remaining three bidders. She had three computer drives in her pocket, but from the early signs they wouldn't be needed. The three men looked hugely hungover and brimming with guilt as to their sins from the previous night.

As Wyatt drove into the meeting area, Kari handed each of the men a thick red Bloody Mary and a vitamin B tablet. Two of the men tossed the celery stick from their drinks overboard, the third retched.

"Well gentlemen, I hope the night was a success. Mr. White will not join us, as he was called away on a family emergency. He left a bid with us, which Ms. Vilano-Lobos will post. First, let us complete yesterday's experiment."

Wyatt nodded, and Kari lifted a sheet of material from the container, which, the day before, had contained the soiled water. The water was completely clear, and it sparkled in the sunlight. Kari dumped the remaining piranha into the water. The fish were agitated, but otherwise seemed normal. Kari produced a Yellowtail Snapper, still wriggling from the hook, and tossed it into the tank with the piranha. Within seconds the fish was gone, and the water remained clear, even though the blood had been evident for a second or so.

Wyatt smiled. "Gentlemen, I hope any skepticism you may have held is now laid to rest. Ms. Lobos, will you open Mr. White's bid and tell our guests where we will begin."

Kari produced an envelope and made a scene of opening it. She then passed the document to the first man. The paper made its rounds and all of the men seemed confident.

"Kari will now accept your initial bids. Please write on the paper in front of you the amount you are willing to bid."

***

As promised, the bidding closed in precisely one hour. The short time-frame worked to Wyatt's benefit, as the men couldn't do much bluffing. It was obvious two of the men had tried to form an alliance and control the spiraling price of the bug, but because they hadn't been able to convince the third man to enter their group, and because of the unknown bid the absent Mr. White might offer, the price finally came to a close just short of eight hundred million dollars.

Because Harry Wyatt had forgone the usual safety regulations, inspections, and permits, this amount would offset the cost of the pipeline rather nicely. Wyatt was very pleased with the thought he would pump oil from the mainland to his legitimate derrick in the Gulf of Mexico with a near-cost free construction. It was like harvesting two crops he never had to plant or maintain. If only the sugar industry had been so lucrative.

The negotiators for the bug disembarked at Islamorada. Both the vanquished and the victor were very happy to be back on solid ground. They walked with downcast eyes past Kari Vilano-Lobos, who stood in the same position she had two days before when she welcomed them aboard. The men were eager to return to their loving and unsuspecting wives and the comfortable lives they had made for themselves. Each would return home with flowers or some such gift in hand, trying to mitigate the guilt of sampling the hostesses' pleasures.

When the last of the men was out of sight, Kari hurried down to Wyatt's stateroom. She found the big man dipping a large spoonful of scrambled eggs from a bowl.

She raised her eyebrows at the sight and sat heavily in a nearby captain's chair. "We have two problems. One is obviously Zan. We can't continue to do this caliber of business when we have a damn psycho-cannibal on our hands."

Wyatt waved the spoon dismissively. "Zan is not *our* problem. Zan *belongs* to me, and I will deal with him. That's nothing for you to worry your pretty head over."

Kari heaved an exasperated sigh. "Our second problem is more imminent and destructive to the whole plan."

Wyatt grunted as he speared a half dozen links of sausage with his fork.

Kari waited for him to ask what the second problem was. When he didn't, she continued. "There is a small leak in the pipeline. It's just south of the main pumping station, still on your land, but it was discovered by some environmental researcher, who was trespassing."

Wyatt paused in his chewing. Fragments of colorful food spewed from his mouth as he spoke. "What about the security? Why the hell didn't anyone catch the bastard since he was trespassing?"

"I don't know, but we can't allow those scientists you have running the pumping facility to deal with it. They would come off worse than a man selling umbrellas in a hurricane."

Wyatt intermittently smacked his food and cursed. "Fuck, fuck, fuck… what do we need to do?"

"We need to get over to the spill, to the pumping station, and put the bug to work."

"Do you think it really works?"

"I damn well hope so. If not, the jig is up and we need to take our new pot of money and find residence in a country without extradition."

Chapter 69

Zan sat with watery eyes in his wooden cage deep in the cargo hold of the *Big Thunder*. Hard times had been the only constant in his young life. Born into a small tribe of people who were farmers, hunters, gatherers of the earth's bounty, life had always been difficult.

His tribe was one that practiced cannibalism. Back in the jungle where he was born, this wasn't as taboo as it was in modern civilization. His people didn't kill for profit, or even to dominate their neighbors. The killing and eating of one's enemies made you stronger. You took into your body their strengths, but you let their soul move on to the next plane of existence.

He hated the fat man. He hated what heinous acts Wyatt made him perform. He hated being a servant. But most of all, he hated what he had become. Even though he was born into the cannibal's lifestyle, he knew each time he killed or fed, it was wrong.

Zan pressed his forehead against the splinter-laden wood of his cage. He remembered the day he came to know Wyatt. The Elder of his tribe had been away for some time, maybe as much as it took the moon to show full. When the Elder returned, he brought Zan to a small thatched hut and had him sit on the floor. The old man wept as he spoke. He was obviously very distressed at what he had done.

In their own language, punctuated with clicks and tics of facial expression, the old man told him his fate. "Young warrior, your life has been sacrificed for the greater good of the tribe. You are not my son, but I have loved you as if you were the same. The Gods have seen fit to give the tribe another year of bread and sustenance. The outsiders are taking our land. They are taking our hunting grounds and our ability to feed ourselves. The tribe will prosper, but the price we pay… is you. I have sold your body to a capitalist. A great pig of a man who I know will make your life into hell. I do not ask your forgiveness; I only ask that you know the sacrifice you make will prolong the life of our tribe. I also remind you, I sold your body. I have no ability to barter for your soul. You must remain loyal to yourself, to the beliefs of the tribe. You will come back to this earth in another life, as a man with much learning and with many more opportunities."

With that the Elder left the hut and gave Zan's mortal life over to Harry Wyatt Sullivan.

Chapter 70

As the furling water swept to the side, the *Big Thunder* passed through Vaca Cut in the Key's town of Marathon. Harry Wyatt Sullivan was speaking on a satellite phone with Larry Red, the man who had made all of this possible.

"Larry, my good friend, everything is proceeding along just as we hoped."

On the other end, Red wasn't as sure of things as his counterpart. "I haven't heard from you in almost three weeks. You know I've been bombarded with police, the press, and even a private detective? And I still haven't received my money."

"Larry, now you knew going in this would take some time. I've been very busy setting everything up. I told you the money would be there, but if you are impatient, then you can just come on down here where the fire is a little warmer, and I will give it to you personally."

"This shit seems to have gotten a little bigger than we first spoke about. You know, one word from me and your whole operation would be overrun by the FBI."

Wyatt enjoyed toying with him. "Larry... Larry, that seems dangerously like a threat. We don't want to get into that sort of territory. You can either wait for things to run their course here, or you can come on down and we'll settle up like gentlemen. I can't very well just send you a check, can I?"

Larry Red sat in his sparse living room. He was watching the fish in a clouded aquarium slowly swim back and forth. "He really was a good friend. I don't know why you had to go and kill him."

"You very well know young Mr. Facon would never have bought into our dream. Let's not get carried away. You just come down to my farm, and I will set all your fears to rest."

Red hesitated then said, "All right, I'm leaving now. I'll be there tomorrow morning. You'll have the money, right?"

"Yes, Larry. Let me give you directions."

Chapter 71

Cloud, Miami

At one o'clock in the afternoon, I exited the bed. I had been sleeping alone for some time by the cold feel of the sheets. I stretched and felt the clean air as only a newly freed man could. I scratched violently at my front and back midsection.

Not so many years before, I remembered waking up the morning after a mission that had been particularly hard on my body. Despite the loss of some human life and the incredible loss of property, the mission was a success. That morning, I felt as if every past sin had been erased, as if every wrong deed was forgiven. In the moment, I felt more alive than ever before in my life. I sensed possibilities that had never occurred to me.

As I looked into the mirror and brushed my teeth, I felt the same sensation, only stronger. Maybe the drugs the men gave me while I was in the dungeon had catapulted my mind into another dimension. Maybe I was in a euphoric trance. But maybe, just maybe, I was beginning to live. Maybe I could put the pettiness of normal life behind me and could search for something unknown.

In the kitchen, everyone was accounted for and there was an intense conversation under way. Ragged piles of paper were on the table—evidently an assimilation of information was at hand. I took a seat at the table. Ahmad pushed an empty coffee cup in my direction. I smiled at him.

Blue looked at Ahmad and said, "Cloud is odd. He doesn't drink coffee."

I motioned for them to continue their conversation. Kirk pointed out several columns of information scribbled in black ink on what appeared to be a used pizza box. "What we know so far is:

1. Someone killed Amul Instad Facon at the Biotechnology Building.
2. Facon was working on a bacterium that could consume spilled petroleum in water.
3. Some group associated or the same group stole the National Championship Trophy presumably as a cover.
4. Larry Red tried to set Cloud up as the fall guy.
5. The night Cloud was kidnapped, a top boss in South Florida organized crime was killed at the Belly of the Beast.
6. There is some connection, because the trophy was sitting at the bar that night and was gone the next day when we went back to investigate the crime scene.

Kirk then paused. "What am I missing?"

I looked at the list. "Unless Larry Red was trying to lead me down a dead-end street, he did say the man lived on a boat."

Kirk added this information to the list and looked up to see if anyone had more.

Blue spoke up, "When you men were on the other side of the world getting Cloud, the only lead I had enough information to pursue was regarding the trophy. The trophy was a prize, and from what I have gathered, I think the man who owns the Alligator Farm and the Belly of the Beast is our best bet. Even if he doesn't still have it, he for sure knows who he bought it from."

Kirk nodded his head. "I agree with Blue. William Barker III knows something that we should. I don't think he could engineer this other mess. He's only a wannabe criminal."

Emma and Bean had been sitting off to the side playing with Jake and Seb. When she overheard Blue, she chimed in. "What about the gas?"

Kirk looked her over with impatience.

"What do you mean?" I asked.

"Well, this whole thing seems to revolve around the petroleum bug. I wonder who might need such an animal."

The question had been so obvious and the turn of events had caused such a confusion that we had all missed it. I looked at Kirk, and his face had turned from frustration to one of appreciation. He spoke to the group. "Well yeah, there's that. Florida isn't a big producer of petroleum. The tourist trade has kept mainland drilling to a minimum and pretty much the offshore interest as well."

I was thinking, but tried something out loud. "Maybe it's not a Florida interest. Maybe it's somebody who's trying to make out by selling the bug to some big outfit out of Texas or Alaska. But maybe it *does* have something to do with the Sunshine State? I think maybe we should check up on what oil is being drilled both on the mainland and in the Gulf."

"I think you might have something. I haven't been fired as far as I know, so I'll follow up on the oil drilling permits. Cloud, why don't you guys see what you can find out about the trophy. I expect I'll get several hits when I pull the permits, so when I do, we'll need to split up into teams and check out each one," Kirk said.

I could tell everyone was being a little cautious in light of what had happened to me. They were trying to make sure I would be surrounded by friendlies no matter what I did. "Listen up, everyone, I appreciate all you've done. But I need to get back in the saddle. I need to feel like I can get control of this thing."

The eyes and nods I got confirmed what everyone had been thinking. Blue walked over and squatted down in front of me, placing her hands on my knees. "I know you need to do this. I know you need to get back some of the piss and vinegar that flows through you. But understand something. Emma and I sat here for days not knowing if we would ever see you again. We aren't letting you out or our sight for at least a little longer."

I understood and nodded. "Earl, Bean, and Silasteck should go over to the Belly of the Beast tonight and see if they can pick up any abnormal vibes. Kirk, you said you would check the drilling permits. Blue, Emma, and me will follow up on the trophy. Let's all meet back here tomorrow morning and share information. In the meantime, stay in touch."

I know Kirk's natural urge was to take over and give out assignments, but he did a good job of letting me take the horns for now.

Chapter 72

William Barker III lived at Morning Glory, a palatial estate he'd inherited from his granddaddy. The grounds were gated and umpteen old Royal Palms towered above the coquina fencing.

Emma, Blue, and I sat on the side of the road and watched the comings and goings of the staff and various people. Kirk had provided us the address and a description of the lord of the manor. He wasn't one of the people we witnessed leaving the estate in over three hours of surveillance.

We passed the time by making small talk during the first hour. We were just glad to be in each other's company once again. Emma sat in the passenger seat of the Durango, Blue was in the driver's, I was in back. After a small silence, Emma with no warning at all threw out a question we'd avoided for nearly a year. "Blue, what happens when you finally get a job with the FBI?"

The airy feel of the confined vehicle suddenly became claustrophobic. Blue looked out the window on her side and offered something to make the discomfort pass from her to the rest of us. "What do you mean?"

Emma shifted in her seat and looked directly at Blue. "You know what I mean. What happens to our... family? We've all been together for going on three years now. I never thought this was what I wanted, but when we thought Cloud was gone, well it just shook me up. I don't want for this to end. I like the way things are."

God, how I wished I were somewhere else. I wished Willy Barker would come down the drive with a dead corpse strapped to the hood of his Mercedes.

I wished he would take the turn in front of us, smile and give us the finger, trying to provoke us into some kind of action. I'm a lucky man, but lady luck was doing her nails when I was wishing.

The silence became loud—deafening. Blue finally spoke up. "I don't know, is the real answer. I'm just as happy as you are right now, but I do think about that Federal badge all the time. When I'm around people like Kirk and his crew, I just know I can do the job. I think I can do it better than they're doing it. I don't want to ruin what we have, but I think one day I will take that badge."

I caught Blue's eyes in the rearview mirror. Nothing she had ever said to me was as powerful as that look. I wanted to look away, to make the whole question go away. Instead, I continued to gaze into her huge eyes and tried not to convey what I was really feeling.

Blue broke first. She shifted her gaze onto Emma. "I love you, I love Cloud, and I love our life together."

Emma returned her gaze. "There's a *but* coming, and that's where we usually leave things. I want to go a little farther. *But* what, and what happens then?"

Both Jake and our new puppy Sebastian were sitting in the back seat with me. I think they sensed the heaviness of the moment and maybe even knew their future was involved. Jake, who is usually Blue's nemesis, the only being in our family who was as hard-headed as she was, left my lap and with a folded tail silently eased into the front seat and Blue's lap.

I saw a tear fall onto Jake's fine pelt. Blue doesn't cry; she sees it as a weakness and will do whatever is necessary to make sure no one ever witnesses her in the act.

She rubbed a rough palm over her whole face. "I guess I've always thought you'd go with me. I'll have no control over where I'm stationed to begin with. It could be the other side of the country, or for that matter the other side of the world. So I guess this isn't a question as to what I'll do. I guess it's a question as to what you and Cloud will do."

The conversation, even though sparse in words, had lasted nearly two hours. I didn't want to be callous to the situation, but I needed some relief. I spoke up. "We can't sit here and wait for Mr. Barker. I have a plan."

Chapter 73

The plan was pretty simple. I knew young master Barker was a single man and had quite a taste for the ladies. It was just getting dark, so I figured since he hadn't been out so far, he was probably making preparations for a night on the town. Emma and Blue were to just drive right up to the house and ask for Mr. Barker. The only question was how to get through the gate, but I noticed when someone came in or out, the gate remained open for an unusually long time. The idea was for them to wait for the next vehicle then follow it in.

Once they got up to the big house, I figured the feminine charms of the two ladies would take over, and Barker would probably fall all over himself to let them in. They would make a cursory search of the house, and if there weren't too many people on hand, then they would suggest a take-out pizza or some such thing. Blue would ring my cell phone, and I would come in.

Blue, being an official law enforcer, would have to leave so she wouldn't run into any problems on the legal side. But I figured once I was in, I could probably handle Barker without them. Emma was a little skeptical of leaving me by myself, but I was pretty convincing.

The plan, as simple as it was, worked like a charm. Better in fact than we'd hoped, as Barker had sent all his house staff away for the evening. He was waiting for a driver, but when the ladies showed up on his doorstep, there really wasn't any need to go out.

About an hour later, my cell phone rang just once. I checked the number and saw this was indeed the signal. When a hustling young lad dressed in red and blue swung a ravaged Pinto into the driveway, I called to him, paid for the pizza, and gave him a twenty for his trouble. He was all too happy to get going for his next delivery.

As I walked up the driveway, I noticed a slight creak to my joints. This was something new. I had suffered several bumps and bruises, a bullet, and more than my share of soreness over the years. But I'd never experienced the deep mud I now felt in my bones. Some people might say age was coming and I should just get used to it. I made my mind up right there, if old age were looking over my shoulder, he would have to fight me every damn step of the way. The week I spent in the Qatari dungeon had left me thin and stringy, not a description anyone would have placed on me before. But as happy as I was to be alive and kicking, I was surely not going to miss out on any part of life because the old chassis couldn't handle it.

A motion sensor clicked a light on. I wasn't really worried. William Barker wanted to be a bad man, but a *real* bad man was making a house call, and I didn't feel much like showing any hospitality.

I didn't knock or ring the bell. I just pressed the lever and the oak door swung open. I could hear faint laughter and forced giggles from a distance. I was intimately familiar with the jovial tone.

As I walked through the marbled entrance, I noticed the National Championship Trophy sitting on a mantle brightly lit from three directions. I reached over and snagged the hardware and continued in the direction of the laughter.

When I got to the rear of the house, I looked through a sliding glass double door and saw Barker lounging next to an ornate pool with Emma and Blue hungrily soaking up every word he said. I tossed the pizza on the floor, the box made a slapping sound as it hit the ground. Barker looked over his shoulder in my direction. He was still wearing the smile of the naïve.

His mood changed. "I'm sorry there, friend. This is a private party, and you're surely not invited."

When Emma and Blue saw me, I saw their façade drop with great exaggeration. The look I got said, "It's about time. How long were you going to leave us with this douchebag?"

Barker realized I was holding the trophy. His confident smile faded, and his eyes got very wide. "I don't know who you think you are, and I'm sure you don't know who you're messing with. I suggest you just set that on the ground, turn around, and get your ass out of my house."

When I just smiled at his bravado, Barker reached for a cordless phone sitting on a deck table. Emma grabbed it first and casually flung it into the pool. Light began to dawn on the rich young man.

"If you people came to rob me, I can tell you, I keep absolutely nothing of value in the house. Furthermore, I keep company with some very tough men, and they'll be none too pleased knowing you forced yourself into my home."

I held up one hand to try and settle him. With the other hand I placed the trophy on the deck table. He stood there trying to seem mean, but I could see a little tic on the left side of his face. I nodded at Emma and Blue, and they departed without a word.

Barker watched the lovely twosome leave, and I saw a look that clearly said he realized he was going to bed without dessert. I took one of the chairs the ladies left vacant and looked at him. He was deciding whether or not to make a break for it. I helped him with his decision by setting my .357 Colt Python on the table. I made a sitting gesture, and he slunk back into the seat.

"Willy, just settle your ass. My name is Cloud, and among other things, I'm here to ask how you came by this lovely cup."

Barker looked away toward the pool—a spoiled child who had made up his mind to be difficult. Superb.

"I take it from your body language, you prefer not to speak with me. That's outstanding. I was kinda hoping it would go this way."

He looked back at me momentarily and gave me a superior smirk. I reached across the table while he was looking away and thumped him on the side of the head. The thump made an audible bark, and he reached to the wound as he stood. I stood up with him.

"That was just to get your attention. Now, where did you get the trophy?"

He feigned a look away, then took a sweeping overhand at my face. I leaned back and the swing took only air. I stepped forward and delivered my first punch since being tortured in the dungeon, directly to his gut. I could almost feel spinal bone.

He staggered backwards and toppled the chair he'd been sitting in. The look on his face said he was missing oxygen to an extreme degree. I was oddly satisfied and just continued to look on as he sank to his knees, then to a fetal position on the deck surface.

The caw of a mocking bird woke me from the trance I was in, watching this man writhe in agony. I grabbed him under the arms and sat him back in his chair. There was a deck-side bar, I walked over and poured him two fingers of Jack Daniels. I did the same for myself. *Pity,* I thought, *no Bulleit bourbon.*

There was a small cedar box on the table. I opened it and retracted a fat cigar. While Barker was finding his breath, I snipped the end of the cigar and took a long minute to light it properly. When I had a quarter-inch of ash and Barker seemed to have regained most of his breath, I motioned at the glass in front of him. He sullenly took it and downed it in one gulp. I pushed my glass over in front of him and he did the same again.

"This is fun. I've always been a little skeptical of the good times one could have in South Florida, but I have to tell you, this is a blast."

With a flash of inspiration and courage, Barker flung the empty glass at my head. It missed by a mile. I casually inhaled and blew a blue plume of smoke in his direction. His eyes regained that *in the headlight* circumference.

"Willy, Willy, Willy...now—that's not very nice. You have to realize this is going down only one way. You're going to tell me who sold you the trophy."

He looked around surveying the possibilities. When he saw there were none, he sat back heavily in the chair. "It's mine you know. I bought it fair and square. I paid a million for it."

"No, it's not yours. You bought it from a man who stole it. It belongs to the university. And after you tell me who sold it to you, I'm gonna walk out your front door with it under my arm."

He was huffy, excreting the aroma of spoiled rich boy. "What's in it for me? I'm not just gonna sit by while some asshole takes something I paid so much for."

I blew another cloud of smoke in his direction. "Yes, you are. And for the last course, you can rest assured representatives from the FBI will be by here tomorrow morning. They'll have some follow-up questions for you."

He was dejected. He fairly disappeared into the cushions of the deck chair. "If I'm already in so much trouble, why the hell should I tell you anything?"

I set the cigar on the edge of the table and gave him my most earnest stare. "Because I'm enjoying beating the shit out of you. It would suit me right fine if we kept at it all night. I'm not so sure your delicate belly could take it, but in about ten seconds, we're gonna find out."

His hand absently found the spot where the last punch had landed. He lightly rubbed it. "Fuck it, the sorry bastard probably deserves it."

"Probably."

"His name is Harry Wyatt Sullivan. I don't know a damn thing about him, except he comes to the club about three of four times a year."

"Does he have a boat?"

"How the hell should I know?"

I made a show of reaching for my gun.

"Hold on now. I told you everything I know. I think he might have a boat."

I tucked the gun in my pants. I hoped it wouldn't fall out since I had lost so much of my ass.

"Alright, he owns a boat. I think it's named the *Big Thunder*."

I put the cigar back in my mouth and spoke around it awkwardly. "Willy, you've been very helpful. I'll pass that on to the FBI. You just sit tight now. They'll be by here tomorrow morning."

I palmed the heavy cup one handed, tucked it tight to elbow, and did a Heisman Trophy impression. I could see the reflection of William Barker III in the doorway glass. He didn't look like he would wait around for the FBI.

Chapter 74

The next morning everyone was sitting around Kirk's kitchen table. It was just the same as the afternoon before, except everyone was eager to report. The pizza box from the day before had been replaced by a large flip chart containing the notes we'd assembled thus far.

I waited for everyone to get at least one full cup of coffee down before we started. *Coffee people*, I've learned, aren't much good until the beans are in their blood. When the second rounds were being consumed, I asked Kirk if he wouldn't mind leading us through the details. My encounter with William Barker had soothed my need for control, and I felt an expert might do a better job this time around.

Kirk asked Earl to tell us all what they'd found out at the Belly of the Beast.

Before he could get started, Bean asked, "While we're getting the details ironed out, I was wondering if it would be alright if I ran and got us all some donuts or something?"

I wasn't all that hungry, but an investigation and donuts went hand in hand, so I told Bean to go right ahead. Before I knew what was happening, Emma and Ahmad volunteered to keep Bean company. The trio grabbed clothes and a handbag and headed out the door.

When the four of us were all settled in again, Earl began. "Everyone already knows the man who got himself killed that night was J.D. Re`bel. He's a big man in crime circles down here. But the word is, he was losing his hold on his crew. The man was a sloppy drunk who didn't do much anymore, just kinda depended on his second-in-command to take care of things."

Kirk nodded ascension. It appeared he knew most of this already.

Earl continued. "The last anyone remembers seeing old J.D., he was in the company of great big fat man. Of course, nobody knows who he was, even though by many accounts he was as big as a barn. A waitress said she served J.D. and the fat man drinks, and it looked to her as if J.D. was getting on the fat man's nerves. A few hours later, the fat man left, but nobody had seen Re'bel for quite some time."

Kirk scribbled notes on a legal pad in front of him. When Earl stopped talking, Kirk said, "As we go through this, you may think I'm asking questions I already know the answers to. You may think I'm shining you on. I'm not. I… we… have to deal in proof, not stories, conjecture or gut feeling. Proof, people. Proof is what we need. Anything else about the fat man? Anyone notice any details which might help us pin him down?"

Earl shook his head and then hesitated. "At least a couple of the people said the fat man didn't walk. He rode around on some souped-up scooter of some sort."

Kirk smiled, made another note on his pad. "Alright, that's real good, Earl. Blue, what did you and Cloud find out?"

I knew Kirk intentionally directed his question at Blue. He wasn't trying to shine her on, but he scored many points with the gesture. Blue sat her cup down and said, "We visited William Barker III at his home—his estate I guess you'd call it. When we were walking through the entranceway, we saw the trophy on a mantle. We made a light surveillance of the house and then called Cloud. He'll have to take it from there."

I reached into a duffel bag sitting at my feet and retrieved the trophy. I set it on the table. I must admit, I felt some great sense of satisfaction at having gotten back the item that I'd been originally hired to find. Blue already knew about it, but the looks from Earl and Kirk were congratulatory.

"Willy Barker said he paid nearly a million for the trophy. Said he got it from a man named Harry Wyatt Sullivan. My bad, I didn't ask for a physical description, but I wouldn't be at all surprised if the seller was a great big fat man who got around on a souped-up scooter. I did think to ask him about a boat. He said the man who sold him the trophy had one. He thought the name was the *Big Thunder*."

Kirk said, "That's what I'm talkin' 'bout. We got a witness—someone we could squeeze." He furiously scribbled more notes.

Just as Kirk finished speaking, the donut brigade made their return. I could tell the group hadn't waited to get home to sample the donuts. Bean was eating a chocolate cream and glazed sandwich. He shoved the last bite in his huge gap as he set down three boxes from Krispy Kreme.

Ahmad had a big greasy smear on the side of his mouth, but he tried to seem a little subtler. When Emma bent down to kiss my cheek, I reached up and gently wiped away a dusting of white powder that sprinkled the faint dark hair on her upper lip. She reddened with embarrassment.

Everyone dug into the donuts—everyone, that is, except Kirk. He pulled a file from his pile of papers and began checking something we'd said with his notes.

No matter how many donuts you get, no matter how diverse the makeup, people will fight—they will feel the perfect pastry has escaped them into the mouth of another. I toyed with a plain glazed and watched the frenzy, but mostly I watched Kirk. He'd made great sacrifices—probably including his career—for me. I only hoped we could solve this thing, then he would be vindicated, no matter what Bureau transgressions he'd committed.

The empty boxes were thrown out, and everyone sat back at the table. Kirk made a swooping circle on two of the pages and sat back in his chair with a satisfied smile. I asked, "What'd you find?"

"Mr. Harry Wyatt Sullivan does have some oil interest. His family has been mining oil from the Gulf for nearly fifty years. They don't have much to show for it, but I think it's the connection we're looking for."

Kirk's cell phone rang, and he snatched it up. While he was mostly listening, I noticed several of the things I'd taken for granted in my life until I was holed up in that dungeon. Earl and Bean were discussing bass fishing with Ahmad. They were animated as they assured the big Arab that he hadn't lived until he felt the fight and pull of a ten-pounder on the end of a light line. Both Emma and Blue held a lap full of Jack Russell terrier. The women were trying to decipher the merits of what Earl was talking about, while gently stroking the ears of two very happy dogs. I thought what a truly lucky man I was.

Kirk clicked off and made a few more notes. "I haven't been completely forgotten. We have a few new developments. First, a high-ranking official within one of the big four petroleum companies has gone missing. He was supposed to come down to Florida to negotiate some huge deal, but he hasn't been heard from in forty-eight hours. Second, a naturalist environmental researcher working on the lip of the Everglades is also missing. The man was evidently studying the effects of sugarcane fertilizer runoff into the 'glades."

Everyone was wondering what this had to do with our case. Kirk, on the other hand, was very happy with the information. I asked him to spell it out for us.

"What I'm about to tell you is classified. We have satellite photo imagery confirming that there are substantial deposits of crude oil beneath South Florida. For several years, we've tried to keep this from the big oil companies at the bequest of several high-ranking politicians who appreciate the votes and support of the tourist industry. The area where the naturalist was last known to do his research is called Scrug Quarter Parrish. It's a huge sugarcane plantation that has been in business way before the United States counted Florida as one of its own."

Earl, Blue, Ahmad, Emma, and myself were beginning to make a connection. Bean had taken to playing with the dogs.

Kirk continued. "I'll give you just one guess who owns Scrug Quarter Parrish."

Ahmad spoke up, "Harry Wyatt Sullivan."

Kirk nodded. "It's folded into a couple of incorporated entities, but yeah, Sullivan's the owner. He inherited the land outright some forty years ago."

I asked, "What about the big shot from the petroleum company?"

"His last know location was Islamorada in the Keys. If you've been there, you know it's a big marina with a couple of bars and hotels."

We all sat there letting the new information take hold in our brains.

Ahmad spoke first. "I must go and find this Harry Wyatt Sullivan. It seems he is most probably the man who had Amul Facon killed."

A look of violence was on his face when he said this. We were becoming organized, and this thing was looking like it was a lot bigger than we first thought. The last thing we needed was a vigilante, especially one from the Middle East.

I looked at Kirk and could tell he was thinking the same. "Okay Captain, what now?" I asked.

Kirk was in his element. He was also preparing for a career outside the FBI. People who are civilians and not tethered to the rank and file of a government bureaucracy don't have to take orders. He thought for a moment and then spoke with conviction, yet caution.

"As I see it, we need to do four things. One, we need to check out Islamorada. Two, we need to find out what's what at Scrug Quarter Parrish. Three, we need to find out where Harry Wyatt Sullivan is now. And four, we need to get the trophy back to the university. The last will relieve some of the press pressure and let us ask for favors if we need them, which we surely will."

Kirk looked at me. He wanted help with the assignments. Everyone wanted to be the one who nailed Mr. Fat Ass, if he was our man. Kirk was trying hard not to offend by giving someone a lower task.

I remembered an Army/Navy game when we were upper class at the Academy. The game was the only time cadets and midshipmen were allowed to show their true colors. All of those tight conservative young men showed their collective asses when the event came around. At a rustic bar full of the Army side of the tradition, after a win by Army, Kirk the Captain of Cadets had stood naked on a table and spewed beer on every female entering the establishment. At the time, we thought it to be the height of manliness. Now, however, I was impressed with his restraint.

I called a recess by excusing myself for a bathroom break. When I turned to shut the door, Blue blocked it. She followed me in and shut the door. "Go ahead, do your business."

"What if I have to go... number two?"

"You don't. You don't even have to go number one. You're just trying to figure out how to tell me and Emma we're the delegates to return the trophy."

Sometimes it's nice when someone knows you so well. Sometimes it's not. I lifted the lid and out of defiance made a little water.

"Process of elimination. Kirk is the FBI. He can't take the trophy back. He'll take credit for the recovery, but I owe him. Ahmad would rather cut his own throat than not be there when we find the bastard. It's my case, but I can't very well take off and deliver the trophy while everyone else fights the battles."

"What about Earl and Bean?"

I knew it was going to come down to this. There was no easy way to say it. "I need the muscle. I need Earl and Bean. That doesn't mean I don't need *you*, but I would prefer to know Emma isn't in a fire fight."

"You know, when Emma asked about me going into the FBI? This is why it's so attractive. I'm just as capable as any of those men, but even *you* see me as a woman first."

There was no good answer. One of things I've come to realize is that a strong woman isn't part-time. You want a little obedient honey at home who vows to love, honor, cherish, and obey, you better hope you don't also want a rattlesnake. I happen to love rattlesnakes, especially the kind with red hair.

"Babe, I don't have the right answer. But for right now, this time, I need for this to be about me more than you. There's no making up for it. There's no "I'm sorry" at the end of any of my sentences. I'm asking you to take the trophy back… for me."

The sullen look was constant. She slowly turned to walk away. I couldn't leave it like this, especially with what I'd discovered about what I treasured in my life. I reached out and grabbed her arm and spun her back to face me. She had the wild look of an animal that would just as soon tear out your throat as look at you. I didn't waver, I looked into those beautiful eyes and tried to make her understand without saying a word.

She looked away slightly. "I know I'm a bitch. I know I'm the most selfish person you or Emma has ever known. I want and want and want. How you can continue to love me is a mystery. I'm ashamed. Let me walk away and sulk."

I loosened my grip and she started to pull away. I grabbed her wrists tighter and pulled her into me. I didn't say a word but looked at her for a full minute. Something passed between us. It was at the chest level, but tugged at our tear ducts.

Chapter 75

The assignments were set. I took Emma and Blue, Jake and Sebastian to the Miami International Airport and put them on a plane bound for the Cable Counties. The goodbyes and other assorted sad stuff had already happened by the time we got to the gate. The only eventful moment was when the trophy set off the contraband detector. There really was no protocol for transporting a two-foot tall metal cup, obviously with some metal in it, so we suffered a little scrutiny, but got on pretty quick.

"When you get back, take the trophy straight to the stadium. Hand-deliver it to Jack Malloy, the Athletic Director. I've called ahead and a man will meet you at the airport. He's someone I trust and can pave the way to Jack without going through the usual red tape bullshit. His name is Paul Washington. Call me when you land and make contact with Paul."

An unusual occurrence, the plane was on time, and the boarding call was quick and easy. There were a few sniffles, but Emma and Blue were soon heading down the gangway, waving goodbye over their shoulders.

For the first time since I had reached good old American soil, an overwhelming sense of meanness came over me. It surely had something to do with the ladies heading out of harm's way. It had something to do with the fact I was finally feeling healthy, not the shadow-shy prisoner anymore. But mostly it had to do with the fact that I was feeling the primal man show his head again. This seemingly normal case had taken, and given, a huge spectrum of emotions. Now it was time to get even. Somebody had to pay for the deaths, the pain, the ungodly unknowing. As I walked through the concourse, an unusually hard rock anthem began to clang. Bells, black bells ringing. AC/DC was speaking to me, if no other human in that airport. This thing was probably getting ready to *Go Country*, and I welcomed it.

Chapter 76

When I left the airport, I found Ahmad standing next to my truck just where the ladies and I had left him. Obviously, no one had dared to ticket me. I motioned and we both jumped in.

As we drove from the two-story concourse, I clicked onto a Sirius XM channel that continued the feeling of manly infinity. I looked over at Ahmad and could tell he was feeling the same intensity. "You were pretty hard on me when we were over there," I said.

Ahmad bowed his head a little and I could hear heavy breath. "I'm sorry. I'm not a man who can be proud of my actions."

"Yeah?"

"That really doesn't matter does it? Now, having seen you and your friends, your true self, I'm ashamed."

"Silasteck…"

"Please call me Silas. That's what Earl and Bean call me."

I tested the taste of that more informal moniker and found it salty. "Silas… Silas, fuck that. Listen, you big ass. I do not forgive you, not yet. We all get out of this alive and kicking, then, maybe… maybe I'll be able to be a bigger man. For now, just know you don't have to watch your back around me. I'll do that for you, if you give your word you'll do the same for me."

Ahmad nodded and looked out the opposite window. I wasn't moved. "That's not good enough. Say it. Give me your word. Before you do, know something. I didn't tell anyone, any of your new friends, Earl, Bean, Emma, or Blue you were one of the men who tortured me. If I did, you could never count them as friends."

He cringed, and I could tell my words were the harshest he had ever taken in without retaliation. He gathered himself. "I give you my word you will suffer no more if I can possibly prevent it."

"Good enough."

***

While I was dropping off Emma and Blue, and making emotional pity-pat with Silas, Earl and Bean were on their way to Islamorada in Emma's Durango. Kirk was going back in to what used to be his office. He was going to see if he'd been fired. If not, then he would use all the resources of the office of the Special Agent in Charge of South Florida to try and locate the whereabouts of one Harry Wyatt Sullivan.

Ahmad and I were now on our way to the obscure Scrug Quarter Parrish. I was trying to settle my mind into thinking only about the case. A Parrish is the equivalent of a county, but only in the state of Louisiana. What could that possibly have to do with a sugarcane field in South Florida? For all of my intense thinking, I got nothing. Sometimes you get what you get. And you make do with what you have.

Chapter 77

Scrug Quarter Parrish, Deep South Florida

"You flinched again, Larry. I'm afraid that means another taste of the lovely Kari's bad medicine." Harry Wyatt nodded, and Kari Vilano-Lobos hit Larry Red with two open-palm smacks to the head, then did a wheeling roundhouse kick that landed with authority in Red's breadbasket.

The three of them, along with Zan, were locked in a small room within the large metal building at Scrug Quarter Parrish. They had arrived some hours before, and Wyatt had instructed his team of transplant bioengineers to release the petroleum bug in and around the area of the leak. Most of the staff was eagerly waiting at the spill site to see first-hand the hopeful validity of the bug. There wasn't anyone around to hear Larry Red's screams.

"Larry, do you need for me to remind you of the ground rules of our little game? I guess so. I will ask a question; you will answer. If you pause or flinch in any perceptible way, then you get more medicine. I think it's pretty simple. Do you agree?"

Larry Red staggered to a metal table in the middle of the room. There were no chairs, so he bent over at the waist and rested his arms against the surface. A slinky thread of blood and saliva clung to his nose and made its way down to the table without breaking. He nodded his head slowly.

"Good. I find it's always better if everyone understands the rules. Now, who did you tell of my involvement in all of this?"

Conscious of the pause rule, Larry blubbered, "Like I said before, the only person I mentioned anything to was that private detective."

"Yes, and what was his name?"

"I don't really remember, but it was something like Clod or Clown, but that's not it exactly."

Wyatt smiled a greasy smile around a mouthful of pork rinds. He looked over at Kari. Before anyone could register movement, she backed off a half-step then got her momentum going forward and punted Larry Red in the ribs. His knees buckled and he sank to the gritty concrete floor. Kari looked down at the pitiful form. His right hand was extended, trying to prop up his bruised body. A hateful sneer crossed her lips as she raised her booted foot and brought the heel down onto his hand. An audible cracking sound rung out with a simultaneous scream.

Wyatt pushed a button on his custom ride and it lunged ahead a couple of feet. "How about now, does that help your memory?"

In the corner of the room Zan's instincts were awakening. Blood, fresh blood was at hand, a wounded animal which needed to be culled from the herd.

Larry Red curled up and hugged his battered hand to his heaving chest. "Cloud... I think his name was Cloud."

"Very good. Cloud what?"

"I don't know. That's all he said. I'm sure he didn't give any other name."

"Larry, do you mean to tell me that you surrendered my name, my involvement, and my very livelihood to a man with only one syllable of a name?"

"I swear, it's all I got. He was big, dressed in dark clothes. He wasn't the kind of man you could say no to."

"You are a pathetic waste of space. I'm offended you suck oxygen from the same pool of air I do. What about that young wife of yours. Did you tell her about me?"

Larry's eyes grew wide, but he tried to hide the answer. "She doesn't know anything; I swear. I didn't tell her anything about you."

Wyatt put on a huge half-moon smile. "I believe you, Larry. And with that I fear you've served your usefulness."

Kari took the cue and headed for the door. She opened it and stood to the side. Wyatt reached to the console and switched a small key. He twisted the handle of his motor cart and it shot forward toward the door. He cut the engine at the door, but continued to look into the outer area of the big metal barn. He uttered a single phrase, and then punched the little vehicle onward. "Zan… dinner time."

Outside, Wyatt spoke up cheerily. "Kari my dear, let us go and see how the bug is doing. I think we can leave Zan to his business for at least the next half hour or so."

Chapter 78

Cloud, SQP

We arrived at the area known as Scrug Quarter Parrish to discover desolation. Empty, harvested cane fields and a huge barn with not a soul in sight. Ahmad wore his retro-fitted overalls, but his air and demeanor was anything but good old country boy. He literally seemed to be smelling for trouble. He walked along the long barn and concentrated on noting things.

His senses were acute. I could feel the enemy, too. To an outsider this piece of farmland would verily be ready for Norman Rockwell's brush. However, there was something *dark* stirring among the homeland scenario. Was it the sweat and blood of so many poor immigrant cane harvesters from the last two centuries? Probably, but there was something more.

A stout farm-hardened man with the sun baked into his skin approached. He hitched his pants and extended a leathery hand. "I'm Cal Taylor, the foreman of Scrug Quarter Parrish. Who might you be?"

Cal Taylor was the kind of man you liked before you even got to know him. The richness and superior standard of living that the middle-class of the United States take for granted was built on the backs of hard-working, sweating, calloused men like Cal Taylor.

"Name's Cloud. That's Silas over there. I was wondering if I could ask you a few questions about the cane business?"

Taylor removed a bright green cap with the Deere logo emblazed in golden yellow. He made a purposeful gesture of combing his fingers through his dusty black hair. "Yeah, I reckon I been expecting something like this for a while."

"Cal, who owns all of this sugarcane land?"

The old farmer looked at me with a bit of surprise in his eyes. "You don't know?"

It was my turn to look quizzical. "Yeah... no. I might have an idea, but I was hoping you could tell me for sure."

Cal combed his hair again. It was a nervous habit. "I'll tell ya right now, I'm probably gonna end up telling ya anything ya want to know, but first I'd sure like to know who I'm talking to."

Salt of the earth, this man. It pained me to think I might deprive him of his livelihood one day by sinking his boss. "I believe the man who owns this land might be involved in some other business. I think he has interest in some illegal ventures."

"Yeah, me too," he said with obvious concern.

"I got myself caught up in this mess almost by accident. I surely wasn't counting on coming to South Florida and turning up... what it seems like I'm turning up. I'm a private detective of sorts. I was hired to find something I believe your boss stole. But in the process, I've stumbled onto something much bigger."

Cal Taylor listened intently. He was fumbling with some loyalty issues, but I could see he knew personal preservation was going to be involved. "I been working this same land for going on thirty years. I was twelve when my family floated across from Cuba on four wooden pallets strapped to a couple of coolers. I don't even know where all this sugar goes, but I tell ya every year we grow more, grow it better, and it's still never enough."

If I'd been in a better mood or if I wasn't so pressed for time, I probably could have sat there all day soaking up the history of this land and of Cal Taylor's ancestors. As it was, I needed some information. "Who owns the land?"

"Mr. Sullivan."

"Harry Wyatt Sullivan?"

"Yeah, he's the one. I never even met him until just a few days ago. Before him, it was his daddy. And let me tell ya, I wish I only had contact with that man once every twenty-five years."

"Didn't care for the man, huh?"

"Man didn't care for us. People of color, I mean. That was back before it was politically incorrect to openly show your hate for coloreds."

I really didn't need anything to make me hate Sullivan any more than I already did. I almost wished I hadn't heard that he descended from enthusiastic racists. "The daddy was pretty hard on your people?"

Cal Taylor stifled a snicker. He repeated the hair comb. "Back then, Fridays were something special. One reason was because it was payday. The other was it was punishment day. One worker, out of a number of them who'd fallen behind during the week, would be chosen at random. Back then, the straw bosses were all white and didn't give a damn who got called out. They'd take some sorry soul out of the crowd during the end-of-week pay out. They'd take him out in the middle of the lot and all of the straw bosses would remove their belts and beat the man half to death. I have to say, it worked like a charm. Everyone was getting paid and at the same time some poor bastard getting whipped right out in front of them. Next week came around, everyone worked a little harder. And Big-Daddy Sullivan was always there, coaching and encouraging the straw bosses."

Before I could catch myself, I said, "Why the hell did you all put up with that?"

Taylor's eyes scratched lit like an old match. Before he could answer, I caught myself. "I'm sorry, bad question. I know... it was that kind of time... in the South."

He nodded and continued to look at the ground.

"What's in that new-looking barn over there?"

Both of us looked over to the shiny tin structure where Ahmad was lingering. As quickly as Taylor had taken offense, his face dawned with anticipation. "I'm not sure. I've never been in there. In fact, it's strictly off limits for all of us cane-farming staff."

"Didn't you ever wonder?"

Oops, I did it again. I rubbed my face and tried to extricate the toenail I had left behind when my foot jammed in my mouth. "Once again," I said, "I'm sorry."

"Barn went up about eighteen months ago. It was during the off-season and nobody even saw the damn thing being built. One week there was the dusty field, the next, there was a bright shiny barn."

"Who comes and goes?"

"That's the damned-able hell of it. Near 'bout every man who works over in the barn is foreign. I don't mean Latino or Black. They look Chinese or Japanese or some *nese*, from parts unknown."

"So you've never had any contact, any conversation with the men from the barn?"

"Awe hell, no… I ain't ever talked to'em, but my boy got a taste for one of the women who comes around ever so often. He told me they're working on some kind of bug. Something having to do with gas."

Ahmad was waving his arms. I looked up, and he motioned me over. I invited Cal to join me. As the old farmer and I walked over I wondered about the name. I asked him, "Cal Taylor… doesn't seem a very Latino name."

He fumbled in his breast pocket and found a toothpick, which he tucked into the corner of his mouth. "My real name is Jose Enrique Lescono. The Sullivans have been calling the straw boss Cal Taylor since that was really his name. The real Cal Taylor died nearly seventy years ago. The Sullivan patriarchs never knew, so my granddaddy was Cal Taylor, my daddy was Cal Taylor, and yours truly has been Cal Taylor for nearly twenty years. I'll be damned if it don't make paying income taxes easier either."

I smiled at the man as we walked through a roll-up door Ahmad had found.

Chapter 79

The inside of the building didn't resemble the outside at all. It was a most modern-day lab. Endless rows of racks lined with test tubes covered the outer walls. Down the center were at least two dozen large galvanized tanks holding water in various shades of green, blue, black and completely clear.

Most of the interior was a huge open bay. A small cubicle of an office was in one corner. As we approached we could hear a low hum and a continuous grinding noise. I pulled the .357 Python from my shoulder holster and pushed back against Cal Taylor's chest. I spoke in a hushed tone. "You stay right here. Let me and my friend see what's in there."

Cal Taylor, a.k.a., Jose Enrique Lescono, was more than happy to yield.

Ahmad tried the doorknob. When he found it locked, he looked to me. I nodded and he stepped back and drove his enormous foot into the door latch. The entire doorframe gave way and fell in splinters.

As the door fell inward, a tide of smell like long-baked battery acid, assaulted us. Taylor clapped his hands to his face. Silas pushed through and I followed. None of us were prepared for what we saw.

A small brown kid, probably fifteen or so, was sitting in the middle of the floor. He had a severed, bloody skull in his hands. He was naked and the blood was everywhere. The kid didn't pause—he hardly seemed to notice we had entered the room. A stubby finger rubbed across a dead eye in the skull. The finger pointed and then scooped the eye out. The young man held it on the end of his finger like some grotesque pudding pop. He looked at us, smiled, and popped the eye in his mouth.

Chapter 80

My gun hand collapsed by my side. Cal Taylor stumbled, and Ahmad half-caught him before he reached the cement floor.

The most disturbing affect was that the young man didn't stop. I felt like the mother catching her son doing the dirty with an open Hustler magazine. The son would cower, would try and make out like he was doing something different than his joystick. This lad was proud. He looked to us and expected cheers.

I reached to my ankle and retrieved my backup weapon—a small Glock. I handed it to Ahmad, who was gaping as much as I was. It was a show of faith that fell on deaf sensibilities. Ahmad held the gun pointed at the cement floor.

As I approached the lad, I expected him to become territorial. He did not. The bloody, scavenging skeleton paused, smiled between a flesh-clutch and pointed a still-meaty thighbone in my direction. I coughed and pushed the retch down. Ahmad pushed the gun sideways into my gut and I took it back from him. He bent down and slowly caressed the bloody face of the smiling young man.

The boy wasn't easily separated from his feast. I left that to Ahmad, the man who had had his way with me in Qatar and owed me at least this much.

I sat in the safe confines of my truck and looked into the rear-view mirror at the big Arab as he tried to compassionately constrain the bloody cannibal. We didn't move for at least an hour. During that time, the bed of the truck rocked with Ahmad's efforts to contain the young brown man.

Chapter 81

As I was sitting in the truck, my phone rang. I picked it up and could hear loud, tangy, reggae music in the background. Earl finally realized the phone had been answered and spoke into the receiver much louder than was necessary. "Cloud… is that you?"

"Yeah Earl, it's a phone, not a CB radio."

"Yeah, I guess I'm not up to snuff. Anyhow, it took some doing, but we got the harbormaster here at Islamorada to talk to us. It's taken half a dozen Rum Runners and some drink they set on fire, but we finally got him to talk to us."

"Sounds painful."

Earl laughed the laugh of a man who'd sampled the bar's wares. When he spoke again his tone was little on the defensive side. "We couldn't let the man sit there and drink alone."

"Yeah, so, what have you found out?"

"The boat we were wondering about, well it was here. The man who's gone missing fits the description of a fella who went on board. Harbormaster says he saw a great big fat man on board the boat, but he never got off."

"Were you able to find out where the boat was going after it left Islamorada?"

"Yeah, harbormaster says it was heading for Miami."

Never send two country boys to investigate criminal mischief at an island bar. I would file that one away. "You and Bean just stay over there tonight.

Get a room and I'll pay you back. Looks like I might need you tomorrow, so try and make it an early night."

The connection scratched and I half-wondered if Earl was paying me any attention. "What… what did you say?"

"I said… I said, thank you for coming half way 'round the world to fetch me. I think I'm getting things figured out, so why don't you and Bean stay there tonight, all expenses paid. I'll give you a call in the morning."

"Cloud, man, you wouldn't believe it. Some sorority honey is up on the table and she ain't wearing a strip of clothes."

I looked in the rear-view mirror at Ahmad and the bloody young man he was trying to hold. My patience was anorexic, even for my lifelong friend. "Tuck a dollar bill in her… awe hell… just do what comes natural. I'll talk to you tomorrow."

I disconnected and called Kirk. A cheery young voice answered. "FBI, Office of the Special Agent in Charge, how may I help you?"

I was still a little irked with the boys for enjoying themselves, even though I had no right to be. "Let me speak to Kirk."

The voice took on a superior tone. "Special Agent Kirk is not available at the moment; may I pass you on to his voice mail?"

The truck rocked and I saw Ahmad in the mirror. He was physically holding the young man by the hair. The blood-soaked cannibal was trying to bite his face. Glistening, pointed teeth snapped at the open air between them. I was just before getting out and shooting both of them. The cannibal because… well hell, because he was a cannibal—and Ahmad for mothering him.

"No, don't you even think about pushing some button on that console of yours. I know Kirk's there, and if you tell him Cloud is calling, he'll answer."

"Sir, I must say, that tone is *not* necessary. I am only following procedure."

The week of being confined in a dungeon, the stress and pressure of the case, and the freak show going on in the back of my truck was too much. The Cloud-world shook, a fissure emerged, and the hot black lava of my frustration melted over the innocent receptionist. "Get him… get him, and *get* him. Get him on the phone, get him on the goddamn-mother-fucking phone, right this goddamn minute."

The line went dead.

I heaved in anger and frustration. I grabbed a leather sap from beneath my seat and in one motion left the truck. Ahmad was still holding the gnashing, pointed teeth at bay. I brought the heavy sap down on the young man's neck with satisfaction.

Ahmad held onto the limp body. He blinked repeatedly. "His name is Zan. He has a name," he said. I sensed he was wondering whether to be sad or to jump from the truck and stomp my ass.

I didn't care, I said, "What the fuck is wrong with this whole fucking world? Why do I get caught up in a ring of death while trying to find some insignificant trophy? Why does Blue get mad? And what in the unholy… for the love of… are you looking at me like that for? Why don't you just bring your big ass down here with your warped values? You just saw that little fucker *eat* another man, and you look at me like you want to kill *me* for hitting him."

Ahmad drilled me with torture on his face. I was ranting and I saw I'd struck a nerve. I drove on with pleasure. "Get down here. You and me… have something to settle and we probably… awe fuck it. Just get down here and let's get it over with."

I vaguely remember setting my feet. Getting ready to give the big bastard the whipping of his life. I don't remember much after that.

Chapter 82

When I came to, it took me a few minutes to get my bearings. My jaw felt like somebody had hit me with a ten-pound sledgehammer about a half dozen times. I would have asked if anyone had gotten the number of the truck that hit me, but no one was standing around. I was lying under my truck and for the life of me I had no idea how I'd gotten there. I rose up and hit my head on the drive shaft, just to confirm I really *was* lying under something immovable.

When I pulled myself from under the vehicle, I saw Ahmad lying on the ground about ten yards away. I leaned forward and stumbled over to his big carcass. As I approached, I noticed a blossom of blood on his upper chest and a twin plume on his leg. I knelt beside him and saw his eyes were wide open. Great, just what I needed, to have gotten another of the Sultan's kindred killed. As I was hanging my head I heard a rasping breath and saw him blink.

"You're alive!"

He struggled, but managed to speak. "I'm not sure whether you sound grateful or disappointed."

In spite of the situation I had to smile. "What happened? Did I shoot you?"

Ahmad started to laugh, but it came out mostly coughing. When he finished he said, "No, no, you didn't shoot me. Why, was that your intention?"

I thought for a moment. I sincerely didn't remember shooting him, I did remember wanting to. "No… of course not. What happened?"

"Right after our little disagreement, a fat man and a dark woman arrived. Between trying to handle *our* situation and restrain the boy, I got surprised. Before I really knew what was happening the woman shot me. The only reason I'm talking to you is that the Taylor fellow came over and tackled her."

I looked around with a sense of panic. "Where's Cal?"

"Cloud, you've only been out for ten minutes or so. This whole thing went down real fast. Could you get me some water?"

I felt a little guilty at having not considered the man was lying here bleeding to death. I stripped my shirt and tore it into halves. I wrapped one half around his leg and the other as best as I could around the wound on his shoulder. I grabbed a gallon jug of water from the cooler in the bed of the truck and held it to his lips. He drank hungrily.

I looked around again and then reached for my gun. It wasn't there. I groped my leg and found the backup missing as well. Even in his weakened condition Ahmad noticed and said, "I took your guns when I dragged you under the truck. I didn't want you waking up and shooting me on sight. I hid them under the front seat."

I ran to the truck and while I was fishing my guns from under the seat I grabbed the phone and hit the redial button. When the same cheery voice from the FBI office answered I took in a whole long breath. I tried to speak in a little higher voice. "Yes, this is Assistant Director Savage. This is a *code red* transmission. Please scramble all frequencies and put me directly through to the Special Agent in Charge."

Of course, this was all made-up bullshit. I wouldn't know a code red from a candy-coated cream corn bowl of mush. Amazingly it worked and two seconds later the phone was answered. "Kirk here, sir."

"Goddamn I'll have to remember that. I think you might have a receptionist problem."

There was a marked hesitation. "Cloud?"

"Yeah, and I wasn't kidding about the receptionist problem."

"I'll call you right back. There's a scramble of epic proportion going on."

I hit the end key and waited. Seconds later the phone rang and when I answered Kirk was on the other end. "Cloud, what's happening?"

"We are right on target. You need to get a team of people out to Scrug Quarter Parrish. I'm not sure what we've found, but it was enough to get Silas shot and maybe some more."

"I'll be there in… twenty minutes. Is Silas dead?"

"No, but he won't make it much longer. He's got two big ones still in him."

"Just hang on, we'll be right there."

"I'm glad to hear you still have a job."

"I don't, but that doesn't take effect until the end of the work day. That gives us at least another six hours." The phone went dead.

That's when I realized Zan, the boy cannibal, was gone.

Chapter 83

As I was walking back towards Ahmad I noticed a lump of denim with a white shirt over on the other side of the truck. I put a rolled-up jacket under Ahmad's head and hurried over. As I approached, I wished for the same reception I'd gotten by surprise from Ahmad when I thought he was dead. I was very disappointed.

Cal Taylor lay askew. The bright green *John Deere* cap was crumpled and looked to have small tire tracks marking it. His body contained at least a half dozen ruptured bursts of flesh made by a very big gun. The condition of his face was the most appalling. It looked as if someone had repeatedly run a wheeled vehicle over it.

Chapter 84

A swirling cloud of dust marked the entrance of two black helicopters. With several heavily armed men in tow, Kirk jumped from the first bird. Within minutes, men from the other chopper and wearing the same black bulletproof uniforms, were canvassing the entire area.

I gave Kirk the thumbs-up. He ran over to where Ahmad was laying and began barking orders at several of the men. Within five minutes Ahmad was loaded on the second chopper and it lifted off with orders to deposit him in the hands of one of South Florida's leading surgeons at Jackson Memorial Hospital in Miami.

Kirk summoned a half-dozen men and put them on the remaining chopper to make a mile-radius sweep from the air. He couldn't tell them what they were looking for, but maybe something would go our way. A couple of moments later, Kirk and I found ourselves alone.

"Let it never be said that knowing you, the mighty storm Cloud, isn't an adventure."

"Sorry about you losing your job?"

"Hell, it's just about the best thing ever happened to me. I told you I've been wanting to get into business for myself. I reckon this gives me the boost I need."

"All the same, I need for you to know, I appreciate everything you've done."

"Game ain't over yet. Thank me when we mount their heads and hang 'em over the fireplace."

Chapter 85

We sat on the ground near my truck and watched a team of emergency workers zip Cal Taylor into a body bag. The back doors of the vehicle slammed, and it headed back toward the city with lights and sirens abloom. I hadn't known him very long—hell, I hadn't known him at all. Ahmad had hardly ever spoken to him, but the man called Cal Taylor, a.k.a, José Enrique Lescono, still found the need to give his life up for us. When this was all over, I was going to make sure his descendants knew what he'd done, and that none of them would carry the name Cal Taylor ever again.

I looked over at Kirk and asked, "Were you able to find anything out?"

"The fat man we keep hearing about is indeed Harry Wyatt Sullivan. We've investigated him a few times for relatively minor things, mostly having to do with land fraud and real estate scams. We've never been able to pin anything on him directly. His family is big sugar, has been for longer than we have records for. I still don't know if we have proof enough."

"Earl and Bean are still down at Islamorada. They got the Harbormaster there to confirm the *Big Thunder* was there right about the same time that fella from the petroleum company went missing."

"I put in a call to the Coast Guard. They'll be looking for the boat. A couple of agents back at the office are calling all of the marinas in the area. It should be only a matter of time before somebody spots him. Thing is, we don't have much time." He looked at his watch and shook his head. "In about four and half hours my time in the FBI will come to a close. I'll probably still be able to call in a favor or two, but for the most part, we'll be going it alone."

I wanted to tell him I was sorry again. But it seemed, at the time, it might only make things seem drearier. Instead I kept the pressure on. "What should we do now?"

"For starters, we need to know what's in that barn over there."

"We had a peek inside. It's a lab. I'm guessing upon further inspection we'll find that Sullivan was carrying out the experiments a particular college student started up at the university."

"You think it's where he's growing the petroleum bug?"

"I do. And I think our missing petroleum company big-wig was down in sunny Florida to make a bid on it. Until a few hours ago, I would have bet big money we would find his dead remains buried out in one of these cane fields."

"What makes you think different now?"

"We found something else when we were in the barn."

"Don't make me guess, what the hell was it?"

"I think it would be better, if I just showed you."

Chapter 86

Inside the barn, Kirk gave orders, and the team of men secured the whole building. When he saw the lab setup, Kirk called in a Hazardous Materials team. As he was putting the phone away, one of the agents called out. He was at the rear of the building in the office. I knew what we were going to see. I moved slowly as Kirk sprinted toward the agent.

As I got close to the door, the agent who'd called came running out looking for sunlight and holding his hand over his mouth. Kirk stood just inside the doorway with his hands on his hips. He looked at me and shook his head.

Kirk said, "I'm guessing this is what you wanted to show me."

I kept my eyes on the bloody mess on the floor and nodded.

Kirk's radio beeped and someone said the crime scene specialist had arrived. "Tell him to come on in. Tell him to bring all of his tools and a big-ass sponge."

Just as Kirk was pulling on a pair of latex gloves, my phone buzzed. I answered, it was Blue. I took a few steps outside the office. She said, "Hey, it's me. Mission accomplished. Your friend picked us up at the airport, and we're on our way to the Athletic Department."

"Thanks, listen. This thing isn't over yet. Probably be best if you kept your eyes wide open."

"Sure thing, Dad. Your friend wants to talk to you."

As the phone transferred I took in the meaning of Blue's clipped tone. She was still pissed about being asked to do the benign part of the operation. Paul Washington picked up on the other end. "Cloud, I'll be damned if you didn't do it, boy. I sure thought we'd seen the last of this here trophy. But you got it back, no scratches, and I'll be damned if you didn't pick a hell of a delivery person."

I could have done without that last compliment. I was sure Blue was seething at having been referred to as the delivery person. "Thanks, Paul. Listen, I would surely appreciate it if you would try real hard to make friends with those two ladies."

Paul was a wise old man. He picked up my meaning and just countered with, "You bet."

As I was turning back toward the office, Kirk emerged. He held something small and bloody in one hand. He raised it up so I could see it clearly. It was a state of Florida driver's license. I squinted to make out the name through the smears. I felt my face become hollow as I read the name. Lawrence C. Red. So ended the life and times of Larry Red.

Chapter 87

I dipped my head and looked at the loose sand. Kirk took the license and put it in a clear plastic bag and wrote on the outside with a marker. He paused and looked over at me. "This is the guy?"

"Yeah, Larry Red, he's the one who gave me the first real lead about the fat man and the boat. He was also Amul Instad Facon's research partner."

"You think he was following up on his friend?"

"I think he was a loose end."

"He was working for the fat man?"

"Something like that."

The HazMat team arrived, and Kirk set them to the task of testing every vat, beaker and test tube in the lab. We could hear the helicopter coming back and went outside.

Through the haze of dust kicked up by the chopper rotors, a group of about twenty or so men dressed in white lab coats appeared, escorted by Kirk's men. As they neared I could make out their features. They all seemed to be Asian. This must be the merry band of scientists Cal Taylor had seen coming and going from the lab over the last several months.

Even though their clothes pronounced them as scientists, their faces were the same as every illegal alien when caught by the INS. Kirk approached and asked who was in charge. The faces all turned from fear to confusion. They looked to one another to exaggerate their lack of comprehension of the English language.

Kirk looked at the men, and I could tell his personal clock was ticking. He didn't have time to do things by the book. It was only a few hours until he wouldn't have any official authority.

We were on the far side of the barn, shielded from all of the scurrying agents and HazMat workers. Kirk told the leader of the escort team to take his men around front and make sure everything was all right. The leader looked at Kirk, making sure he'd heard his superior properly.

"Sir, shouldn't I leave some of my men here to secure the prisoners?"

Kirk looked at the man with a bolt of clarification. "I'll take care of the prisoners."

The agent made a swift gesture and all of the escort team followed him to the opposite side of the building. I myself was wondering what in the hell Kirk was planning now.

Kirk looked at me, shrugged his shoulders, and pulled his Glock from a shoulder holster. He made a show of ejecting the clip, then sliding it back in. Smiling in my direction, he said, "If they can't talk English, then I don't have no use for the wormy little bastards."

With that, he grabbed the white coat nearest him and with one quick jerk had the man down on his knees. Kirk put the gun close to his own mouth and spoke to it like a long-awaited lover. "Okay Ruby, baby, let's make the world a better place." He put the gun to the man's ear and pulled the trigger.

A metallic click was all it took for a flood of English to pour out.

Chapter 88

The scientists all spoke at once. I could decipher part of what they were saying, but most of it just ran together. Kirk pointed the Glock in the air and squeezed the trigger. Three loud shots rang out and the men fell silent. Kirk again asked who was in charge, and there was little hesitation as everyone pointed in the direction of one man cowering at the edge of the pack.

Kirk had him sit on the tailgate of my truck and then began to question him. "Who do you work for?"

The answers came without pause. "Mr. Harry Wyatt Sullivan."

"How long have you been in his employ?"

"One full year."

"What are you working on in the lab?"

The answer came in scientific language that neither of us understood. Kirk asked him to make it simpler. The man thought for a moment. "Petroleum-consuming bacterium."

"Does it work?"

A wide smile stretched across the scientist's face. "Yes. When the men in the helicopter found us, we were watching the first experiment. I believe it is a total success."

"You speak English rather well."

"I was educated and worked in Hong Kong before it was returned to Mother China in 2000."

"What is the bug to be used for?"

The scientist looked at Kirk with sincere confusion. I helped him out. "The bacterium, what's it going to be used for?"

His features relaxed. "For oil spills from tankers and drilling rigs."

A young nerdy-looking Federal Agent came running around the side of the truck. He was winded but enthusiastic. He spoke to Kirk. "Sir, we have something we need you to see."

Kirk and I, with the scientist in tow, hustled into the barn. The agent led us to what appeared to be a storage area. There were several crates and pallets of large industrial-looking equipment. In the center of the room was a large cylindrical-shaped structure which gave off a constant low hum. Kirk looked at the agent and asked, "What is it?"

"I believe it's a nuclear generator. Like one you might find on board a submarine."

Kirk's face pinched with weariness at where all of this could be headed. "It seems to be running. What is it supplying power for?"

The agent led us to the back area of the room where a large pump, the kind you would see at oil fields, was steadily dipping up and down. Kirk looked at the agent then at the scientist. "Is that what I think it is?"

"It's an oil derrick sir. And by the look of these gauges, it's pumping raw crude oil at full capacity."

"From here to where?"

"I don't know where the oil is going, but it's coming from directly below us."

"We're sitting on a pool of oil?"

The agent gave a small smile. "I think it would be fair to say we're standing on a small *ocean* of oil."

Kirk shook his head then told the agent to continue monitoring the pump and especially the nuclear power source. He grabbed the scientist by the elbow and roughly pulled him from the room. I followed.

Kirk checked his watch then looked severely at the scientist. "What's going on here?"

The man was shaky. He said, "We only monitor the nuclear device. I knew, of course, that oil was being mined, but I know nothing else."

Despite all that was being discovered, the scientist didn't seem like some criminal mastermind. He was an employee. I don't think he even knew that what was going on was illegal. Kirk handed the man off to an agent and asked me to follow him outside. He walked straight to my truck and got in the passenger side. I got in the driver's side and started the engine. He leaned over and put the air conditioner on full. We sat for the next few moments in thick, thinking silence.

Chapter 89

Finally, Kirk looked over at me. "I'm gonna run the plan by you, and I want you to see if you can improve on it."

I nodded.

"I figure it's about an hour and half until the end of the business day. I'm going to check with the Coast Guard, the Miami P.D., and every federal agency I can think of. I'm checking first to find out if they know what the hell I should do, finding a real live oil well here, this close to the Everglades, not to mention an unlicensed nuclear reactor. Then I'm gonna get a team out here to track the pipeline, try to find out where the oil is being pumped. And most of all, I'm gonna find out if anyone knows where that fat fuck Sullivan is."

I looked out the front window at all of the men around a barn out in a desolate sugar cane field. I thought about a trophy and a tiny spark that was now a raging forest fire. I looked back at him. "No, I can't think of anything else. That's just what I'd do, if I were you."

He said, "I'll bet you a case of hundred-year-old scotch, just about the time we do all the hard work, about the time we figure out where the oil is going and where the bastard is, my time will be up. That's just not good enough. We aren't going to let somebody else accept the credit for the game we've played. If you're up for it, I got something I need you to do."

I nodded.

"I need you to get us a boat. One probably, thirty-foot. I need—"

I cut him off. With everything he had on his mind, at least I could do some of the thinking. "You want me to set up the contingency plan. You want vehicles, supplies, and men enough to follow the fat bastard wherever we need to."

Kirk looked at me with a slim wave of relief. "I reckon I don't need to tell you every little detail, do I?"

Thinking back to a small book every graduate of the Academy is required to read, I winked. "Captain, I am your Rowan. Consider the Message to Garcia delivered."

Chapter 90

The Overseas Highway, U.S. 1, is a well-worn stretch of black-top which takes you from Florida City to Key West. About an hour's drive into it is Islamorada. During my drive, I called home and got no answer. I couldn't decide whether this was a good thing or not. I next tried Paul Washington at his home, and again got no answer. I could feel the tension build in the grip I had on the steering wheel. One more place. I called the Athletic Association.

The cheery voice of Mary-Ann Lemke greeted me, confirming I had indeed reached the office of the Athletic Director. I wanted to give a little sparing flirt, but kept the professional in my tone. "This is Cloud. Could you please pass me through to the Director?"

Instead of the chilly reply I expected, I got a rather warm response. "Yes Mr. Cloud. The Athletic Director has been expecting your call."

I waited, listening to the canned music, which was not quite as soothing as the hum from the mud-grip tires on my truck licking asphalt. After only about a minute, an excited voice greeted me. "Cloud, you lucky son of bitch. I can't believe you found the trophy. Legions of university fans will bow down before you when tomorrow morning they read the trophy is back home all safe and sound."

I could hear music in the background. In fact, it sounded like a three-alarm party was going on. "Have you seen Blue and Emma?"

"Seen them? Hell, they're right here. We're having a hell of a time celebrating the return of the trophy. All we need is for you to be here."

"How about Paul and Mame Blake?"

"They're here, too. We got the head ball coach and even the governor up here in the skybox. Here, wait a minute and I'll put you on with Blue."

"No thanks, Jack. I just wanted to make sure they were back there safe and sound."

"They're safe from the really bad guys, like you and whoever you got the trophy from, but I'm not so sure you'd appreciate the moves our starting quarterback and a couple of the linebackers are putting on your women."

Jealousy sunk one fang in my neck. I reached out more than metaphorically and slapped the greedy devil down before he could sink the other fang. "Well, I'm just happy the trophy's home." Sarcasm was the replacement for the jealous beast. "I just give thanks to God and my teammates, and we'll just keep trying to win them one game at a time."

There was silence on the other end. Then Jack said, "What... what the hell are you rambling on about, God, team...?"

"Just take care of my women. I'll hopefully see you in a couple of days."

Before he could answer, the frizzle of a lost connection set in, and I set the phone in the cradle.

I pulled the truck into a parking space flanked by totem poles carved out of palm trees. The sullen faces of wooden gods spoke to my heart. Locking the truck, I walked toward Islamorada's Tiki Bar. The signs outside pronounced it as the "World-Famous Home of the Rum Runner." I was sure to find my two country friends awash in the dark pink liquid.

In any bar, it doesn't take long to spot Earl and Bean. They are usually towering above the last scene from Sodom and Gomorrah. What I saw was even spectacular for this twosome. Both men were wearing industrial-strength bras on their heads as caps. Each had a welterweight, thirtyish broad on shoulder. They were facing an ancient man, complete with Skipper's cap turned backward, who sat at the bar trying desperately to swallow some foamy liquid from a large jar. Everyone was chanting, "Drink, drink, drink!"

Earl saw me first and immediately looked like a man-child caught with his pickle outside the jar. He tried a bashful smile and let the legs unwrap from around his thick neck. He walked over to the corner of the bar where I was standing with his eyes studying the ground.

I'm the last man on Earth to serve harsh words for someone experimenting with pleasures of the flesh. I kept this in mind as I spoke to the hung dome of Earl's head. "Seems like you're having quite a good time."

Even as his head was hanging he reached out a huge black paw and settled in on my forearm. "I'm sorry, Cloud, I'm sorry as hell for…for I don't know all what." He caught a flash of remembrance and looked at me with a sway to both his body and his eyes. "Hey, I thought… I thought we were supposed to see you tomorrow. What the hell are you doing down *here*?"

I smiled past him, and he looked over his shoulder to see what he was missing. I took a bottle of Tabasco Sauce, stripped the plastic stopper, and poured it into his pink drink. When he looked back in my direction, he remembered the guilt he was supposed to be feeling. He grabbed his drink and furiously stirred it, then downed what was left. I waited, smiling.

His face began to contort. He grimaced and tried to hide the pain. Then he looked at me with the beleaguered eyes of one who has seen his Judas. He first grabbed a mug of beer from a couple sitting at the bar and drank the whole thing. Then he reached over the bar and fumbled with the drink spout until he had a full stream of bluish black liquid spraying his entire face.

The man next to us, the one who had his drink taken hostage, was smoking a big cigar. I nudged him and said, "I like how that stogie smells."

He reached into a breast pocket and produced a leather case. Sliding the top off, he moved the pouch in my direction. I took a cigar from the case, he clipped the end for me, and I lit it with a bar candle. About this time, Earl was spewing a rancid gush of toxic waste on the barroom floor.

Bean turned to see what was happening with his brother. First he saw me, smiling. He walked over with the bra on his head and the girl still straddling his neck. The girl bumped her head on at least three of the rafters as Bean approached the bar.

"Cloud, what…what are *you* doing here?"

I helped the lady down from her lofty perch and told the bartender to give her another of whatever she was drinking. By this time Earl had managed to gather most of himself and walked over to us bent over at the waist, rubbing his belly. He became Robert Mitchum in *El Dorado*, "My friend, my real-long friend…you dirty bastard. Cloud, what the hell did you put in my drink?"

I cupped his chin and pointed it in my direction. Bean was already looking at me for the next move. "Gentlemen, we have a problem, and we need a boat."

The two big country boys on loan from hayseed glanced at each other and actually smiled.

"What's the rube?"

Earl tried, but Bean put a hand on his brother's head and said, "Well, we might just know somebody."

***

An hour later I was steering the *Half Naked* through Vaca Cut. On board were the partially-sloshed Earl and Bean and the fully and completely sloshed harbormaster. Evidently, some Dot Com big wig had moored a sixty-foot Bertram at Islamorada some sixteen months prior and had never paid his bills. By the rules of the marina, the Harbormaster had rights to the boat and could sell it to make back whatever was outstanding on the bill.

I wrote a twenty-five-thousand-dollar check for the outstanding bill and now found myself the owner of a plush luxury yacht worth fifty times that amount.

I'm not much of a sailor. I needed a lot of guidance, especially in the winding channels surrounding the Keys. The Harbormaster's name, I learned, was Abe West. His intense state of inebriation required us to use a couple of bungee cords and a whole reel of duct tape to fasten him to a chair beside the steering consol.

I had loaded the armament from my toolbox onto the boat before we set out. I wasn't really sure if it would be enough, but things were looking up. I used my sat-phone and called Kirk. He answered his own phone this time. "Kirk, South Florida SAC."

Kirk's time in the FBI had expired. We both knew this as he answered. I detected a marked difference in his voice. There was a wild boldness he hadn't exhibited when under the rule of the FBI.

"I got what we talked about. I'm coming 'round the horn. What do we need to do, Captain?"

"That's the last time I'll ever answer the phone that way. I hadn't really thought about it until just now. This is a good country, just a little spoiled. The grand old man fought in WWII and kept reminding me that we, the afterbirth of the 'Great Generation,' wouldn't and couldn't ever be that brave or honorable again. In a way, I think he was right. You and me won't ever again lie in a mud hole in any god-forsaken country. If and when we fail, it'll be long distance. Now, we're all just settling for shopping for shit on TV."

I prodded him for more useful information at the moment. "Captain Jesse James Kirk. The newly named *USS Enterprise* is drifting off the coast of Armageddon. Please confirm and issue new orders."

I think this shocked the life back into him. Kirk breathed in a sound that could only be described as determined. "*Enterprise*, the Captain is well. Set course for star base Joke Cove. I have the bogey on radar. I will rendezvous with you at ten hundred hours. Heat up the phasers and tell the horny green bitches to get their mean asses ready to cum. Kirk out."

I knew the Captain had waited his entire career to utter those words.

Chapter 91

I picked Kirk up at Joke Cove, a small marina on the western side of the Everglades. I had to use the dingy on a count of the water was pretty shallow. Heading back into the Gulf with Kirk on board, I saw the boat I had just become the owner of. It now looked to be at least sixty feet long and even in the dim light left of the day, it was a white, shiny, magnificent beast. Perhaps I'd underestimated my haul. I now reckoned the twenty-five thousand I'd paid for it wasn't shy by fifty times her actual worth, but more likely a hundred times.

As we drew nearer, Kirk looked over at me with concern on his face. "You do see that big-assed boat don't you?"

We were in the fourth quarter now and I was the only one who knew what play was coming next. "Yeah, I see it."

"If you don't veer a little left or right, we're gonna find ourselves plastered to the side of it like so many of our little crustacean friends."

I let a small evil smile curl my lips. "Yeah, well, *that's* the boat. That's what you wanted, wasn't it?"

Kirk duplicated my evil smile. He produced the Glock and spoke to it again. "Ruby... Ruby my dear, sometimes it's good to know our old friend Cloud."

In my absence, Earl and Bean had scraped the old name off the vessel. Curls of sticky plastic letters carrying the words *Half Naked* rode the waves or became fish food. In their place one of the boys had painted in a droopy hand scrawl, "The Enterprise."

On board, Kirk got right to the task of giving orders. He had Earl work the anchors, and within five minutes, *The Enterprise* was headed west northwest with everything she had.

Kirk sat at the steering console and the rest of us waited behind him. After he got the bearing right and made two radio and one cell phone call, he chucked the cell into the ocean and spun his chair around to look at us.

"With the aid of some of my sources and the U.S. Coast Guard, I've determined the *Big Thunder* is on its way to some blip on the screen that's been identified as an oil derrick. The last official information I'll probably ever get was from a team using sonar to follow the trail from the pumping station at Scrug Quarter Parrish to the edge of the Gulf. It looks like our friend Mr. Harry Wyatt Sullivan was industrious enough to build a pipeline all the way from the Glades to this remote drilling rig out in the Gulf."

Kirk said all of this to me. He knew Earl, Bean, and our Harbormaster friend, Abe West, would've long ago lost the significance of what he was saying. He looked at me and continued. "This means Harry Wyatt intends to pump oil from the mainland to his legitimate derrick, then haul if off in tankers at an incredible profit."

No one really cared. I didn't even care. One day soon I would look back and see the forest for the trees, but at this point, I just wanted Harry Wyatt Sullivan's big ass turning slowly on a spit.

Chapter 92

We dropped anchor just after three a.m.. We were five miles from the blip on the screen that the considerable radar and navigational equipment on board *The Enterprise* told us was our destination. Checking and rechecking our weapons, Kirk and I backed a Boston Whaler craft off the forward deck of *The Enterprise*. Earl and Bean were busy inflating a rubber raft and decking it with an outboard motor. When all of the equipment and weapons were loaded, we gathered on the aft deck. Kirk supervised as all of us painted our faces with black-green camouflage paint. He then painted his own face and looked at us like the hell-sent demon he was.

"The FBI and other authorities are on their way. If the bureaucratic engines grind at the pace I've been used to, they'll be here in a few hours. If the legal channels take them, the bad guys, they'll stand trial. It's fifty-fifty as to whether they'll pay. That's why we've got to get them first."

Every man was hanging on the Captain's words. It was very reminiscent of their covert operation used to recover their last treasure—me. Kirk used a grease pencil to draw a diagram on the deck the way a basketball coach would draw out a last-second play.

"Earl, Bean, you'll approach from the rear. Circle the derrick and come in from their blind side. Cloud and I will use the Whaler to approach from the east." He looked at the slowly recovering Harbormaster. I could tell Kirk was sure the old man would blow his assignment. "Abe, when I call back and give you the word, I want for you to set a course for the center of the derrick. We'll already be on the rig by that time, so hopefully you'll just give us a minute or two of distraction. I want for you to get real close, maybe a couple a hundred yards from the derrick before you veer off. By then, we'll either have them, or they'll have us. Don't much matter then. You just steer back to the Florida coast, and at least you'll have one hell of a story to tell."

Abe West was much more awake and aware than any of us realized. He stood and said, "I was on a rescue boat that fished soldiers and sailors out of the harbor back at Pearl, was only fifteen years old. I'm nothing but a salty old drunk now, but there was a time I was knee-deep in bodies on a bloody rescue skiff in that damn harbor. So don't go telling old Abe to bring up the rear like a fucking washer-woman or something."

Kirk reached for his backup sidearm and withdrew it. He checked the chamber and then tossed it to Abe West. "I'm sorry, I didn't know."

West caught the weapon, looked at it, and tucked it into his waistband.

Chapter 93

Taking the bottom level of the derrick went very smooth. Kirk had reconnaissance that told us only nine men lived aboard the rig full-time. Harry Wyatt Sullivan must have believed his operation, so spread out into the Gulf as it was, couldn't be detected. Earl and Bean met us on the lower deck and together we had only to subdue four guards. If Kirk's intelligence was correct, this only left five more men, plus whatever Harry Wyatt had brought with him.

The first shot rang out as Earl was halfway up the scaffolding to the second story. Bean was right behind his brother and they both folded into the metal supports as if they were a part of it. Kirk hustled up the opposing side of the metal structure. Automatic gunfire rang out like chimes at St. Christmas day. The deflections of bullets against metal frame flashed like so many fireworks.

My job was to secure the boat, the *Big Thunder*. As I stepped onto the deck, a burst of automatic gunfire erupted from the cabin. The backdrop of a flare shot from the rapidly approaching *Enterprise* lit up the dark morning. Just for a second, I saw a man's form in the cabin of the *Big Thunder*. I lobbed a flash-bang grenade inside and instantly saw the blue brilliance of a torch ignite. As the figure retreated, he was stung with fire from above and toppled into the sea.

Between the gunfire, I heard signals being passed between Kirk, Earl, and Bean. By the time I was on board the *Big Thunder* and searching for some moving life, I registered three more men from the derrick had been subdued.

With no warning, all of the lights on both the derrick and the *Big Thunder* lit up. I was temporarily blinded, which I'm sure was the whole point. While I was rubbing my eyes to get the blindness out, I felt what appeared to be a dull spear slam into my back. My legs went weak, the MP5 sub machine gun I held clanked against the railing and fell over the edge of the boat.

As my mind searched to tell me whether I been shot or not, a grinning female appeared above me. Her face was bent into an ugly contortion of rage and satisfaction. The dark woman raised both hands over her head and brought a silvery glint down towards my heart. At that very moment, a substantial wave, a rarity in the Gulf, must have struck the bow. The knife missed and dug itself into my left arm.

Even as the pain came, I bucked my hindquarters and lifted the grinning woman off me. It took both of us a moment to realize I wasn't dead. The woman bounced off the railing and charged again with blood and hate in her eyes. At the last second I pushed a boot in her direction and saw it glance off the knife and ricochet into her opposite shoulder. I rolled with the kick and her lithe body thudded against the deck.

The knife tumbled from her hand and fell overboard, too. I got to my feet bleeding and ready. The smear of hate on her face and the evil in her eyes was striking. It was as if she was hungry for the battle, fancied the pain, and longed for my bloody death. I felt the same. I needed her to die, not just to experience a little pain, but to die—hard. I looked to my bleeding arm, and a wicked smile swept over my face.

"It's unfortunate that you are a woman who's become a monster."

The expression which shrouded her face was one I'll never forget, but I wish I could. Seldom have I witnessed a human lose their mind. But without a doubt, that's just what happened to the hateful witch I was battling. For a second, it occurred to me that I'd never had such a terrible opponent in battle—man, woman, or beast. The part of me that I'm not particularly proud of was happy—was as ready to scratch the itchy red whelp of hate as any serial killer. Then she came. It was fast, but seemed slow-motion. No weapons, just grit and fury barreled towards me. She was unarmed, but I wasn't. Still, I didn't reach for any of the backup weapons. I stood stock-still and when she was within arm's reach, I struck out with one hand and grabbed her by the throat. The meat of her neck slapped against my palm. She flailed her arms and scratched and kicked and tried to bite. I felt the corners of my mouth turn upwards. I loathed the feeling and embraced it at the same time. I tightened my grip and saw her already huge eyes bulge even more. The devil inside hungered and was lusting for more. I fed him.

I gazed up and saw the stars for the diamonds they were. Her knees buckled then stiffened, searching for one last thrust. The devil begged for more torque. As I looked out into the beautiful night sky, I gave him his due and felt a snap in my palm. Her body became dead weight, and she hung at the end of my arm as if from a hangman's tree. My face was still tilted skyward, and I remember thinking that I'd never seen so many stars in all my life.

***

I don't remember meeting the deck, but I looked up, laying on my back, to see Earl, Bean, and Kirk escorting three men away.

I hustled into the interior cabin of the *Big Thunder*. It was the most gruesome, and intoxicating site of my life—I hope.

An enormously fat man held what appeared to be a silver key chain above his head. He was continuously pressing some unseen button and yelling at the same brown young cannibal, I'd previously captured at Scrug Quarter Parrish.

Bolts of lightning seem to hit Zan with every press. I was stone-stricken into immobility. Zan seemed to take every bolt of electricity as a need to continue stalking Wyatt.

Harry Wyatt Sullivan's vocal cords hummed with disbelief, right up to the point where Zan sunk his beveled teeth into the fat man's neck.

Kirk came into the room, looked, and then lunged toward the carnage. I pushed a single boot in his direction. He tripped and fell flat on his face.

Chapter 94

Kirk pushed himself up off the floor and looked at me with surprise and a little anger on his face. I drilled back at him with a sincere command in my eyes. There was now a continuous howl coming from the direction of the fat man and Zan. Kirk and I continued to look at each other. Sick, wet sounds began to leak out between the screams. I pushed up on an elbow. Kirk rolled on his side and did the same. The law enforcer part of him was struggling with this. The *mean* part of him was not.

Kirk reached into a pocket and removed a cigarette and a Zippo lighter. He lit the cigarette and took a long drag. The screams stopped abruptly and were replaced by a ripping, crackling sound. As he exhaled, Kirk spoke. "How long we gonna let this go on?"

I pulled myself to my feet then reached my hand out to help Kirk up. "I reckon that's 'bout long enough."

Earl and Bean came bursting through the doorway. The look on their faces made me a little ashamed, even though I was sure they thought we were doing everything possible to prevent this.

It took all four of us to separate Zan from the bloody carcass of Harry Wyatt Sullivan. When Zan began to struggle a little less, Kirk and I released him. Earl and Bean somehow got him out of the room.

I leaned over and looked at what was left of Harry Wyatt Sullivan's face. His eyes were wide open in horror and shock. Then I saw a half blink. The fat man was still alive. I pulled the Randall Fighting Knife from its scabbard at my lower back. Kirk took another long drag on his cigarette and walked out, shutting the door behind him.

"I'm actually glad you're still alive so we can have this little talk. You caused a lot of pain, fat man. And you'll keep causing pain, just in a different way. All of us, mostly that little brown boy, were pretty innocent until your life crossed ours. I'm not sure any of us had seen pure evil until now." Another wet, half-blink told me Harry Wyatt was still hearing me.

"You see. Good people… us humans, we'll feel bad 'bout killing you, even though you deserve it. I'll have to wrestle around with my conscience for a long-assed time over this. As for the boy, well, I think you can rest assured that you warped his mind forever. If the boy thought he had a soul, he probably thinks you took it from him."

A spurt of black blood shot from Wyatt's neck and his mouth formed a big 'O' as he struggled to pull air. He looked like a dying fish somebody discarded on a bloody pier. He struggled to make sound. I bent low, looking into his dying eyes.

He said, "Please… please have mercy. Please kill me."

I looked deep into his eyes making sure my face and what I would say would be burned into what was left of his memory of life. I slowly stood up and put the knife back in the scabbard.

"No. Suffer."

Chapter 95

As I walked out onto the deck of the *Big Thunder*, I could see the lights and hear the air being violently stirred by several helicopters. The hull of a Coast Guard ship loomed on the not too distant horizon.

Half of the beautiful yacht, which for a short time was *The Enterprise*, grated its fiberglass hull against the frame of the oil derrick. That wave that I thought I felt, the one which let me escape the knife-wielding dark woman—well, I reckon that was really Abe West keeping the yacht on course to the very end.

I went to the edge of the *Big Thunder* where Earl and Bean were furiously trying to force air into the lifeless corpse of Abe West. Captain Jesse Kirk stood over them. He knew it was futile. He also knew they needed to keep trying.

Twenty minutes later, a cavalry of FBI Agents and Coast Guard personnel swarmed the derrick and the *Big Thunder*. A team of rescue workers looked after the body of Abe West.

Kirk and I stood silent at the railing. Earl and Bean joined us. We avoided eye contact with each other. We all beheld a giant orange ball of flame—the sun—rising from the east.

Chapter 96

The next day in Miami was eventful, but with much less intensity than the days before. The Director of the FBI flew down from Washington D.C. and reinstated Kirk as the SAC for South Florida. He also pinned several ribbons on Kirk and handed him a half-dozen awards for all manner of bravery and conduct.

As the Director and Kirk left the press conference, Kirk turned and offered his hand, which the Director took hesitantly. After a silent, firm shake, Kirk reached into his breast pocket and handed the director a single piece of paper.

After the ceremony, I drove over to Jackson Memorial Hospital and met Earl and Bean, who were helping Silasteck Ahmad eat all the contents from several gift baskets. I walked over to his bed and looked at Ahmad. He handed what was left of a half-eaten banana to Bean, who promptly ate the rest. Ahmad got a very sincere look on his face and said, "Thank you. I will always call you my friend. One day... one day soon, I hope... you will call me yours."

I smiled, reached out and shot him with thumb and forefinger, then walked out of the room.

Back at Scrug Quarter Parrish, I found Cal Taylor's widow and three sons. We used the tailgate of my truck for a table as we ate yellow rice and spicy black beans. I told them the whole story.

Chapter 97

A month later, I was in the back yard lying in my hammock. I had just finished reading *Catcher in the Rye* for the sixth time. At once, I felt the satisfaction at having read another book and the emptiness Salinger always seemed to leave me with. Perhaps that was his point. I would probably have to read it again to make sure.

Jake and Seb were enjoying the swinging breeze in the hammock beside me. Without any warning, they both heard something and jumped from the hammock. Blue's official SUV came over the hill. She wasn't running Code, but the cruiser was closing the distance with considerable speed.

Earlier in the day, I had been over to Carter Wells' office to collect my fee. There was a disagreement about the amount, and I had to get rather *strong* with Carter to make sure he saw it from my point of view. Ever the politician, Carter tried to make light of the trophy recovery. He said I had as much to gain by its recovery as a citizen as he had. Besides, he pointed out, he couldn't be expected to pay for "all of my runnin' 'round after criminals, committin' crimes other than the theft."

He actually had a point there. I didn't really feel like bargaining with him, so we settled on an amount to be donated to the university's English Department, Emma's department, in the name of the Cal Taylor Foundation. This way, Carter felt he was being magnanimous and I was happy enough so's I didn't feel like I had to take one of his toes. I did make him pay for the *Bare Naked/Enterprise* though. More like the real value, not my cost.

I was pretty sure this was what Blue was in such a hurry to confront me about. The Cable Counties Agent-In-Charge would probably have gotten a call the moment I left Carter's office, accusing me of extortion or some such thing. I left the hammock and walked over to the driveway.

As Blue got out of the cruiser, I lit a fat cigar I'd received courtesy of Cal Taylor's widow. I leaned against the front of the cruiser, and Blue rested her elbows on top of the SUV on the other side. She gave a little smile. "I don't suppose you'd know anything about an almost-robbery which occurred at Carter Wells' office this morning, would you?"

I tucked the big stogie into the corner of my mouth and held my hands up, face out. "I'm sorry, Agent. I haven't heard a single thing, but I'll keep my ear open."

"That's not why I'm here. You're something of a celebrity, bringing the trophy back and all. The AIC told Carter he'd gotten a call from you before you even went to his office. He also told Carter he'd be following up to make sure that donation reached the English Department."

"Well, Mac's a good man. I think his tastes are improving at an alarming rate. To quote my mentor, Mark Twain, 'When I was but ten years old I thought my old man was dumber than a fence post. But, by the time I was twenty-one, I was surprised by what the old man had learned.'"

Blue chuckled. "You're a strange piece of fruit, Cloud. But at least you know it."

I rolled the cigar around getting the taste on both lips. "What're you here for?"

"Judge ruled today that the Petroleum Bug was the duel property of the university and the heirs of Amul Instad Facon. The company that bought the bug from Sullivan was ordered to redirect their money into the accounts of the university and the Sultan."

"Well, if I was gonna get half-killed, it's nice to know that the university can continue to prosper. As for the Sultan... no amount of money could heal that poor man."

Blue walked around the front of the car, reached out and took the cigar from my lips. She put it to her mouth and took a deep drag. She then tossed the cigar on the ground, where Jake and Seb found it a great toy. I found it a great waste. Emma's bright red Durango came over the hill at that very moment.

Blue looked at me with a nasty, cunning little smile. "I told Emma what you did. I told her about the donation to the English Department and what would be coming to the university on account of the bug."

"Well, I appreciate that."

Emma got out of the Durango and walked over to us. She looked at the cigar the dogs were sniffing and wrangling over. "Cloud, are you teaching the babies to smoke?"

I felt that all too common punch in the jeans and smiled with more than a little lust. "I don't remember when both of you were here... at the same time... on a weekday afternoon. Perhaps an afternoon delight... If you would."

EPILOGUE

I was taking a run around the property with Jake and Seb when I saw a plane circling the field at a very low altitude. By the time I reached the back area of the property, where my little homemade landing strip was, the plane was not circling, but lining up for a landing. My guess was a wayward drug runner who needed an out of the way place to set down. I hustled over to my little hanger where I formerly kept my own plane.

I reached under a stack of perfectly cared-for Playboy Magazines, dating back to the early seventies, and grabbed an ancient Colt pistol given me by a former client as a bonus. I leaned against the doorjamb and watched the plane come in for a perfect landing, much better than I could have done.

The plane taxied up to the hanger and began to shut down the engines. I checked to make sure the pistol was loaded.

The engines finally came to a halt and the door opened. An enormous man unfolded from the cockpit and was followed by a fellow of more average size. The big man was wearing a pair of denim overalls, and his partner was wearing a long flowing white robe.

I set the pistol on my desk and walked out to greet my friend. Silasteck Ahmad shucked aside my outstretched hand and lifted me off the ground in a crushing bear hug. When I was again touching the ground, I looked deep in his eyes. There was a change from the last time I'd seen him, lying in that hospital bed.

He grabbed my face in both of his huge hands. "I have missed you, my friend."

Despite some of our history, I was very glad to see him. "Silas, what... why didn't you call? I was getting ready to shoot, thinking you were a drug smuggler or something."

He looked sternly at the man in the robe and extended his hand. He handed him a small key. Ahmad dangled the key in front of me, grabbed my hand and put the key in it. "The Sultan sends you this gift. He sends his apologies again, and his thanks. He asks that you accept this airplane as a token of his limitless gratitude."

I rubbed the key between my thumb and forefinger. I looked at the twin engine Beechcraft. It was obviously brand new and the most current model. I patted Silas on the arm and smiled.

"How 'bout you and me take a ride in my new plane..."

The End

Become a Cable Native!

If you liked **BUG TROUBLE**, you'll love **SCREAMING JACKASS**, book four of the Cable Counties Thriller series.

Visit HartleyStevens.com to become a **Cable Native** and receive the latest updates, short stories, and special offers.

About the Author

Hartley attended the University of Florida, studying exercise science, and played football for the Florida Gators. A stint in the United States Army followed with postings in Oklahoma, Indiana, Georgia, Texas, and South Korea.

His education continued as a world traveler. He and a friend set out on a one-year odyssey covering North America, Australia, the Pacific Islands, Southeast Asia, and both Eastern and Western Europe.

He lives in North Central Florida with his wife Jeanie, his son Brendan, and Maximum-Ready-Set-Go, an energetic pug/yorkie. His older son, Justin, is a United States Marine, stationed as an infantryman with 1/6 Hard, Camp Lejeune, North Carolina.

Acknowledgements

I thank, Alisa Jeanine Stevens, my wife. I love my art more every day, but all fades in the shadow of your compare.

Andy Sherrard, I'm a constant student of complicated thought. You are the teacher, thank you.

Jani. Yours is the loudest voice when I write.

Mind-Benders, the experiment is working. Let us all continue towards the light.

Thank you Kate. The Cable Counties brand is solid, and I'm very proud.

Lieba, thank you for first reads, edits, and brilliant conversation.

Cowbell Brothers, in real relationships, it's good to know the difference between sand and stone.

Some readers have a friend like my John. Thank you Johnny Pants, thank you.

Graeme Hague, the copy-edits teach more than they fix, if that's possible. Jessica Holland, thank you for the sanitation of your proofread. Your edits prevent a rookie moniker. Jason and Marina Anderson, Polgarus Studio, I'm forever grateful for what your company has done for me.

Sharon Julien, thank you for the evolution of the website.

Jeff Goins, Leader of Tribe Writers, thank you for the fundamentals and inspiration to build a tribe.

THE ORIGINAL Tribe Writer's Pro-Team: Amy Crumpton, Shaunta Grimes, MaryEllen Miller, Jeff Blackburn, David Villalva, Dr. David Ball,

Karen Love, Katherine Martin, Aram Boyd, Colleen Valles, Nicole Bianchi...
I learn more from our conversations than I can say. Thank you. Steady On!

I would like to thank my two sons, Justin and Brendan, I wouldn't ask for
the lessons, but I'm glad I'm learning them.